LOVING LILY

Lily was too tired to resist. Part of her exhausted brain knew she shouldn't lie down near him, that he was no longer so ill. Yet Lily wanted his comforting presence as much as it seemed he wanted hers, so she slipped in next to him.

He stayed awake no longer than the few moments it took to adjust their positions. She quieted, surrendering herself to his comfort, his strength, the reality of him beside her, and slept.

Hours later Lily rose to the surface of consciousness. She was snuggled up tight against Adam now, and the warmth she felt was not merely physical. The sensations rippling through her were myriad, unexplored, delightful . . . and confusing.

Was she dreaming? Yet she seemed to be lying in her own bed, with Adam's face inches from her own. Whether dreaming or not, his warm mouth had to span the merest distance before it claimed hers. With a ferocity that surprised her, Lily hoped that he would . . . and that this was no dream.

Then, with great care and tenderness, he joined her lips to his, and Lily thought nothing in her life had ever felt so wonderful.

Dear Romance Reader,

In July we launched the Ballad line with four new series, and each month we'll present both new and continuing stories set everywhere from medieval England to the American West—the kind of passionate, romantic stories you love best, written by the most gifted authors. At the back of each book, we'll tell you when you can find subsequent books in the series that have captured your heart.

Martha Schroeder's atmospheric *Angels of Mercy* debuts this month, chronicling the dreams and desires of three women stubborn enough to join Florence Nightingale on the battlefields of the Crimean War. In **More Than a Dream,** a young woman of privilege wants nothing more than a life as a healer—until a brooding physician tempts her wish for love. Next, Corinne Everett begins the *Daughters of Liberty* series, in which three young women chart their own passionate courses in the wake of the War for Independence. An ardent Patriot meets her match in a dangerously attractive man who may be Loyalist—and who threatens to steal her heart—in **Loving Lily.**

Next, rising star Tammy Hilz continues her breathtaking *Jewels of the Sea* trilogy with **Once a Rebel.** When a woman who despises the nobility's arrogance encounters a handsome aristocrat, she never imagines the adventure that awaits them on the high sea—or the thrilling fulfillment she finds in his arms. Finally, the second book in Kate Donovan's *Happily Ever After Co.* series presents a Boston society beauty and a widowed sea captain marooned on a tropical island—and the once-in-a-lifetime love that results when they're **Carried Away.**

Kate Duffy
Editorial Director

Daughters of Liberty

LOVING LILY

Corinne Everett

ZEBRA BOOKS
Kensington Publishing Corp.
http://www.zebrabooks.com

ZEBRA BOOKS are published by

Kensington Publishing Corp.
850 Third Avenue
New York, NY 10022

All Kensington titles, imprints, and distributed lines are available at special quantity discounts for bulk purchases for sales promotions, premiums, fund raising, educational, or institutional use.

Special book excerpts or customized printings can also be created to fit specific needs. For details, write or phone the office of the Kensington Special Sales Manager: Kensington Publishing Corp., 850 Third Avenue, New York, NY 10022. Attn. Special Sales Department, Phone: 1-800-221-2647.

First Printing: February, 2001
10 9 8 7 6 5 4 3 2 1

Printed in the United States of America

*To fellow author and friend Neesa Hart,
and to my agent Pam Ahearn
for advice, support, and
endless encouragement*

One

I have here only made a nosegay of culled flowers, and have brought nothing of my own but the thread that ties them together.

—Michel de Montaigne,
Essays, 1595

Crouching ignominiously in a flower bed was not Lily Walters's idea of what Williamsburg's first florist should be about. Those men so sought after in London by the nobility for their expertise in the new art of flower arranging surely were not sent to gather small flowers suitable only for sprinkling in porcelain bowls.

Yet here she was, hunched over in the rich Virginia soil, immobile only because the words floating over the boxwood hedge concerned Peter. Eavesdropping, in a word. Her best friend and someone she did not know were gossiping about her younger brother, rousing all the protective instincts toward the boy—really, now a man—whose mother and father she had been for the past five years.

"Was that Peter Walters's sister I saw entering your house?" the stranger said to Lily's best friend, Mary Hardison. "I hear she has become a merchant, of all things."

Lily clenched her teeth in annoyance but dared not utter a word.

"There's nothing unseemly, Alicia," Mary said loyally. "While you have been in London these last few years, their parents died at sea. Lily had to support herself and Peter. She has become a florist, which I hear is all the rage in London. She's quite successful too. Lily is arranging the cut flowers for Mama's assembly tonight."

"Indeed," Alicia said in a bored tone. "She should have found herself a husband to take care of her. She is what, twenty-three, twenty-four, by now? Well, 'tis her brother who interests me. I saw Peter when we first returned a few weeks ago." She sighed. "How handsome he has become. I would have enjoyed a few weeks' flirtation with him. 'Tis a pity my own dear betrothed arrives soon with the new army contingent from Britain."

"Hush, Alicia, you are very wicked." Mary sounded quite scandalized at the other girl's forwardness.

Lily balanced precariously on her knees, wishing she could see what this Alicia looked like. Ugly, she hoped.

"Besides, his sympathies are decidedly Patriot," Mary continued. "Your parents would be most distressed. My mother says that soon Peter Walters will not be accepted in respectable homes. How could you think of flirting with him, when you are about to marry a British officer?"

"Oh, Mary, this is only March," Alicia said, then laughed. "I am not to wed until May. Much as I would have loved to marry in London, my betrothed has been seconded here to the Colonies to watch over these rebels."

"Whatever do you mean?" Mary asked.

Lily's legs started to cramp. She put a hand down into the flower bed to steady herself, feeling the moist earth against her palm, reassuringly warm and familiar. She could not move without noise from the crushed-oyster-shell path giving her away. She hoped the girls would go inside soon.

"I returned with my parents ahead of William. He is charged with finding these Patriots who call themselves the Sons of Liberty. Once they are discovered, they will be charged with treason."

Alicia paused, apparently bored with a conversation not centering on herself. "I myself shall want someone to arrange flowers for the wedding. As you said, 'tis quite the latest style in London, you know. Do you think Peter's sister is up to my standards?"

"Oh, goodness, yes," said Mary, sounding relieved at finding a safe topic. "Only come see in the salon what she has done."

Their footsteps crackled on the shell pathway. For a moment, Lily feared they would round the corner and stumble upon her. But the noise receded in the other direction as the two women headed toward the house.

Lily straightened, her back aching from the awkward position. Suppose Alicia's words meant that Peter was in danger? Lily was as staunch a Patriot as her brother, but she did not like the idea that he was involved with the Sons of Liberty without her knowledge. Yet Peter was no longer her baby brother, she reminded herself. At eighteen, Peter was a man, and she was only his sister.

Could that horrid Alicia know something that she, his very own sister, did not? Indignation stained Lily's cheeks rose-colored as she made her way back inside. Mary and Alicia had gone upstairs, their voices floating faintly down the hall stairwell.

Lily quickly placed the pinks and the sweet william in the bowls Mary's mother had shown her. She did not stay to admire her handiwork but headed home at once, her empty split-oak basket swinging vigorously from one arm.

* * *

Dusk mantled the landscape by the time Lily reached home, but Peter was nowhere to be found. She thought she heard noises from the dining room—odd, since no cooking smells emanated from the kitchen. Lily struck a tinderbox and lit two wall sconces in the hall before she pushed open the dining room door and stepped inside.

The room was in total darkness, but she was not alone. In the dim light from the hallway she made out about a dozen shapes, men, since the odor of tobacco wafted toward her. What was happening in here?

One shadow detached itself from the mass and moved toward her. About to cry out, she recognized Peter immediately when he seized her hands and shushed her quickly.

"Lily, forgive me. I neglected to tell you I would meet my friends here before venturing out tonight," Peter said too quickly. "I shall take them to Chowning's Tavern with me, and you need not feed this hulking lot."

Lily was not so easily pacified. "If you do not need me to feed you, surely you do not need me to light your candles for you," she said. Her mood did not improve upon hearing a low chuckle from one corner of the room.

"What are you doing here in the twilight with these 'friends'?" she asked, pulling her hands free. No matter how old he was, she was still the only mother and father he had.

"The lass has spirit, Peter," a deep, amused masculine voice said. The voice was utterly unknown to her, but somehow his words settled deeply into her, where her breath caught. A tall shape stepped out of the shadows. Lily saw only a white shirt—the stranger wore no coat—gleaming in the near dark.

A large, strong hand moved into the circle of light cast by the candles in the hall and clapped Peter on the shoulder. "Rest easy, young Walters. None shall contribute more than they are able. Certainly not your sister. We will take our leave now and meet you . . . shortly, where we agreed."

Several men took advantage of the speaker's words to leave, slipping by Lily in the dark, three-cornered hats jammed low on their heads. She was unable to make out any faces as they dispersed. With the others gone, the man who had spoken turned, and Lily thought he meant to speak to Peter again. Instead, the candles fluttered faintly at his movement. She could have sworn he sketched a bow in her direction.

But he seemed to see her well enough, for he took her hand in his. "Your pardon, mistress, for disturbing you," he said in cultured tones that carried no trace of mockery. But instead of brushing the top of her hand with a light kiss, as custom dictated, he paused.

He boldly turned her hand over and kissed the sensitive palm. In her confusion, Lily felt a brief surge of relief that he had not kissed the hand she had earlier pressed into the flower bed. She pushed aside the absurd errant thought and snatched her hand away, grateful that no one could see her burning blush in the dim room.

Before she could frame a coherent phrase, another low chuckle escaped his lips. "Spirit indeed," he murmured, but she detected not a hint of remorse for his forwardness in his deep baritone voice.

Then Peter reached for her, and the stranger slipped away.

Lily waited for Peter to speak as she poked angrily at the banked fire warming their evening meal. Among the volatile emotions swirling inside her was a strange excitement set off by the stranger's kiss, a reaction she tried severely to repress. As Peter laid dishes on the table, she stole glances at his face. He was obviously groping for a way to approach the subject of the strange meeting held in their house. Well, she was not about to make it easy for him.

Lily finally broke the silence as they ate their mulligatawny stew in silence. "Those were not your college friends. You held a meeting here a-purpose because I was at Mary's. What sort of plotting are you involved in, Peter?"

Peter shook his head ruefully. "Lily, please do not press me. I do not want to conceal this from you, but 'tis safer that you do not learn of my activities."

"You have never kept anything from me before," she said, frowning.

Peter glanced down. "I know," he admitted. "But the choice is not mine," he went on stubbornly.

Resentment stole through Lily. She had no doubt that the commanding stranger was the reason Peter would not confide in her.

"Are you involved with the Sons of Liberty?" she asked without preamble. Startled, Peter looked up, alarm flashing in his green eyes. "And that man who . . . who spoke to me has something to do with all this?" she added.

"Can nothing be kept from you?" he muttered in exasperation.

"Better you should tell me than alert the town," she said with asperity. "Aye, I am not jesting. You are not so discreet as you think." She leaned toward him, the meal forgotten in her intensity. "I came back early from Mary's to tell you that I overheard Mary and a Tory friend of hers discussing you."

His eyes widened in surprise. "You and your support for the radical cause," she went on implacably. "They said that soon you would not be welcome in respectable homes. Of course, they mean Loyalist homes," she added with scorn.

She told him the rest then, except for the feminine gossip about his looks. By the frowning concentration on his face, she knew her news about the British Army and its intent to stifle the Sons of Liberty was of intense interest to him.

Yet he remained silent. Finally she left Peter to put the dirty bowls into a bucket of water, then went upstairs to dress for the evening.

Lily feared for her brother, yet she was also fiercely glad he was involved with those who had vowed to take the Colonies' destiny into their own hands. Now she had only to devise a plan to do something helpful herself. . . .

She brushed her hair absently, fretting anew. For the first time, she played no part in something important to her brother. That stung, as did the fact that his secrecy kept her from a cause she believed in herself.

She struggled into her clothes, grateful she was able to tie the front stays herself, since they had no servants. Her gown, though simple, was well cut. In exchange for weekly flowers to grace the tiring-room of her shop, the milliner had sewn a lovely gown of bronze silk. Settling a paisley shawl of wool challis about her shoulders to ward off the early spring chill, she found Peter pacing in the hallway below.

"You look lovely," Peter said. He beamed at her with brotherly pride. "You shall be the fairest of them all, Lily."

"Hardly!" She laughed, reaching up on tiptoe to smooth away his frown at her dismissal of the compliment. Peter was sweet to think she was special, but she knew better. She was small and her figure was trim, but other than that she was no beauty. Her skin was not white enough, her hair was too honey-colored to be fashionably pale, and she had a lamentable trail of freckles across her nose and upper cheeks, which she rarely remembered to dust with powder.

Peter offered her his arm as they set out to walk up Duke of Gloucester Street toward the Hardison home. They had no choice but to walk, since they could not afford a carriage, but Lily did not complain. She merely slipped the wooden patens over her brocaded shoes and kept pace with her brother.

"You are not staying, I take it?" she asked when she realized he had not changed his attire.

"No. Can you forgive me? I know I've often railed that you have no suitable escort, and here am I abandoning you, but . . ."

"I understand," she said. He still looked distressed, so she reassured him. "Truly, I do not mind, Peter. Mary Hardison's home is almost as familiar to me as our own, or it used to be. . . ." Her voice trailed off.

Invitations had not been so forthcoming after Lily set up her business, but Mary still was loyal to her. Even though she and her family were all staunch Royalists.

"You will tell your friends about what I overheard?" Lily asked neutrally, gratified when Peter nodded.

"Good," she replied. "Perhaps tonight I may learn something more."

Peter stopped in the middle of the road. "That had not occurred to me," he said. "Mayhap 'tis a mistake not to attend the assembly tonight."

She squeezed his arm, smiling. "I do not think they will say such things in front of you, Peter. After all, I was eavesdropping."

Peter chuckled. "You are a forward baggage. But there could be no better sister, unconventional as you are."

"I am the only one you have, after all," she returned lightly. For the moment, their quarrel was gone. They were allies again, narrowing the divide that had sprung up between them for the first time in their lives.

Yet the divide was real. Lily promised herself that she would bridge it by learning more about Peter's activities.

"Lily, I will leave you here." Peter stopped just before the entrance. "I'll be back at eleven. Enjoy yourself," Peter urged. He kissed her forehead, then left.

Lily stood on the steps alone, lost in the heated memory of a different kiss. She felt the stranger's kiss on her palm like a brand. Could any gentleman at the ball tonight reproduce a sensation such as the one that now shivered through her? What forward thoughts! Still, she wondered what he looked like, the tall man with the disturbingly low voice. Lily was convinced she would recognize that voice if she ever heard it again.

Even if she happened to be eavesdropping.

Two

Forever, Fortune, will thou prove
An unrelenting foe to Love,
And when we meet a mutual heart,
Come in between and bid us part?

—James Thomson,
Song, 1730

". . . and the Massachusetts Committee of Correspondence urges its sister colony to follow suit in opposing Lord Grenville's Coercive Acts and to refuse the importation of British goods." Adam Pearson, late of Boston, surveyed the dimly lit barn as he finished the speech he'd begun earlier in the Walters home. Small wonder he could deliver the speech without looking at the letter, given the weeks on the road he'd had to practice.

The men arrayed before him were a disparate lot. Some were landed, some merchants, while others were laborers, students, even apprentices. Peter Walters, the lad sent to meet him that afternoon, could be no more than eighteen or nineteen.

Definitely too inexperienced to realize he should not have held a clandestine meeting in his own home, Adam thought, not unkindly. Especially not with a discerning sister, one who possessed a sharp mind and tongue to match. He tried to push to the back of his mind other thoughts concerning the woman he had seen so briefly by candlelight, but he was too intrigued to let thoughts of her fade completely.

Later, he told himself, willing the well-disciplined side of himself to assert control. Still, he listened with only half an ear to the debate that sprang up after he finished speaking. He was not surprised to hear the Virginians arguing, knowing that the southern Colonies were not all agreed on independence from Great Britain. Personally, he was convinced the rebellion would end in war, for he knew firsthand that Britain did not let its sons and daughters go lightly from its grasp.

These colonists would learn England's lessons in their own time, however, not at his behest. 'Twas important they accept him as one of them. Adam wanted no doubt in their minds about his loyalty, which his past would inevitably provoke.

After all, he had started life as the son of a titled aristocrat and became a British Army officer. He was still supposed to be in Boston, infiltrating the Sons of Liberty there. Although the British must be making discreet inquiries, since he had not reported in so long, he did not think his former commanding officer knew he had left the Massachusetts Colony. He wanted as much time as possible here before Colonel Ware was alerted to his presence elsewhere. So he would employ disguises.

"Why should we bring down upon ourselves the same wrath Boston suffers?" a barrel-chested man asked. Heads nodded in assent.

"Virginia can forge its own path," a young, chestnut-haired man said, casting a thinly veiled look of challenge at Adam. Growing murmurs accompanied this assertion.

Jack Cameron, the leader of the Williamsburg Sons of

Liberty, spoke up. "We need only accept this 'gift' from Massachusetts. We are not yet committed to Boston's ways, now or ever, if we do not so choose."

He pushed to the head of the throng, standing beside Adam to make clear his acceptance of the "gift," the Patriot leader from Massachusetts. Adam was grateful for the support. Peter Walters and several other young men rose at once to stand by him and Cameron.

"While we yet have our freedom, let us make the most of it," Cameron continued. "We are *not* all agreed that war is inevitable. But we have all agreed to support the merchants' boycott, and there will be consequences from our defiance. We may as well learn all we can from the experience of Massachusetts."

"My thanks, Cameron," Adam said, moving to resume control of the meeting. "You men can take what I have to offer—training, tactics, knowledge of the British military—in the spirit in which they are intended: to better prepare yourselves. Whether to move beyond defensive measures remains the decision of the sovereign Colony of Virginia, one that is not mine to make or even encourage."

He passed a hand over his eyes, rubbing his fingers tiredly through his thick dark hair. Sleeping in barns and haylofts through the long weeks of moving southward had taken its toll. He'd decided to use the life into which he had been born as his ally. It gave him money and a base from which to operate. To cover his trail, his movements, the activities he planned here, he would hide in plain sight.

Returning his attention to the men before him, Adam shoved the three-cornered hat lower on his forehead. Only Peter Walters had seen him in daylight, when they'd met that afternoon. Adam hoped he would have no cause to do something about that one lapse in his precautions.

Time to end this meeting. He finished with warnings

to be discreet. "Never speak my name aloud. We will meet at night. The locations and times of our meetings will vary. You will drill either by night with me, or together in daylight without me. For those of you in the militia, this should pose no problem. The rest of you may need to make some arrangements to be away. Any of you fight in the French and Indian War?"

A few older men nodded assent.

"Then you'll have seen the British fight. For the rest of you, you should know 'tis difficult to oppose them in open terrain. In mountainous or forested areas, however, 'tis they who are at a disadvantage. The Tidewater country is broad and flat, as you know. You have a lot of work ahead of you."

"How shall we communicate with you?" a man asked.

"Leave a message at Raleigh Tavern for a traveling vendor named Knowles, on days when the Royal Governor takes audience. The man will see the messages get to me," Adam said, not revealing that he himself would be the traveling peddler.

At this, several men snorted. Adam paused, surprised.

The barrel-chested farmer said derisively, "Here now, you must not know our new Royal Governor, the Earl of Dunmore, does not have 'days' of audience? He meets with petitioners but once a week, and then upon his fancy."

"I see." Adam thought hastily, then set a fixed day and time for messages to be delivered to the tavern. It was not as safe—falling into a regular routine never was—but he had to set up something now, and nothing else useful came to mind. Peter volunteered to act as courier.

When the men dispersed, Adam was alone and able to let down his guard for the first time. He climbed into the hayloft, cursing softly as he stretched out his long legs in

the scratchy straw. One more night of the itinerant life.
One more night of insects and moldy straw. His material
comfort would be assured as of the following night, although nothing could alter the uncertainty of his under-
cover activities.

Adam fully appreciated the irony of what he planned
to do in Williamsburg. The money, the power, the privilege—all the things he had shunned for so long—were all
to be his again. Everything he had rejected when he left
his ancestral home years earlier to become a green lieutenant would again be his.

His good humor fled. Could he assume the trappings
of privilege now and not become what he had left behind?
Could he avoid becoming like the pompous aristocrats he
despised?

Adam pushed the unwelcome thought to the back of
his mind. He would be aping his aristocratic origins deliberately, not returning to them. His needs were simple
and few, and they were not about to change. He mentally
added one new item to the list: a comfortable bed.

Amend that: one without fleas.

His last waking thoughts were of sharing the bed. With
a far more pleasant bedmate than a bug. Tantalizing
glimpses of tawny locks and a sultry, indignant voice came
to mind, along with the imprint of a delicate palm and
fingertips that were, surprisingly, roughened as if she
worked with her hands.

His imagination filled in the details of her figure. It
pleased him to be generous.

The next day a vision in scarlet and lace visited every
trade establishment in Williamsburg. As Adam waited
near the courthouse, word spread quickly of the rich Tory

squire who had arrived to outfit Oak Grove, a plantation along the James River near Williamsburg. Peering out upon the world through his newly donned spectacles, Adam could almost see the news spread through Williamsburg as each person met a neighbor and shared the information he had planted. He'd chosen to become Squire Adair Sotheby, a man of indeterminate age under the fashionably large powdered wig, blue-tinted spectacles, face powder, and stylish lace dripping at his neck and cuffs.

Adam stood back a moment, pleased by the speed with which his lie ran through the town. Then he plunged back into the character of his creation, swinging his walking stick and examining a silk-shod leg with an air of boredom.

A polite but uncomfortable clerk of the Court of Assizes told "Sotheby"—who by this time had acquired a considerable following of townsfolk, including a small mob of young boys to carry his purchases—that things were not so simple.

"Squire, this property was registered in the name of one Adam Pearson, Esquire, a solicitor resident in Boston." The clerk lowered his voice. "He is wanted, 'tis said, by the Admiralty Court, for certain offenses against the Crown. The property at Oak Grove is subject to seizure by officers of the court."

Lest alarm take hold, Adam reminded himself that the "trouble" in Boston had been deliberately contrived. Colonel Ware would see to it that no consequences would fall on Adam's head—at least not until he learned what Adam had actually done. And by then Adam hoped it would be too late.

Pausing to take a pinch from an enameled snuffbox, Adam remained in character. "My good man, that hapless solicitor is no doubt being run to ground somewhere in

Delaware. At least that is where he was when he sold me this property." Removing a parchment from his frogged and embroidered red waistcoat, he flourished it before the entranced crowd.

"The unrepentant radical was forced to flee for his life from Boston and had little on his person to keep body and soul together when I chanced upon him." Adam paused to sneeze politely. "The fellow was gambling, and his last stake was this property he said he owned," he continued, pushing the spectacles up his nose. "I have come to see if 'tis of any value." He looked around with a condescending air and proffered the deed of "sale" to the clerk.

That should do it, Adam thought to himself. No one would have any reason to think a rich Tory like himself would be connected to a Bostonian hunted by the law, thus throwing off any pursuit. As no one in Boston knew about the plantation he owned in Virginia, there was no reason for anyone to be suspicious of the plantation's new owner.

Best of all, he thought, easing himself carefully into a hired carriage as if his bulk were large and his body flabby, he would sleep in a comfortable bed this night. He must be getting old, he told himself ruefully, if the prospect of a bed, even at the price of playing so ridiculous a fop, was appealing.

"Ahem, your squireship, ah." A local youth, Will Evans, his new majordomo, had only his youth and eagerness for a paying job to recommend him. Adam smiled behind one gloved hand, knowing his mother would have sacked the lad in minutes for failing to address a person of his consequence properly.

The memory of his mother brought a frown, and he realized he had flustered the boy further. Well, he was not the Earl of Dalby here on Virginia's soil, merely a rich planter entitled to the rustic honorific of "squire."

Adam shook off the pall of memory. " 'Squire' will do, Will," he informed the young man.

"Thank you, your sirship, ah, I mean . . . ah, your squireness." Will twisted his hat between his hands, gulping a deep breath. He tried again. "If you wish to acquaint yourself with all of Williamsburg's better trade establishments, may I recommend you visit Lilies of Francis Street, uh, sir?" he asked. Much better.

"Certainly, Evans. Lead on, there's a good fellow," Adam said in the nasal voice he affected as the squire, not really caring where they went for the moment.

Soon he realized they were pulling up to the house he'd visited the evening before. A carved wooden sign bore the insignia of a lily, painted white.

Bloody hell. He could not afford for Peter to recognize him. Thank God he had met that inventor Franklin last year in Philadelphia. The spectacles he'd purchased at least covered his eyes, and he hoped his outlandish dress would do the rest. Adam pinched the lenses with their tiny metal bridge tightly on his nose as they entered the shop.

Satisfaction with his disguise vanished at once. For there, dressed in a simple moss-green gown that enhanced her golden complexion and the green flecks in her amber eyes, was the strong-willed woman he had briefly glimpsed the previous night.

Peter Walters's sister, Lily.

Will had called this place "Lilies of Francis Street." Now Adam realized he meant "Lily's." Of course. He groaned inwardly. Just his luck to see her again when he looked like a simpering fool.

Behind the counter of her shop, Lily saw only a dandified man standing behind Peter's friend Will Evans. He

sported a hideously bright vermilion coat that reminde⟨
her instantly of a British Army officer's uniform. Who bu⟨
a Royalist would wear such a shade, she thought. And h⟨
was a macaroni to boot, all gotten up with lace to hi⟨
fingertips. She had seen spectacles before, on a near
sighted friend of Peter's who read law at the college, bu⟨
she'd never seen colored lenses. The total effect of th⟨
squire, for all his height, was of a fussy, crabby, middle
aged man.

But a customer is a customer, she reminded herself
She pasted on a bright artificial smile before addressin⟨
them. "Good morrow, sir, and welcome. How may I hel⟨
you?"

Adam hastily remembered to pitch his voice upwar⟨
before replying, and then his first act was to prod hi⟨
majordomo ungraciously. "Well, Evans, this was you⟨
idea," he said in an appropriately peevish voice.

"Mistress Walters," Will Evans began. Adam notice⟨
the young man's eyes were a little glazed. It looked as i⟨
he had a *tendre* for her. "This is the new plantation owne⟨
in town. I told him he should visit your shop. The squir⟨
has let furnished lodgings in town as well, and require⟨
your skills to ornament . . . to decoratize, um . . ." h⟨
trailed off.

"He wants to receive visitors and needs the finishin⟨
touches for his lodgings," Lily finished, favoring Will wit⟨
a radiant smile. Seeing this, Adam could have cheerfull⟨
ground the lucky young man into the floor. "Your thought⟨
fulness in bringing the new squire here is most appreci
ated, Will. Sit a moment, gentlemen, while I prepare som⟨
flowers for you to seal our contract."

She moved swiftly around the shop, gathering bloom⟨
from small oak barrels half filled with water. She tosse⟨
comments over her shoulder as she worked. "May I as⟨

sume, sir, that you wish the visiting rooms of your lodging kept supplied when you are in town? You have but to inform me when you are ready to receive visitors at Oak Grove, and I will be happy to provide you with suitable flowers and greenery there."

A pretty little formal speech. Having heard her speak so unguardedly the night before, Adam knew she could be far more passionate and much less polite.

He grunted his assent, peering above the lenses to follow her lithe figure. As Lily reached for a pedestal vase, he saw the topmost swell of her breasts above her modest bodice.

Lily chose that moment to look at him, her amber eyes catching his gaze. Hastily, Adam looked at her through the lenses once more. Fortunately, there was no sign of Peter. Still, he could not be too cautious. He'd been told often enough that he had unusual eyes the hue of aquamarine that could easily identify him.

He remembered his role and dropped his gaze to his pocket watch, which he withdrew from his waistcoat on a thick gold chain. Harrumphing loudly, he announced they would take their leave. He would not approach her, although she held out the vase of flowers toward him. Adam knew that if he touched her, he would be tempted to repeat the kiss of the previous evening.

Turning on his heel abruptly, he left with no more than a muttered word of thanks flung over his shoulder. In truth, her work was delightful, her artistry considerable. He forced Will to take the vase, but the flowers reminded him of her every blessed mile out to Oak Grove plantation.

This was going to be a damnable deception.

Three

A military operation involves deception.
                                    —Sun-tzu,
                        The Art of War, 4th century B.C.

"You are going to the library again? You've never studied this hard in your life, Peter."

"And never will again, Lily, I assure you, since I finish my studies next year," Peter said uneasily, hoping the lie didn't show on his face. He hated lying to Lily, but Pearson had been clear: *Tell no one of your activities.*

Not for the first time, he wished he knew more about Adam. There was no doubt the man was a military genius, but why all the secrecy? Training in a militia was not illegal—at least not yet—although it was obvious the British trusted their "American cousins" less and less. Governor Dunmore had even considered moving the powder and arms out of the magazine that stood uncomfortably close to the Palace Green.

Peter shouldered his pack, which Lily thought contained books. Actually, he was learning to fire a musket. Inside the pack were the disassembled parts of the weapon that he already knew was inferior to the Pennsylvania long rifle. But few Tidewater residents had weapons like the frontiersmen who lived on the dangerous edges of colonial

America. Acquiring better arms was one of the deficiencies he suspected Pearson was working to remedy.

Lily saw the weapon's stock poking out of the canvas bag. She longed to confront Peter with his lie but suspected he would keep the same stubborn silence as before. Once she closed the door behind him, however, she ran to fetch her cloak.

If Peter thought he was going to sneak out without her knowing and tell her tales, he could think again. Lily was sure Peter's sudden, prolonged absences at night were connected with the mysterious stranger, and a surge of anger and jealousy reminded her that the divide between her and Peter had widened again.

When she reached the forest outside town, Peter turned off the rutted river road into dark boughs of sheltering pine. Lily continued to follow him, her cloak picking up burrs and twigs along the way, but she paid them no heed. Soon Peter came to a clearing. She drew back into the protection of the trees. Two dozen or so men were grouped in various postures near the sheltered glow of a fire.

One man held a lantern aloft, and by its light Lily saw a tall, broad-shouldered form standing near. A long wool cloak swirled about him, and a three-cornered hat covered his hair, but Lily was certain this was the deep-voiced man who had so brazenly kissed her hand.

Voices were low throughout the clearing. She did not hear him speak but knew he directed the activity. The lantern light flared fitfully; the fire was banked not to reflect in the direction of the clearing's entrance.

Peter, she saw, had found a place among a group of men assembling and disassembling weapons. Others filled powder horns or shoved the charge down the gun barrel. Several were engaged in sword fighting, while others stabbed bayonets into bales of dried-out hay. Only their soft grunts indicated the effort they were expending.

Grateful for the sturdy low boots she wore and the sheltering cloak, Lily leaned against a tree trunk, fascinated by the quiet, purposeful scene before her. So this was why the stranger was here.

To help the Patriots prepare to fight the British.

Nothing brought home to her the possibility of war so starkly as this. She knew the northern Colonies were rife with rebellion and that the Quartering Act allowing redcoats to take over people's homes had been extended throughout the Colonies. The royal governor of Virginia went nowhere these days without a company of grenadiers.

And here she was, watching her brother methodically learn tasks associated with the killing of men, placing his future and his trust into the hands of a man she had yet to meet face-to-face.

Fear mixed with a curious excitement ran through her. The cause was not the stranger's easy assurance, his authoritative air of command, his commanding figure. She told herself her eyes were *not* straining to see his hair, pulled back in a neat queue under his precisely cornered hat. She was *not* hoping he would turn around so she could see his features by the fire's glow.

So she told herself, and knew she lied.

Two hours had passed. Lily was growing stiff and tired. How much more tired must the men be. They had scarcely paused, changing tasks when the Patriot leader had a word with them. She recognized most of the men by now—Jack Cameron, many of their neighbors, even Will Evans.

She wondered briefly why Will had gone to work for

that atrocious Squire Sotheby she had met last week but shrugged. Will's parents had been indentured servants once, and even now they only scraped by. A fat, rich Tory probably paid him well.

Startled, Lily rubbed her eyes. Had she dozed off? Only a handful of men occupied the clearing now, and someone extinguished the fire as she watched. She must go as well. Though moonlight dipped silver radiance into the clearing, back amid the pines and oaks, it was dark indeed.

Lily eased away from the tree trunk, moving quietly back onto the path that led out of the woods. Suddenly a hand covered her mouth, while an iron arm encircled her waist. Lily jerked her head, trying to sink her teeth into her captor's hand. "Do you make a habit of attending meetings to which you are not invited?" a low voice said.

There was a thread of humor underlying the exasperation in the deep voice. But though his hand dropped away from her mouth, the restraining arm did not, and he spun her to face him.

Excitement spiked through Lily. His voice could melt icicles, she thought before recalling she should be outraged at such familiar handling. Somehow, she could not summon up much outrage. After all, she *was* sneaking around in the darkness, which surely exceeded even eavesdropping as a social gaffe.

"What do you find amusing, Mistress Walters?"

"I would say your social graces leave as much to be desired as mine, sir," she pointed out. "You are . . . ?"

"No one whose name you need to know."

The abrupt reply irritated her. "Do not think you can come into our lives and disrupt them just because you are a Patriot, sir," she said in a huff.

He touched his finger to her chin, tipping it up toward him as if he could read her expression in the dark. "*Our* lives?" he inquired in a rich voice that flowed through her like honey.

"Mine and Peter's," she managed to say, feeling warmth spread from his touch.

"Ah, I see," he said. The tenuous connection between them vanished when he took away his hand. "So you are your brother's keeper?"

"No!" Lily sputtered. "But Peter is still a boy, and . . ."

"Peter, my lady, is a *man* who handles a musket as well as any in this group." He went on before she had time to wonder about being called "my lady." It had sounded so . . . British.

She had no chance to say anything, because he started striding down the path. He hooked his elbow firmly through her arm and hustled Lily over the forest floor at a remarkable pace.

"Did I mention your deplorable manners?" she asked in a breathless voice.

"I believe you did," he replied. But he did not slow his steps until they were within sight of Williamsburg. Then he eased his pace to a more civilized one she was able to match.

"Stay at home, Mistress Walters," he had the audacity to say. "Peter is safe enough, and soon the time will come when even your devotion cannot help him."

"Why?" Lily asked, but she already knew the answer.

"Because there will be war with Britain."

They were almost at her house. Lily turned to face him defiantly. "What makes you think this war will be fought only by men? Surely you know that the women of Boston have made gunpowder as well as knitted socks? This freedom we seek is not for men alone."

"I said you have spirit, and by God, you do." His tone was one of reluctant admiration. "There will be opportunities for women to contribute, and I am certain you will find them." His voice dropped, becoming stern. "But not now, and not here. Stay away from what I do."

Forgetting they were standing in the street, Lily lost her temper. "Who are you to tell me what I may and may not do? You have not even told me your name!"

His name. Somehow, Adam thought, it would be only her first step toward learning all his secrets. He looked down at her, this sparkling topaz gem that had cast its light across his path. She was independent, no doubt about that, and possessed everything that attracted him most about Americans: courage, tenacity, and candor.

But those very attributes could put him in jeopardy if this little wench got her way.

He could not pretend he was indifferent to her, and just then he was not in the mood to try. Adam captured her chin with one hand, while the other swept back the hood of her cloak, brushing the softness of her hair. Before he had time to stop the irrational impulse, he kissed her.

He was not sure what he intended, but rational thought fled the moment his mouth touched hers. Her lips were cool and soft. They quickly warmed under his touch, heating his blood. When her lips parted in outrage or surrender, Adam did not stop to determine which. He merely took advantage of the opportunity.

Angling his mouth over hers, he dropped his hand from beneath her jaw to encircle her waist beneath her cloak. He tasted the inner sweetness of her mouth, touching her tongue.

After a brief hesitation, she rose to the challenge, meeting him, her fiery spirit channeled now into passionate exploration. Desire twisted and exploded in him like rifle shot. The urge to repress it died when a tiny moan emerged from Lily's throat.

Pressed against the small of her back, Adam's encircling hands felt her spine begin to soften, her body to flow into his. He tasted the nectar of her innocence greedily, like an insect burrowing into a fragrant bud to absorb its sweetness.

But when her hands crept up to his shoulders and began to caress his neck, he knew she had turned the tables on him. He was in danger of forgetting everything he had to keep secret. Hell, he was in danger of telling her his name for the sheer, selfish pleasure of hearing it whispered from her lips.

Selfish pleasure. The thought brought him back to reality. He silently recited the familiar litany while reluctantly disengaging his mouth from Lily's. *He would use no woman, love no woman, leave no woman. Because a woman, for the sake of her own selfish, heedless pleasure, had betrayed him, his family, his father.*

There was not a female in the world who was worth that kind of pain.

Lily's breath was ragged when he pulled his mouth away from hers. She came back to herself slowly, clinging to him like a vine, before she regained her scattered wits. She felt his arms tighten briefly, as if he did not want to let her go, then drop away.

She stared up at him in the dark. Still cloaked and hatted, he remained a cipher, an enigma he obviously intended she should not solve. He tasted of warmth and strength and pure, unexplored masculine appeal. She knew him by voice and now by touch, yet she did not know his name.

Whereas she was open and exposed to him, her hood pushed back, her hair tumbled down around her shoulders. The moon's reflection in her eyes must have shown him something he did not want to see, something she did not want to give away, not to a stranger.

Too much of herself.

He spoke as if he knew her thoughts. "Do not give up your secrets so readily, fair Lily," he whispered across the few inches of space dividing them, the air warmed from the heat of their bodies. "Not to strangers, and especially not to me."

The space between them widened, vast and cold like the night. Then he was gone.

Lily did not follow Peter again, though she let him know he should stop making up excuses for her benefit. She told herself the reason was not the warning of one deep-voiced stranger.

Spring was full upon them, and with it Lily's busiest season. Alicia Chalmers had contacted her about her forthcoming wedding. Lily was working even now on the meanings underpinning the flower arrangements she planned.

Many clients never asked, but if they did want to know what flowers she used in her bouquets, she gave them a card with both flower names and flower meanings, with her lily insignia written in the corner. Lily did not care what her clients thought, since she performed this work largely for her own satisfaction. She sat now, poring over her notes, various texts she had obtained over the years, the Bible, and other sources of information for the special art that she liked to think made every one of her creations unique, no matter how small or large.

"White lily for purity, white lilacs for youth," she murmured to herself, pushing back a tendril of curling hair from her brow. "Ranunculus: 'your charms are radiant';

China rose for young beauty. For the greenery . . . let me see. Ivy for fidelity and marriage . . . ferns for sincerity."

Peter, entering the shop from the house, overheard her last words. He knew Lily arranged the meaning of her creations as carefully as the flowers themselves, endowing each with an ensemble of meaning as eloquent as any poem.

". . . and lady's slipper for capricious beauty."

Peter heard a small, satisfied chuckle and knew at once what she was working on. Alicia Chalmers's wedding. Perhaps it was best that Lily generally kept these cards for herself.

"Lily, I am going out. I have a small chore to do," he called from the shop doorway. He saw her abstracted nod. Peter breathed a sigh of relief. Absorbed in her work, Lily had not so much as given him a sharp glance. He closed the door quietly and stepped out into the warming sunshine of the March day.

Peter was off to place a message at Raleigh Tavern for Adam. These notes were getting to be a problem. Scrutiny of the activities of those known to be Patriots had increased. Lately Peter often felt he was being watched. Redcoats lounged about street corners, ostensibly keeping public order, but he had felt the stare of hidden eyes.

What Lily had overheard from Alicia Chalmers about hunting down the Sons of Liberty worried him. If only he could find out who the officers were and tell Adam, he would feel he had made a real contribution to their cause. Peter occasionally wondered just what Adam did during the day. They were grateful for his knowledge and his commitment, of course. Any of them would have gladly followed him into battle by now, but there was an aloofness about Adam that for all his cordiality, none could breach.

As long as he continued to train them so diligently at night, Peter really did not care what Pearson did during the day.

Four

. . . these troublesome disguises which we wear.
—John Milton,
Paradise Lost, 1667

This business of disguises was a damned bloody nuisance, Adam thought. He hastily removed the squire's fine clothes and pulled on the stained homespun of an itinerant tinker. He kept the clothes stashed in a hidden compartment of an armoire in his Williamsburg town house. Despite his exhaustion, he had to see if there was a message for him today at Raleigh Tavern, but all he really wanted was a good night's sleep.

This was getting to be a regular refrain. At least the night of drilling provided him with a growth of beard to aid this temporary disguise. Adam stripped off the squire's heavy wig. He rubbed grease into his hair to make it lank and greasy. From the bottom of a low chest filled with blankets, he unearthed the type of worn leather pack a tinker carried.

On his way out the door, his eyes lit briefly on the bowl of scarlet poppies, snapdragons, and greenery that Lily had delivered for the squire earlier that week. He saw a scrap of paper near the edge of the bowl with a lily design in one corner. Her bill of account, perhaps.

Possessed of a sudden and unaccountable longing to
keep a small bit of Lily with him, he stuffed the note into
his pocket. He would give the bill to Will Evans—occupied
with enough tasks to keep him out of Williamsburg all
day—when he returned to Oak Grove later.

Adam let himself out of the town house, bowing and
scraping his way backward from the door in a suitably
fawning manner. "Thank 'ee, yer lordship. Thank 'ee."
No one was there to see, but should anyone passing in
the street observe the scene, it would seem the squire had
received a visit from the tinker to show his wares.

Adam set off down the street at a brisk pace. The
sooner he got this over with, the sooner he could get
some sleep.

Colonel Randolph Ware, British Army, watched the
serving wench called Meg sloshing ale as she moved two
pewter mugs from her tray to his table. The heavy wooden
door pushed open and she looked up to see who left behind the warmth of the spring day for the tavern's cool,
dark interior. Her eyes lit up when she saw the handsome
young student enter.

Ware watched in disgusted admiration as she hitched
her bodice around to better display her ample charms.
She had not done that for *him*. She sighed, causing the
flesh above her bodice to ripple in a way guaranteed to
attract men less devoted to their duty than he—and his
suspect.

He had watched the lad seek out Meg before to deliver
his pieces of paper, and he suspected her eagerness to
please him had little to do with why she had been chosen.
He realized quickly that the wench could not read. Any-

thing given to her to pass on, then, would be safe from prying eyes.

Ware nudged the corpulent sergeant next to him. "That one," he muttered in an undertone, indicating Walters.

"Aye, Colonel, I see 'im," said Sergeant Corcoran of the perpetually red face.

"Call me Randolph while we are here," Ware said in an even voice that belied his anger. They were supposed to be two ordinary fellows there for a drink and a bite at the popular tavern. They were not supposed to look like a British Army colonel sharing a table with an enlisted man in his command.

Yet he feared that the two of them looked just like what they were. Ware was not accustomed to sneaking about; he was a king's man and a senior officer. But he had assumed personal charge of this mission and would see it through. He had not earned his reputation for thoroughness for nothing.

The two men watched in silence as the young man approached the tavern maid with a ready smile and a coin. Meg accepted the missive, tucking the note deep into her bodice. Her look made it plain that she would offer more, but the youth apparently declined. With a nod and a word of thanks, he left.

"Colonel, right in front of us 'e did it," Corcoran crowed. Ware smiled. In the days they had been there, this was the best evidence yet of a Patriot plot. He did not yet know what was in the note, but that would come in good time.

Ware had tumbled to the pattern quickly. The boy was no longer careful enough to cover his actions by sitting down and enjoying a drink before making his move. He had become too used to dropping off messages in this fashion.

An error Ware planned to exploit. Finding out the boy's identity in a town this small should not be difficult. His would be the first arrest in Ware's campaign to break up rebel conspiracies. The youth was a known Patriot sympathizer with suspected connections to the Sons of Liberty. But he could not arrest the boy just yet. Randolph wanted to see who picked up that note. If it was a former army officer named Pearson, he would . . .

Ware veiled his eyes, briefly savoring the sound of the lower-class expression in his mind, aware that the sergeant would enjoy hearing it, equally aware that he would never permit himself to say it aloud. Ware prized his control every bit as much as his former adjutant, the efficient, brilliant, disloyal Adam Pearson.

He would have Pearson's guts for garters. Amid the pain of betrayal, the savage thought comforted Randolph Ware. Drawing and quartering was still legal in the British Army, even if rarely practiced. Should Pearson prove to be a traitor—even now Ware still hoped he was not—he would indeed have his guts for garters.

Adam saw Peter walking down Duke of Gloucester Street and assumed he had just left Raleigh Tavern. There was no point in exposing himself to young Walters again in daylight, so he kept his battered hat low upon his head and lounged against a building on the other side of the street.

When Adam arrived at the tavern a short time later, he deliberately hesitated upon the threshold, as if sizing up the place for prospective sales. In reality he surveyed the room to see if he or Peter were under watch.

Adam's eyes slewed around the room under the battered

tradesman's hat. He saw the unlikely pair in the corner and knew them instantly for what they were.

King's men.

Adam stiffened, stifling a groan. Bloody hell. That wasn't just any army colonel. Of all the capitals in all the thirteen Colonies, what the hell was Randolph Ware doing here?

He withdrew, trying to remain unobtrusive. Since he had seen Peter just a few minutes ago, he knew they had not bothered the lad. No, he thought grimly, Ware was undoubtedly waiting for the man who would pick up that note.

They were all in danger now, and though it was the last thing he wanted, he would have to go to the Walters home. Not only did he need to know what was in the note Peter had left, he had to tell him not to deliver any more. If the British grew tired of the cat-and-mouse game, waiting for him to pick it up, they might seize the note from Meg, who would be easily intimidated.

Back at his Williamsburg residence, Adam pulled off the greasy clothes with distaste. The only good thing to come of the day so far was that he did not have to continue wearing them.

He kicked the grimy pile into a corner, then sloshed water from the ceramic pitcher into the bowl on his dresser. He felt cleansed, if not much refreshed, by splashing the brisk water on his face. He decided to shave and clean his hair as well.

Remembering the soiled clothes, he bent to retrieve them with a sigh. He could not afford to leave traces of his other disguise for his manservant to find.

Adam stretched and yawned. He was not happy about waiting until dark to seek out Peter, but odds were the boy was at his classes by now. No point in increasing the danger by going to his house in broad daylight. The prospect of a nap was welcome, considering how little sleep he was getting. He swore briefly as he cut himself shaving. Dammit, he was getting used to the advantages of the soft, rich life again.

He recalled the hungry look in his former commander's eyes. If Colonel Ware did not know he was there, he must at least suspect it. Adam didn't want to believe he was important enough for his former colonel to come after him personally, but he was afraid he knew Ware too well to believe otherwise.

Some hours later Adam quietly edged his way along the clean packed-earth streets toward the Walters house, keeping to the shadows. Dusk had left purple and peach fingers of light glowing faintly in the evening sky. He let himself in at the garden gate, quelling the ball-and-chain mechanism with one hand so the gate hinges would not creak.

He dropped to a crouch. No need to alert anyone to his presence. He made his way slowly through the garden. He saw the gazebo that stood halfway between the back gate and the house, and headed for it.

Lily was in the garden, sitting in the gazebo on a cushioned bench, enfolded in the peaceful quiet of the garden. Her unbound hair streamed down her shoulders, her cap lying atop the flowers she had gathered in a shallow basket. The serenity was broken only by the sounds of birds descending to roost.

Adam wanted to minimize his contact with Lily for her own safety but knew he could not get past the gazebo into the house unseen.

Lily became aware of someone approaching the gazebo from behind a moment before Adam vaulted the railing.

She whirled and rose from the seat, but the intruder was lithe and powerful.

He moved too swiftly. Before she could complete a turn in his direction, he pinned her against him in a firm but gentle grip.

What was it about Lily Walters that he kept running into her this way? Adam thought. The curves of her body pressed against him. His hand spanned most of her waist, his other covered her tender lips.

"Hush, mistress, I pray you," he said. "I am your brother's friend." Dear God, he hoped she could not feel the desire that ran through him in a rushing wave.

Into the silence fell a trill of birdsong. The mockingbird, who could imitate almost every bird. "And your friend," he said haltingly.

"Strange friends my brother has, sir, to come calling thusly," she hissed in an outraged voice.

"I am a friend of liberty, then, if you prefer." He admired her ability to give such ready vent to her feelings. He was so tired of submerging his own.

"Then why do you deprive me of mine?" she returned. Surprising her, he chuckled. Lily had guessed who it was from the first touch of his hands, but his deep voice evoked in her all the wild, ungovernable feelings of his kiss.

"You," Lily breathed.

"Aye," he acknowledged softly. "I regret approaching you this way, but I seek to assure your safety as well as my own. I must talk to your brother." He paused for a moment. "It seems to be our mutual misfortune to meet in awkward situations."

" 'Tis no misfortune, sir." Lily's voice was a whisper of sound in the scented garden as she spoke the truth.

His lips were very near her ear. He still held her but

not so tightly that she could not flee had she wanted to. One strong hand caressed her waist, while the other lightly touched the curling tendrils of hair near her shoulder.

Lily was intensely aware of his impressive height, the breadth of his shoulders, the iron strength of his arms. The echo of his deep voice seemed still to be trapped inside her, and she swayed as if to let it free.

Stepping back, he released her. " 'Twould not be good for any of us were I to be seen here, Lily," he said in a remote voice. "Or seen by you, for your own safety. You will understand, I hope, that sometimes secrecy is necessary?"

Dropped from heaven to earth so quickly, Lily fought down unreasoning disappointment and straightened her back, keeping it to him as he had requested. "I will fetch Peter," she said, stepping out of the gazebo with her flowers.

The urge to turn and look at him was overwhelming. How could she be so attracted to a stranger, someone she had seen only in shadow, someone who had taken substantial liberties with her person. But her heart sang, and blood raced through her veins like mulled wine, filled with the richness she heard in his voice, and his forbidden, potent appeal.

"Peter," she called, outraged when her voice quavered. But was her outrage at the stranger, for the effect he had on her—or at herself, for her too-swift response?

Five

The Alphabet of Flowers.

—John Donne,
Poems, 1633

"You were observed," Adam said to Peter a few minutes later, his control fully restored once Lily disappeared. They sat down together in the gazebo. "The British could have arrested you, but they probably hoped to catch a bigger fish. I did not retrieve the message," Adam continued. "Now we need another way to communicate."

Peter took the reprimand like a man. They fell to discussing other ways to pass messages. As they talked, Adam toyed idly with a scrap of paper in his pocket. He drew it out to fold and pleat between his fingers, forgetting what he held.

The paper spun out of his hand when a breeze swept the gazebo. As he bent down to retrieve it, both men saw the unmistakable lily design in one corner, gleaming in the gathering dark.

"I see you have one of Lily's vocabularies there," observed Peter. "She doesn't often share those."

"She left it behind," Adam improvised. "I . . . ah, startled her when I entered the garden. What do you mean 'vocabulary'?"

"When Lily makes up a flower arrangement, she does not just place flowers together by hue or shape—although she does that well, mind you," Peter added with brotherly pride. "She also concocts a meaning related to the event or person. For a wedding, for instance, she chooses flowers that symbolize joy and purity and other appropriate emotions." Peter smiled, thinking of the flowers for Alicia's forthcoming wedding.

"Let me see what you've got there." He leaned over. Adam held the paper while Peter read the words.

> Scarlet poppies—extravagance
> Snapdragons—presumption
> Lad's love—jest

Peter looked startled. "Did she give you this?"

" 'Tis not flattering, is it?" Adam asked wryly, deflecting the question.

"No, and I cannot believe she meant for anyone to see it. She is not usually so . . . so . . ."

"So bold as to suggest a client is a laughingstock and a popinjay?" Adam replied, conscious of amusement rising that he could not express. The little minx was making fun of Adair Sotheby, and it did not bother him in the least.

"Well, yes." Peter continued to look troubled, but his explanation gave Adam an idea. Adam slipped the card into his pocket, not wanting Peter to pry too closely into how he had acquired it.

There might be something useful in this habit of Lily's. Adam knew the most common meanings of flowers— anyone who had ever given them to a woman had to know the rudiments. One did not give a debutante red flowers, denoting passion, unless prepared to be called out by an irate father, just as one did not send yellow roses unless one's mistress had been unfaithful.

Unfaithful. He pushed aside the bitter memories, forcing himself to concentrate on the matter at hand.

Could messages useful for his purposes be conveyed through Lily's flowers? He stumbled over one obvious flaw: Notes such as the one he had seen would do little good, for the meaning was revealed in them. Suppose instead . . .

"Peter, what if we had a key or legend for these designs, so that someone receiving a bouquet might find a message in it?" he asked.

Comprehension dawned in Peter's eyes. "You're right. Anyone finding such a key at our house would not think twice about it, since flowers are Lily's occupation."

"A particularly interested client might request one, I assume? The key meanings most important to us, such as signaling for a meeting, or indicating danger, can be hidden in full view among the usual designs common to such bouquets," Adam said.

"What could be more harmless than a vase of flowers?" Peter agreed.

The simplicity of it hit Adam with a welcome sense of rightness. Like his disguise, here was an opportunity to find safety in something so public that no one would bother to seek below the surface. The messages could be hidden in full view.

"Do you know of the new plantation owner in town, a Sotheby fellow?" he asked.

"Why, yes, Lily supplies flowers to his town house every week," Peter said. "But the fellow is a notorious Loyalist. How could Sotheby figure into a scheme to transmit information about the cause for independence?"

"That is how we will communicate, Peter. I have a man

in Sotheby's house." Adam smiled in the near dark at the understatement. "He can tell me what flowers have been placed there. I understand the squire is about to launch himself socially and wants your sister's arrangements for his upcoming soirees at Oak Grove."

Peter nodded. Adam trusted the novelty of the plan diverted Peter from thinking about how Adam Pearson, a Patriot in hiding, would know about the squire's business.

"I think 'twill work," Peter said excitedly. "Obviously Sotheby has some Patriot servant with whom you are in communication."

Adam arched a brow at him, remaining silent to allow Peter to draw his own conclusions. The less Peter knew about Adair Sotheby, the better Adam could protect his secret.

"Oh, I know you cannot say who 'tis," Peter said, evidently realizing Adam planned to say nothing further on that score.

"Lily's flowers would be visible, so that anyone passing by could see them and there would be no suspicion about that," Peter said, reasoning out loud. "Using a Tory's house would mean plenty of British about, but none on their guard. Sotheby's place would almost certainly not be watched. But my sister? Is there any danger to her?"

Adam saluted the lad mentally. He had considered this already, but there was no harm in seeing if Peter had a way around the problem of keeping Lily safe. "Is there no way for her to be unaware?" Adam asked.

"How can there be, Adam, if she is to place certain flowers in her bouquets?" Peter batted absently at an insect. "She will not take advice from me on her craft! Besides, between us, I doubt we know more than half a dozen meanings."

"And those not of the sort we need." Both men chuckled a moment, Peter with feigned worldliness Adam had not the heart to pierce. Something in him ached, though, at the thought of using Lily in this plan. He had also concluded that there was no alternative.

Lily had heard enough. She'd hesitated, wrestling with her conscience. She was eavesdropping, after all. But now she had decided: If they wanted her handiwork to help them, they had best consult her.

Armored in righteous indignation, she approached the gazebo. "My brother is right, sir, I need no advice in my craft," she said boldly.

Instead of reacting with anger, Lily watched Adam lean over the stair to the gazebo and draw her up to stand beside him with easy, untroubled grace. "We do have need of your counsel, Mistress Walters," he said.

When he asked like that, what could she do but acquiesce? "Then you may be sure of my assistance," she said.

"I shall hold you to that, mistress." Lily was put slightly off balance by this gentle flirtation. She did not protest as he led her to the cushioned bench, where he helped her to sit as if she had been part of their conversation all along.

The three of them sat together in the dark while Adam asked about meanings for the most likely messages that they would require: danger, escape, war, meet me, and the like.

"Rhododendron means danger, nasturtium is for patriotism, and yarrow signifies war," she heard herself saying. "I can write these down for you and Peter. I have all the meanings in my head, but there are texts I consult from time to time."

They agreed that an iris, which meant message, would be the signal that there was a meaning within the bouquet.

As before, though, the communication was only one way. They could contact him, but he would contact them only in person, and he had just said that this was dangerous.

What if something happened to Adam, who was all alone? Who would help him?

Six

. . . take my votive glass;
Since I am not what I was,
What from this day I shall be,
. . . let me never see.
—Matthew Prior,
*The Lady Who Offers
Her Looking-Glass to Venus*, 1718

Lily adjusted her stomacher nervously, wondering if anyone besides Peter would think it too low. Were bodices lower here because so many of the women were wealthy, or did it have something to do with political convictions? she wondered a bit giddily. There was Alicia Chalmers, surveying her coolly, her blue silk gown looking as if a strong wind would blow it off her bare shoulders. Not one freckle marred Alicia's white skin.

Lily admonished herself to gain some control of her fleeing wits. If accomplishing her purpose meant feeling drafty, that was a small price to pay.

"Why did you come tonight, Lily?" The voice in her ear echoed her thoughts so precisely that Lily almost jumped. Still, she could hardly afford to do that in her current gown, so she tugged at her shawl and turned to smile at Mary, whose familiar brown eyes and dark hair were so welcome in the crowded room.

"After your parents' soiree, and with Alicia choosing me to design her wedding flowers, I thought I should circulate more," Lily said in what she hoped was an offhand manner.

"But here?" Mary's voice had a lamentable tendency to squeak when she was anxious, but at the moment Lily thought it was the sweetest sound she had ever heard.

"With so many folk following the merchants' decision to boycott British goods, there are fewer social occasions in Williamsburg among . . . ah . . ." Lily licked lips suddenly gone dry.

Mary giggled, dimples appearing in her round cheeks. "You need not fear saying the word that starts with *P* to me, Lily, just because I am a Loyalist, not after all we have been through together. But you are right to guard your tongue among these . . ." Her voice trailed away as she watched Alicia Chalmers glide across the room, interested male eyes following the progress of the willowy blonde the entire way.

"Cats?" Lily suggested softly before pasting on her best smile as Alicia approached. She waited, knowing the next few moments would advance or destroy her scheme to help the Patriots.

"Mistress Walters," Alicia trilled, "how lovely to see you."

"How kind of you to allow Mary to bring me," Lily returned politely. "I must thank your parents."

"Yes, well, since Mary could not find an escort, and it amuses her to bring a female friend, why not?" Alicia said. Lily winced for Mary.

"Lily has been my best friend for years, you know, Alicia," Mary said bravely, ignoring the insult, "and now she is to do your flowers. How lovely that everyone could meet."

"Yes, it is," Alicia said, but Lily could tell her mind wasn't on Mary. "Where is your brother tonight, Mistress Walters?" Alicia continued, the look in her pale eyes sharpening. Lily knew now that Alicia had not been malicious to her because she was interested in Peter.

"I could not have presumed on your invitation to Mary, Mistress Chalmers, by bringing another uninvited guest," she said carefully.

Alicia seemed appeased, but her eyes remained narrowed. " 'Twould have been no bother, Mistress Walters," she said pleasantly enough, but Lily knew there was command rather than charm beneath the friendly facade. "Your brother is always welcome."

The approaching British officer had nearly arrived at Alicia's shoulder. "As your escort or Mary's, of course," she said, then turned. "William dearest, have you met Mistress Hardison?" she said in a voice turned suddenly sugary.

"And her charming friend?" William asked blandly, but his eyes lingered at her bosom, and Lily wished she had not let the milliner talk her into such a fashionably low neckline.

Alicia introduced Lily and Mary to a half dozen British officers, all friends of her fiancé's. Lily was glad for Mary's sake that the men were polite enough to ask her friend to dance as well, but for herself, she tired quickly of the frequent glances at her bosom.

Fortunately, Alicia's fiancé did not ask her to dance, although she encountered William on the dance floor several times with unattractive women, all cousins of Alicia's, according to Mary's whispers between sets. His glances were heated enough to make her blush, yet his behavior remained outwardly proper. Lily steeled herself to remember that if she planned to walk into the enemy camp, she would have to develop stronger nerves.

A voice from behind her called out, "Mistress Walters, Williamsburg's fair florist. What a pleasure to see you here!" The voice was high-pitched and annoying, like the whine of a mosquito.

As Mary's eyes widened and she clapped a hand over her mouth to stifle a giggle, Lily turned, grateful for any distraction from William's intent gaze. She was surprised and oddly relieved to realize the man addressing her was her erstwhile client, Squire Adair Sotheby.

Straightening from the elaborate leg he had made her, she saw his eyes were steady and more intelligent than she remembered from their encounter in her shop some three weeks before. He was tall and at least part of him was well formed, judging from the long legs encased in turquoise silk breeches and white hose.

But there his virtues ended. The rest of his body was large, flabby around the stomach, and his age was indeterminate. His complexion was dead white, coated with face powder. A large black beauty patch on his cheek, and a heavy wig tinged a delicate blue to match the lenses perched on the bridge of his nose, distracted her attention briefly. She muttered some polite inanity.

He took her arm and propelled her onto the floor with more strength than she expected from such a flabby man. About to protest politely, she remembered Alicia's lecherous British fiancé.

Then she realized he was talking to her and she was paying him no attention whatsoever. "I beg your pardon,

Squire," she said politely, smiling up at him with another cheerful smile on her face.

Adam indulged himself briefly in the fantasy of erasing that perfectly adequate, hideously social smile with a deep kiss. Remembering his role, he poked at his spectacles, then pitched his voice up another notch to say peevishly, "I say, I'm complimenting your work, my dear. Those lad's love and snapdragons—was that what they were?— in my town residence the other day. Why, they were simply spectacular."

Adam watched a secret spark lighten her artificial smile until it reached her eyes. There was humor in it but no malice. She thought her little jest well concealed, and knowing how ridiculous his disguise was, Adam did not begrudge her a laugh at his expense. Judging from her uncertainty around the British officers dancing attendance on her, she had little experience in being carefree.

Suppressing the thought that he could easily spend the evening contriving ways to make her smile, he plunged ahead. "Oak Grove is ready for entertaining now, m'dear, and I should like you to provide flowers for all my entertainments there. Time to show this town a little life, I say." Time to enter the Williamsburg social scene, to garner what information he could.

" 'Tis too solemn around here, what with all these rumors of trouble and discord, eh?" Lily moved away from him, as the minuet prescribed.

Then the dance brought her to face him again. "I am at your service, Squire." She smiled at him a bit more genuinely this time. "Three days' notice should be sufficient for me to obtain whatever you require. As long as it is in season."

In season? Adam thought dumbly for a minute, feeling

the blood race through his body in a response beyond the control of his intellect.

"As long as the flowers you desire are in season," she amended, looking a bit askance at him. Did she know what she had said? Adam wondered. It did not bear thinking.

Adam relinquished her at the end of the dance with less grace than he liked, but if he stayed with Lily a moment longer, he would have her out on the terrace and in his arms. Surveying the padding around his middle and below, he thought ruefully that at least the stuff helped camouflage his much-too-primitive reaction to her innocent remark.

A blue-tinted glance at his frame sobered him quickly, reminding him that Lily would hardly want to be in his arms given his present role. As he asked her friend Mary to dance next, he wondered why Lily was attending a Tory soiree, this most Patriot of women.

"Lily, you cannot be angry at me for sneaking out, then turn around and do the same yourself!" Peter faced her, arms akimbo, as she locked the front door behind her some hours later.

"Ah, so you admit you've been sneaking out?" Lily vowed not to lose this round.

"Do not try to put me off the scent. *You* have been out."

"Aye, and what of it?"

"Lily, 'tis nearly midnight, blast it, and you have been out alone. 'Tis not proper."

"I was not alone, Peter," Lily said, brushing by him on her way toward the stairs. "I was with Mary."

Peter lowered his arms to his sides, yet he still looked suspicious. "Then why were you out so late?"

"She and her parents took me to a supper party." Standing on the third step, Lily turned back to brush a kiss against Peter's cheek. "Surely you do not begrudge me an evening's pleasure. Ask Mary, little brother. We did nothing scandalous."

Lily ran up the stairs in a rustle of silk, knowing she dared not risk Peter noticing her gown, hoping she had manipulated the lad into silence. After urging her so often to enjoy herself, he was most unlikely to gainsay her now. She had also reminded him none too subtly who was the eldest. From force of habit, he would not challenge her.

"Tonight was a good opportunity for business, Peter, since my work is becoming more widely known after the Hardisons' ball and Alicia Chalmers's forthcoming wedding," she said from the top of the stairs.

She had not said that to manipulate Peter. It was true. She was too old and too unconventional to be marriage material. Nor did she want to flirt with British Army officers unless she gleaned information from the contacts. To that end she would pursue this course of action and succeed, she vowed.

There was more at stake here than her personal happiness. Silence pervaded the hall as she entered her room. Peter blew out the wall sconces before coming upstairs. She had won this round, but she was sorry she had to lie to her brother. One lie hardly justified another, remembering how upset she had been at learning of Peter's secret activities. But now that she had something to contribute, something to do besides merely arranging flowers, she would not stop until she had learned something useful.

Actually, she already had. Tonight she had learned that the good squire would soon be entertaining and she would soon have easy access to Oak Grove. Peter would be able to leave messages for Adam, and she would not worry about Peter being followed or, worse still, arrested.

Satisfied that her first night's foray into Tory territory had not been in vain, she folded the silk dress carefully away in her clothes press, then quickly readied herself for bed.

Sleep came unwillingly, for some reason. All night she felt the gaze of many eyes upon her. Sometimes they regarded her with knowing warmth. At other times, hard brown eyes stared at her while red-clad arms pressed her up against a wall.

Then somehow she knew that eyes the color of the sea in summer regarded her. They watched her, waiting, for something she could not fathom, could not guess. Swirling helplessly, she followed the steps of the dance like a marionette, moving from one man to the next, unable to distinguish friend from foe.

Seven

O, I have pass'd a miserable night.
— William Shakespeare,
Richard III, 1591

Her fourth evening out this week. Lily sighed, no longer able to appreciate the rich surroundings of the Tory home.

"Are you enjoying yourself, m'dear? You look as fresh and charming as your flowers."

Lily rolled her eyes, while the squire's face moved in a half-smile as if he found her reaction somehow both painful and amusing. Tonight he wore a bag wig tied with a ribbon to match his fuchsia frock coat. Even his ridiculous lenses were rose-colored.

She was no longer surprised to see Adair sail up to her at moments when a British officer became too forward for her taste. He might have perfectly awful judgment in his clothes, but his sense of timing was impeccable.

This was purely coincidental, of course. Why would the squire think a British officer offended her, when she attended these events so often? Inwardly, she merely thanked providence each time it occurred and smiled sincerely at her accidental rescuer.

She had grown used to the squire's crankiness and extravagance. After Sotheby began to entertain, he extended a blanket invitation to her and to Peter. He even made certain to invite Mary, though whether to please Lily or from a genuine sense of kindness she could not tell. She thought he was a kind if odd man under his fussy and crabby exterior, but he took pains to hide it.

"Why does a charming young thing like you look as if you could use a bit of cheering up, eh?" he asked with more insight than she credited him.

"Surely, Squire, you are not so old that you would call me young?" she asked, hoping to deflect a question she had no intention of answering.

"You are only a girl," he said with the upper-class British pronunciation that turned the word to "gel." He sighed heavily, pinching the glasses that rested on his nose. "Besides, 'tis how one feels, fair Lily, and at times I feel as if I have lived enough for two lives," he said. She dismissed the notion that there was something genuine beneath his lighthearted words, yet there seemed to be something bleak in his tinny voice.

Her secure invitation to the squire's soirees, plus knowing she could attend with either Peter or Mary, increased her confidence. Despite his oddities, Sotheby was her favorite person at the Royalist soirees she attended. Tonight was the first time she had been in his house, which was large enough for her flower arrangements to be shown to advantage.

Then there were other evenings when Peter left her at Mary's door and she promptly scurried off without knocking. So far, she had been lucky. Neither Mary nor Peter knew what she was doing. Squire Sotheby had appeared at every Loyalist event she attended, and without knowing why, she felt a sense of safety around him. He was never forward, never looked down her dress, never stared at her in an improper way.

Unlike the man with whom she was currently dancing. She didn't know what it was about William Dodgett, Alicia's fiancé, that unnerved her. Although he did not trespass on the proprieties, she had the feeling he held them in contempt, as if he would cast them aside when it suited him.

He was very careful to lavish attention on Alicia when she was present, but he sometimes appeared at events without her or her parents, and Lily felt his regard on her too often for her comfort.

After dancing with Adair, she moved toward a window. "What is on your mind tonight, poppet?" William approached her as soon as Adair left her to greet another of his guests.

"Where is your fiancée tonight, Lieutenant?" Lily countered, aware of her boldness but exasperated by the man's insinuations.

"She is well, I thank you." So he also intended to avoid answering questions. He took her elbow, steering her away from the window and toward a terrace door that opened onto the back gardens.

"Lieutenant, I do not think . . ."

"Yes," he said, "do not think. Why trouble such a pretty head?" As far as flowery compliments went, she thought, she much preferred the squire's.

Before she could reply to his outrageous statement, they were on the balcony, and the scent of roses drifted toward her as a welcome balm.

"How lovely," she exclaimed, forgetting her company.

"Just like yourself," William slipped in.

Lily was paying him little attention, so entranced was she by the cool garden air mixed with the most beautiful and complex of fragrances. She barely heard his last remark, so she did not immediately react when his hands closed around her shoulders.

By the time she became aware of William's intentions, it was too late. He turned her to face him, and his mouth came down bruisingly on hers. Lily tried to jerk away, but William's grip tightened. "Little tease," he muttered, lifting his mouth from hers, "you know you want me."

His lips fastened on her neck while his hands went to her bodice.

"Stop," Lily said, fear and anger stiffening her body. "Stop at once. You . . . you are affianced."

"Mmm," he agreed against her neck. "What of it?"

Lily tried to bring her hands up to push him away. He dropped the hand that was groping in her bodice, easily gathering her wrists within his hold. His other hand jerked her chin up, capturing it painfully for another kiss.

This time he tried to force her lips apart with his tongue. Lily bit down hard, and he released her with a muttered oath. "You little tart. What do you think you're doing?"

"What are *you* doing?" Lily cried, pulling her hands away when he raised them to his mouth against the pain. "You have a fiancée, Lieutenant, who would not be happy to know of your behavior."

He laughed. "Who do you think she will believe, Mistress Walters? A colonial tradeswoman set on bettering her place in society or her trusted, beloved fiancé?" His teeth gleamed a mocking white in the darkness.

This time Lily's hands moved faster than his. She smacked him hard against the mouth. "You are despicable," she hissed.

He yelped with pain. "You brazen wench!" he gasped. "You are just another tiresome Colonial who does not know her betters. But you will, girl. I will . . ."

Lily stayed no longer. She scrambled over the low railing, dropping the short distance onto the warm, welcoming turf of the garden. Had she remained, she had been about to do far worse than injure William's pride.

The thought of him bent over in pain helped ease her flight through the squire's scented gardens. Her mouth felt bruised and tender and her shoulders ached where he had grasped them too tightly. Despite her distraught state, some part of her registered that Sotheby's garden was not as beautiful as the fragrance had first indicated. Some of the rosebushes bloomed, but many were tangled and overgrown.

After tripping over a tree root that nearly plummeted her into the spiny embrace of a large climbing rosebush, she saved all her attention for negotiating the garden in her delicate dancing slippers.

Twenty minutes later, a coach rumbled up to the side of the river path. Lily had stopped running and was now plodding along the road in her ruined slippers. Her patens had been left behind in her flight, along with her paisley shawl. She turned to flee into the woods.

A familiar voice called out, "Mistress Lily, 'tis me, Will Evans."

Lily let out a deep breath where her side ached. "Thank goodness," she said. "How did you know I left?"

"The squire was bringing you food and couldn't find you. He wondered if you had gone, but we found your things. I didn't think you would leave without your wrap and all, but he was most particular that I should take the carriage and look for you."

Will leapt down from his post, reins in hand. "Climb up, Mistress Lily, I am taking you back to Williamsburg."

"You need not, though I am grateful."

He snorted. "Grateful don't enter into it. The squire

would have my hide if I didn't help you once I found you."

"All right." With a sigh, Lily allowed herself to be assisted to the high coachman's seat. She refused to enter the interior of the coach. She had had enough confinement for one night.

Lily was glad the night hid her features from Will. There would be trouble if she returned to Oak Grove and saw William Dodgett. She would not be able to control her temper, and her favorite mental picture had William writhing in pain from a well-aimed kick.

Then, to her surprise, she found she was shaking.

"Are you cold?" the boy asked her.

"A . . . a little," she confessed, hoping Will would take it for a chill and no more.

"Here is your shawl." Will handed it to her from a small bundle next to him on the carriage seat.

She looked at him, amazed. "How sweet, Will. Thank you."

"Not me. The squire, he can be so peculiar. One minute, he is as peevish as an old maid, then he can turn around and be so generous, it fair takes your breath away. I don't understand him."

He would get no argument from her on that point. Whatever instinct had prompted the squire to send her things with Will on the uncertain chance he would find her on the road was a blessed one. She settled her skirts, pulling the shawl around her. Her only wish at this point was to stop trembling.

Adam saw the look on William Dodgett's face when the British officer returned from the outside terrace. Half-smug, half-chagrined, the callow army lieutenant kept one hand near his jaw, rubbing as if it hurt. It had not taken Adam long after that to figure out that Lily was the woman to put that look there, along with the bruise that was rapidly becoming evident.

Jaw clenched tightly, Adam ordered Will out with the carriage to look for Lily. Though he wanted nothing more than to take Dodgett outside and beat him to a bloody pulp, there were too many reasons he could not. Internally, he cursed each reason as he set about complaining of stomach upset to extricate himself from his guests.

"Dear Mistress Potter, do you have a receipt against colic? I fear I have overindulged this night and am feeling quite weak."

First, as the flabby Adair, he had not the strength to fight a strapping young officer like William May-he-live-in-Hell Dodgett.

"Forgive my rudeness, Master Galt, but I must withdraw for the night. I have a severe indigestion plaguing me."

Second, as a Tory, he would never challenge a fellow Loyalist.

"Please, do not leave early on my account, Mistress Baggott. I would like someone at least to enjoy the evening," he said to a stout lady who was starting to tell others that their host was indisposed and guests should leave.

Third, he could not accuse Dodgett without a witness. If Dodgett had half an ounce of cunning, surely he would have tried to seduce Lily on the dark terrace when no one else was around.

As word of his troubled stomach spread, Adam made his way out of the ballroom, lurching and taking short breaths against his supposed pain. He accepted good wishes for his health, invited his guests again to stay, then headed for the stairs.

Fourth, as a crotchety middle-aged man, it would be unseemly for him to call someone out over a woman in no way related to him and in whom he had no sexual interest. As Adair, that is.

He took the stairs two at a time the moment he was out of sight of those below, stuffing the irritating spectacles into the pocket of his frock coat as he went.

Lily sat alone in her own familiar garden. Moonlight poured down silver radiance on her flowers, giving them a luminous sheen. She had looked in on Peter, who slept quietly upstairs. Restlessness and fear that her unsettled dreaming would return had driven her to seek solace in the gazebo her mother had so loved. She leaned back against the railing, breathing in the cool night air and the scents that drifted through it.

"Are you well?" The words, spoken low and deep, seemed a part of her reverie, as if that voice had somehow found lodging within her.

She was reluctant to break the spell by answering, and even more reluctant to relive tonight's memory. The voice, when it next spoke, was closer. Close enough for her to feel a warm breath near her cheek, to detect a vaguely familiar scent.

"Are you well?" he repeated.

"Aye."

"What is it, Lily?"

Now, where had she noticed that particular scent before? She did not associate it with him.

"I don't want to think about tonight," she replied.

"What did he do?" he asked, his voice resonant with anger.

"How do you know about that?" she countered. Then

she realized where the scent originated, and it made sense that he knew.

"You have been in the squire's home, haven't you? 'Tis how you know."

"What?" He sounded startled.

"You smell of that cologne water the squire uses," she said. "You must be one of his servants. Were you there tonight?"

"Yes," he said guardedly.

"Don't worry, I shan't pry, although I wondered how you knew about me and that . . . that man. I didn't think there was anyone to see."

"Dammit, Lily, you are driving me mad. What did that bastard do to you?"

Her composure vanished. The memory of William assaulting her, his hand pawing at her breast, his harsh breath against her mouth, swept through her in a rush.

Adam vaulted over the railing, dropping down onto the cushioned bench beside her. He gathered her into his arms, pressing her head against his shoulder in a fluid movement.

" 'Tis all right, little flower," he said softly. "Tell me."

"I don't want to. I feel . . . unclean."

She felt the muscles of his chest tighten, although his arms remained gentle around her. "Unless you want me to find him and kill him on the spot, you had best tell me."

"Oh no, you could not do that," she said in a rush of concern. "You might lose your position at Oak Grove."

"Among other things," he agreed. His hand rubbed her back soothingly. "Tell me now," he insisted softly.

"He . . . he kissed me. And he tried to—" She fell silent, embarrassed.

"To touch you?" he asked. The picture that his mind

conjured of Dodgett's hands on her creamy skin filled him
with fury.

"Y-yes." To her mortification, she found she was trembling again. "Oh, I wish I could stop this."

Adam's only reply was to gather her more closely into
his arms. "I will kill him," he said eventually in a tone
that contained only certainty.

"Absolutely not," she replied, her voice muffled against
his chest. Adam began to stroke her unbound hair, not
reacting to her statement in the least. Lily sat up, pulling
away from him, even though her whole body ached to be
enfolded in his comforting embrace. "Absolutely not, do
you understand me?"

"Understand you? No." Something in his tone told her
he was not used to being crossed. "An officer in my . . .
in my employer's house tries to take advantage of you and
I am supposed to let that pass? I think not."

"You are a stranger here, recently hired, and in a pre-
carious position because of your connection to the Sons
of Liberty. I would not dream of letting you jeopardize
all you have come here to accomplish over something
so . . . so insignificant."

"Insignificant? You think your honor is insignificant?
All the better, then, that I should have a high opinion of
it." His teasing tone failed; he sounded furious.

"Your presence here is important for one reason only,
and that is what you are doing for the Sons of Liberty. I
simply do not enter into your calculations."

He was silent for so long, Lily had not the least clue
to his emotions. She saw nothing but shadows and the
hands that held her shoulders. Oh, but not as William had
held them. Not at all like that.

"My calculations," Adam said softly, as if he were talking to himself. "No, you did not enter into them. But that

no longer matters. What matters is that I cannot abide seeing a woman so used."

"You will not fight him, Adam. You must not. I could not forgive myself if anything happened to you on my account." She could think of only one other way to deter him, since her words had had no effect. She leaned toward him. "You can make amends if you must, but they will have to be . . . with . . . with me."

Adam's hands fell away, and for a moment Lily thought she would melt through the wooden floor in a sodden puddle of embarrassment. If Adam did not understand her wildly forward, wholly improper invitation, she could not take the initiative herself. She had already been far too bold.

Adam understood, and for a moment surprise held him paralyzed. Then his body reacted before his mind could leash the impulse. His arms swept around Lily even as his mouth sought her lips, accepting her invitation.

Lily felt Adam's lips unerringly meld with her own despite the darkness. The ugly pall of William's touch receded. Instead, she recalled the night Adam had kissed her in the road. Tonight his mouth caressed hers softly, without pressure, a touch as cool as the moon's silvered radiance.

As she relaxed and leaned into him, his hand smoothed up her back, lifting her hair until his palm found the sensitive nape of her neck. Tilting her head back against his palm, he raised his mouth from hers. "You should not ever have been bruised, little flower."

Had he seen the marks on her arms? Lily stiffened for a moment in panic, until she realized he'd been speaking figuratively. Then his lips found her throat and her head fell back against his cradling palm. She did indeed feel like a flower, opening and responding to his touch.

The kiss grew warmer. So did Lily. Adam's lips trailed along the edge of her muslin nightgown, tender kisses warming her shoulders until her skin felt rosy. His palm rubbing her neck sent exquisite sensations down her back. Strangely, those shoots found deeper root in places she hadn't known existed.

Her breasts brushed his shirt, feeling the heat from his chest beneath. She felt her nipples tighten and a little moan issued unbidden from her throat. Adam's voice continued to rumble indistinctly, murmuring caressing words between kisses on her skin.

He found the hollow of her throat, the tip of his tongue tracing it with such exquisite precision that she found herself arching against him, offering him more. When Adam's hands moved slowly to just under her breasts, she remembered William's groping. Her back stiffened and she jerked away from Adam reflexively.

His hands lowered to her waist, his head lifting until she felt his regard on her face. She wished desperately to have a better idea of what he looked like. "Are there more amends to be made?" he asked in the softest of voices. She did not miss the steel will that underlay it.

For answer, she rested her head on his shoulder, nodding miserably against it.

"Ah," he breathed softly, not moving his hands, although she felt the muscles bunching in his arms. They sat for a while in silence, his hands occupied with nothing other than smoothing her gown against the indentation of her waist while she struggled to forget the touch of other hands upon her. At length, he resumed the soothing stroking of her hair that had so calmed her earlier but made no move to seek the skin beneath the tumbled curls.

After some time he tugged lightly on the ends of her hair. In response, she raised her head. He brushed the barest of kisses across her mouth. "I would still call him out if I could, little flower," he murmured. Reverberating inside him despite his quiet tone were fierce anger and a longing to avenge her.

"I would gladly kill him for making you fear a man's touch, but I cannot. I can only make the 'amends' you suggested." She felt relief when she heard the hint of a smile in his voice at his last words.

"But tonight, I think, is not the time," he said. Adam called on all the restraint he had learned over the years in leashing his passions. Setting her away from him with reluctance, he rose, taking her hand.

She stood. "Will you be able to sleep now?" he asked.

"I think so," she whispered.

"Then we have repaired the worst of the damage. Go now, and I pray you sleep well," he said in that formal tone Lily had heard him use once before.

He vanished back into the night without a trace, as if there had never been a midnight visitor to her silvery garden.

Eight

Though she be but little, she is fierce.
— William Shakespeare,
A Midsummer Night's Dream,
1595

The pace of night drilling stepped up. Adam told himself the restlessness that consumed him was due to the unsettled conditions in Williamsburg—where the haughty royal governor had dismissed the House of Burgesses—and to the rumors of strife in British-occupied Boston. Yet he knew that was not all.

He'd wanted to call William Dodgett out that night two weeks ago. Worse, he had wanted to ease Lily's fears, had been livid that the lively, passionate woman he so desired had stiffened at his touch.

He ached still with the desire to remedy her fears but was tortured by the knowledge that his safety and hers meant she must not learn who he was. With Ware in town and Dodgett's spies everywhere, he could not jeopardize his position.

Logical thinking did little to cool his body's heat when he retired to the squire's comfortable bed each night. Passing her flowers in the downstairs hallway brought vivid memories of the scent and feel of Lily in his arms—and a reminder that when he changed disguises, he had also better remove the squire's scent. The woman had a remarkably keen nose.

Lily also had an uncanny ability to slip under his defenses. He had been aroused at the feel of her in his arms, yet he had also experienced the urge to simply hold her in his arms, to soothe her. He, who had regarded all women as Lilith, the corrupt temptress of that first Adam, had discovered an untainted Eve.

Lily was sweet and untouched, like the apple blossom listed in the flower vocabulary she had written for him. It symbolized temptation but also the pure, fresh joy of spring.

He glanced at the flower arrangement sparkling in the bright hallway. It stood in a Chinese porcelain bowl on the gleaming Queen Anne table in the hall he passed each morning on his way to breakfast. Fortunately, the squire's sloth dictated he rise late. Otherwise Adam would get no sleep at all.

Adam stopped, allowing the tinted spectacles to slip down his nose as he looked more closely at the flowers. The blue iris, the signal of a message, was unmistakable. He had seen Peter just last night, so he knew there was no message from that quarter. He had not seen Lily since the evening he had entered her garden to comfort her. He frowned, wondering what Lily knew that Peter had not. And how she had learned it.

There had been no soirees at his house these past two weeks, partly due to his increased nightly activities, partly because he was on the horns of a dilemma with regard to Dodgett. He did not want to keep inviting the bastard to his soirees, yet he knew Dodgett's exclusion would be a subject of conversation. Despite his dislike of the man, Adam also needed to keep Dodgett in his social circle because he knew the man's mission was to ferret out the Sons of Liberty. Any opportunity to get the man in his cups or to hear him boast could be an opportunity to acquire further information about the army's plans.

He tried to suppress a sense of pleasure that her message gave him a chance to see Lily. He couldn't completely succumb to good humor, of course, as that would be unlike the fussy squire. Adam laid down the damask napkin to signal he'd finished breaking his fast.

After downing the last swallow of tea, he answered Will's question. "Yes, yes, do find out if Mistress Walters can handle both the Chalmers wedding and the reception to be held here the night before it. Well done, Will. I shall be in town tonight, so you may have the evening off."

Adam strode off toward the stables, crop swinging vigorously from one hand before he remembered his disguise. Reluctantly, he slowed his steps to the squire's awkward gait.

Although the day stretched ahead of him, he would tolerate its length because he would see Lily tonight. The anticipation was so strong, Adam knew his defenses were almost breached where Lily was concerned. At the moment he had no wish to repair the chinks in his armor.

In her shop Lily laid moss in shallow water-filled trays to keep it moist. She hummed absentmindedly, thinking about the information she'd acquired. Tonight she would tell Adam and Peter. She wasted little time considering why she had not simply told Peter, then asked him to pass it on to Adam.

She told herself that she only desired to make her own contribution to the Patriot cause. Nor would she admit to herself that she had missed him since the night in her garden when he'd held her with such tenderness. Her damp palm holding the moss prickled in a sudden thrill of anticipation. This time thoughts of William Dodgett did not spoil the tingle of desire.

Lily chided herself for such giddiness. She had important information to impart. That was all. When she left her shop to deliver flowers, even the sight of Jack Cameron's daughter glaring at her could not dispel her good mood.

The redheaded daughter of the Sons of Liberty leader had always been a friend to her, but this morning she did not acknowledge Lily, even though they both entered the apothecary at the same time. Lily followed Amy outside after the redhead finished her business.

"Amy, what is the matter?" she asked.

Amy turned, astonishment written across her piquant features. She was even more petite than Lily, odd considering her great bear of a father. "I cannot believe you are so bold to ask, Lily Walters," she sniffed, adjusting her straw basket over one arm, then moving away.

Lily caught up to her, carefully keeping the remaining bouquets in her arms from shifting. "We have always been friends, Amy. I know nothing that I have done to offend you. But I would know the cause."

"I hear that you have been going to Royalist soirees and dancing with redcoat officers." Lily knew Amy had a *tendre* for Peter. Perhaps Amy thought she was being disloyal to her brother.

"And?" Lily inquired, struggling to keep her voice even. "What business is that of yours?" She could have phrased that more politely, but she was increasingly irritated with the other girl's judgmental attitude.

"You have apparently been having quite the best time." Amy's brown eyes flashed indignation.

"I go to these affairs in order to keep up my business."

"You need not dance with Loyalist fops, laughing and smiling," Amy returned.

Lily laughed. The picture Amy's words conjured up was so absurd. "You mean that ridiculous man Squire Sotheby? Have you seen him up close?"

"No," Amy said, looking down as she scuffed the toes of her shoes in the dirt.

"I have, and I can assure you there is nothing attractive about him. Why, he must be forty if he's a day, he wears silly wigs and face powder, and he is as big around the middle as a horse. Really, Amy, you are being ridiculous." Lily's laughter escaped again, causing several heads to turn as other women out doing their morning shopping passed them on the street.

"You may laugh, but there are others, I hear."

"Others?" Lily heard the uncertainty in her own voice and notched her chin up higher.

"Young British Army officers," Amy said slyly.

"If you go to one of these assemblies, you have to dance. A social courtesy, that is all." Lily kept her voice firm and matter-of-fact. If someone gossiped that she had been alone with William Dodgett on the terrace, she could forget the wedding commission from Alicia. Besides, Amy had said "officers," not "officer," so surely she was casting her net in the dark.

Lily did not want more tongues to wag. "I have a business to run, even if I do not like the fact that the Loyalists are more given to entertaining than those who observe the boycott. I cannot force Patriots to hold entertainments just because I prefer them and their politics."

"I hope that's all there is to it," Amy said ominously.

"Do you have reason to doubt my word? Are you speaking for your father or yourself, Amy?"

The slender girl tossed her auburn braid. "For all of us," she said cryptically. Then she lifted the hem of her blue-sprigged cotton dress and crossed the street. Lily looked after her for a minute, noticing that she herself had attracted a lot of attention. Even though she was accustomed to little more than brisk courtesy—few women were in trade, after all—some of the looks in her direction were frankly hostile.

She reminded herself that she was helping the Patriot cause. If she had to attend Loyalist events and pretend interest in vapid British officers, she should expect people to question her loyalties. She just had not anticipated how much it would hurt.

Rainfall pattered on the roof at dusk as Lily went to the gazebo. Perversely, she insisted Peter accompany her. She had been forward enough.

"Lily, why did you drag me all the way out here?" Peter complained.

"You said you wanted to help."

Peter sighed. "I do not mind helping you plait the frames for your baskets, but there is no reason to do it out here in the rain."

"Your friend will not come if we are inside," Lily replied.

"What makes you think that?"

"Has he not prevented anyone from seeing him?"

"But . . ." Peter began. He stopped curving the damp reeds she used to weave baskets. "Wait, I believe you are right, Lily. After I met him on the edge of town that first day, I've seen him only at night. He usually wears a cloak and hat then, so I am not sure anyone else would recognize his clothes, much less his face. He must intend it that way."

"If you do not curve these while they are wet, they will be of no use," Lily said, reaching a hand toward Peter. So her brother *had* seen the mystery man, but Peter realized he had another secret to keep. He would not describe Adam to her now. She closed her eyes, struggling to master her impatience.

Someone took the lengths of curving reed from her hand. "Peter! What are you—" She stopped when she became aware that the hand covering hers was not her brother's. Adam's arm brushed her shoulder as he leaned over her from behind. She caught a trace of his masculine scent.

"You are remarkable," she muttered with annoyance but made no move to pull her hand out from under his. He squeezed her hand but did not speak.

"You do come and go rather quietly," Peter remarked.

Adam chuckled. Lily had no defense against that voice. She fought to keep from brushing her cheek against his arm like a cat seeking a caress.

"I would not still be alive had I not learned to move like an Indian," Adam said.

"Were you in the French and Indian War, then?" Peter asked.

"Aye, as a very young, very green lieutenant." Lily sensed rather than saw Adam's restless movement behind her. He did not want to talk about his past.

Echoing her thoughts, he bent down until his nearness drove all thought from her brain. "Distract your brother from this topic, little flower," he breathed into her ear too low for Peter to hear. "We have other business tonight than the past of Adam Pearson."

Did he know he had gifted her with his name? Excitement lanced through Lily. The topic of his past disturbed him and his careful control had slipped.

"Quickly, Lily, I do not wish to forget we are with your brother." He straightened, his fingertips brushing her cheek and lips before he withdrew. The intimacy of the gesture, coupled with the knowledge that Peter sat five feet away, brought a hot blush to her cheeks. A renewed wave of longing washed through her.

Lily cleared her throat. "Peter, what I wanted to tell you and . . . and your comrade"—she paused, reminding herself not to use Adam's name—"is that the redcoats plan to withdraw the ammunition from the magazine. They fear the militia might seize it in case of an uprising against the Crown."

"The governor has agreed to this?" Peter asked, his voice incredulous.

"I believe 'twas the governor's idea," Lily said. "You have seen how he has surrounded himself with British Army troops. He fears the mood of the people."

"As well he should. He has earned no loyalty at all by his behavior," Peter said.

" 'Twas never wise for us to count on being able to steal it," Adam said. "I've been concerned about that for some time. A ship will arrive at Yorktown soon. If the governor intends to load the ammunition onto it, perhaps we can stage a raid."

"May I help find out?" Lily asked.

"If it means partnering more redcoats in dance, certainly not," Adam said instantly.

"But Mary is always with her," Peter said. "I cannot think Lily will come to any harm."

Adam was silent a moment. Lily's heart raced, wondering if he knew about the soirees she had attended alone. Some had not included the company of very respectable

women, although she had been very careful after the incident with William.

Adam seethed with the desire to shake some sense into
Lily once he realized she had been out at night without her
brother's knowledge. That did not surprise him too much,
for he knew Lily took full advantage of being the eldest.
Peter was not really in a position to tell her what to do.

But, dammit, neither was he. The knowledge galled
him. He could not betray his knowledge that she went
about unchaperoned, because he saw her only as Adair.
With her belief that he was a servant in Sotheby's household, he would have no reason to know about any activities
outside Oak Grove.

"No," Adam said firmly. "She may not seek to learn
more about this. I will not have her taking risks. We have
the flower vocabulary. That is quite enough from Mistress
Walters."

How she hated it when he became so clipped and British sounding! "That is enough," Lily said, rising. "I will
tolerate no interference with my activities, nor will I abide
being addressed through my brother as if I am not here."

"Lily," Peter began, a pleading note in his voice.

"Walters," Adam interrupted. "Your sister may be as
independent as she likes so long as her activities do not
jeopardize my mission." He knew he was going to infu-
riate her with his high-handedness, but she had left him
no choice.

"When those activities become a threat to the Patriot
cause," he continued, "then I require every Patriot, man
or woman, to cease. Without exception." Would she accept
the concession he had offered, his acknowledgment that
she was contributing to the cause?

No, it had been too much to hope for. "Until I am a
member of the Sons of Liberty," she said, her voice trem-

bling with emotion, "I do not do your bidding." With that, she swept down the gazebo's steps, heedless of the rain. The distinct slamming of the back door a few moments later could be heard.

"Forgive my sister, Pearson." Peter's voice was anxious. "She has a will of her own."

"I know," Adam said ruefully, "and were she a man, I would cherish her adherence to the Patriot cause. In this case I wish she had more of the timidity usual to her sex."

Forcing his mind back to the reason for his visit, he and Peter prepared the outline of a strategy that both agreed Lily was never to know about. Or so they hoped.

Nine

Necessity hath no law.
—Oliver Cromwell,
To Parliament, 1654

"Do you mean to tell me you have made no more progress than that?" Colonel Randolph Ware exploded in pent-up frustration at the young lieutenant facing him in the study of the house he'd commandeered under the Quartering Act. This Williamsburg operation had Pearson's mark all over it, Ware thought—seriousness, secretiveness, professionalism. But which side was Pearson on?

He knew better than anyone how Pearson operated. He had been Adam's commanding officer in 1759 when General Wolfe had ordered British troops to climb the cliffs below Quebec. A fifteen-year-old youth had grown up in one grim night, the decisive battle of the French and Indian War. Pearson's leadership of his company had surpassed Ware's expectations. He'd sought to have the younger man under his command ever since. He had acted almost a parent to the lad, considering the circumstances under which Pearson had joined the British Army.

He did not want to believe that Adam had truly gone over to the Colonial side. Ware had come all the way from Boston to find his missing officer, wondering what had gone wrong with the mission to infiltrate the patriots of Boston. Pearson's activities in Boston had been approved, dammit, but this wasn't.

Why hadn't he heard from Adam since he went secret? Surely he had not taken their Patriot drivel to heart and actually become one of them. It did not bear thinking.

The lieutenant before him had a difficult mission, and he lacked Pearson's wit and drive. Frankly, Dodgett was an idiot. "You have not been able to penetrate the group," Ware said.

"No. Sir, I . . ."

"You have not been able to follow the men to their meetings," he went on implacably.

"No, Colonel. Sir, I . . ."

"You do not even know where they are held."

"No, sir."

"Or who they are."

"No, sir."

"What have you done, then, Dodgett?"

"Sir, these Colonials are a tight lot, and they do not give up information freely. I have not learned a single useful thing in the time I have been here."

"You are getting married, are you not?"

"Er, yes, Colonel." Dodgett looked puzzled.

"Unless you want to spend your honeymoon in India, Dodgett, I had best see some progress from you and your men. After six delightful years in London, I hardly think your bride, or her well-off parents, would care to see their daughter shipped off to that distant, disease-laden land." Ware studied the pearl-handled letter opener in his hand, satisfied that his threat to the ambitious young social climber would motivate him better than fear of a bad performance rating.

"Now," he said, summoning a semblance of affability, "what have you learned from the tavern maid?"

"No one came to pick up that note, sir. In fact, the note itself seems to have disappeared. My men searched her thoroughly." Dodgett smiled.

"You mean someone bedded her."

"Er, yes, sir."

"Do try not to get the clap before you marry, Dodgett. 'Tis bad form to go to one's marriage bed in such a condition."

Dodgett's fair coloring suffused an angry red. Ware silently dared him to take him on. He was itching for a fight.

" 'Twas not I, sir," the young man said tightly.

"Good. Glad to know your brains are not entirely located between your legs. Now, has there been any further traffic with the tavern wench?" Ware tapped his immaculate fingernails against the sharp point of the letter opener.

Dodgett composed himself with an effort. "No, sir. No one has approached Meg, er, the woman. From the reports I have received, she has rather wondered about it herself."

"And the boy?"

"Sir?"

"The Walters lad, who brought the message to the tavern."

"Sir, he goes to classes at the college, meets with like-minded friends at the tavern, and engages in seditious political discourse there. Of course, they think they have their freedom here. I have found nothing out of the ordinary otherwise about his behavior, sir."

"What about the sister?"

"Sir?" Dodgett sounded alarmed. Christ, Ware thought in disgust, if the lieutenant was trying to seduce every available maid, he would be lucky to make it to the altar at all. Ware had given him one warning. He would not get another.

"I mean," Ware enunciated precisely, "do you think the sister knows anything about her brother's activities? Does she carry messages for him, that sort of thing? The rebels might have found a different courier if they spotted your men's surveillance. Few would think a woman involved."

Dodgett wore an almost palpable air of relief. "The odd thing is, sir, she spends more time with Loyalists than with the rebel riffraff her brother frequents."

"Oh?" Ware's mind engaged the situation swiftly. The sister frequenting Loyalists could mean two things. Either there was friction with the brother that might be exploitable, or she was a spy for the Patriots, who thought a woman's activities would go undetected.

"I want her followed, Dodgett. Unobtrusively, mind you. She might be the clue to their activities. Remind me what it is she does."

"She owns a flower shop, sir. Her business takes her all over this colonial burg. Her clients are both Loyalists and rebels. She goes to many Tory homes. Of Patriot entertainments, of course, I cannot say," Dodgett finished stiffly.

"She certainly has the opportunity to work for the rebels, since she moves about so much. Very well, then." Ware interjected a note of brisk dismissal into his voice. "Have her followed. But discreetly, mind you."

Dodgett saluted, turning smartly on his heel to leave. "And Dodgett? Keep your hands off the girl," Ware called after him. "She will only become wary of you."

Judging from the dull red flush spreading above

Dodgett's collar, Ware thought his warning might already be too late.

Damn. Perhaps he needed to become involved himself. He had largely remained out of view since his arrival, trusting Pearson's senses to remain as keen as ever. He had not wanted his treasonous officer to know he was here. Dodgett's lack of progress caused Ware to rethink his approach.

He cursed Pearson's defection once again. *Adam, why have you left me to deal with idiots like these?* He slammed the letter opener into the blotter, watching its point quiver, embedded in the rich green felt.

"This is the plan." Adam spoke to the men who had assembled inside the barn the night after he asked Peter to pass the word. The building offered some protection against the spring rains that had continued on and off for nearly a week, but he was glad he had a snug, dry bed waiting at Oak Grove. Lonely, perhaps, but dry.

Damn, he hadn't noticed loneliness in a decade. He would not surrender to it now. A part of his mind wanted to reach out for Lily, but he suppressed it. He could afford distraction now less than ever.

"The ship to receive Williamsburg's ammunition docks in Yorktown Thursday night," he said, his voice rough. "An evening's entertainment is planned at Squire Sotheby's." The good squire would simply develop indigestion again. " 'Twill occupy many of the redcoat officers sent here. Unfortunately, not all. There will also be a contingent of marines aboard ship to guard the stores when they arrive. Surprise remains the essence of our plan. If they are expecting trouble, we will lose the advantage of surprise and most of our ability to seize the ammunition."

The night passed in a haze of plans and debate, even some outright opposition. Cameron handled those objecting with a combination of bluff and sheer Scots cunning. There was much less opposition than on the night Adam first arrived, however, for which he was thankful. Drilling together had instilled a greater sense of unity in these independent Americans, and Adam had used it to cement his leadership.

As he knew from his army days, accepting the responsibility of leading men into a fight during which they might die was a heavy burden, one he took seriously. He asked a militia leader, the German-born minister Muehlenberg, to lead the group in prayer at evening's end.

Then he returned to the squire's sumptuous bed at Oak Grove, conscious as never before of the cold elegance that permeated the place. It reminded him too much of Dalby Hall, his ancestral home. His gut tightened at the thought. Was he becoming the Earl of Dalby, the title he had rejected, the life he loathed?

No, a thousand times no, he answered himself. He might not know how to transform a house into a home, but he knew who did. Every time Lily was here, the place sparkled, reflecting her liveliness, her warmth.

All his suppressed emotions rose to meet the challenge of her verve and joy in life. She would never be like his mother. She would not betray him. He knew that with a certainty that banished the worst of his ghosts.

Yet he was restless, throwing back the sheet and going to pace by the window in his detested nightshirt. He still could not woo Lily. Not as the fop Adair, and not as the fugitive Adam.

He had found the first woman he had ever wanted to

offer anything real of himself. How much, he did not know. Yet he could not even court her.

Adam cursed his many identities. He'd thought they would protect him. Now they had become his prison.

As they finished a light supper at home, Lily sensed Peter's suppressed excitement. It had to be related to Adam's plan, and that plan must mean preventing the ammunition from being loaded onto the British ship. As she prepared to go to Sotheby's for the first time since the night Dodgett had forced his attentions on her, she wondered how she could find out what Adam intended. None of the British contacts she had made indicated anything so extraordinary as resupplying the garrison—but then, they were hardly likely to mention it to her.

The very fact that Sotheby had planned one of his soirees, which were invariably large and lavish, suggested that nothing would happen tonight. Half the British officers and most of the Loyalist citizens of Williamsburg turned out for these events. Yet her uneasy feeling persisted.

A few minutes later she climbed into the carriage that pulled up outside their house. Because her secret outings had almost been revealed under Adam's probing the other night, she had asked Mary if her parents would mind collecting her.

Mary's father had not minded at all. He gallantly offered her a hand into the interior as Lily gathered her yellow satin dress in her other. He and Mistress Hardison had become noticeably warmer since Lily's forays into Loyalist society. After Peter had seen her safely enter the coach, he darted back inside the house as if he couldn't wait until she left.

The strangeness of the evening persisted even after they pulled up outside Oak Grove. Once inside, Adair was nowhere to be seen. Nor was William Dodgett, thank goodness.

"Mary, are there as many British officers here as usual, do you think?" Lily asked as they walked together toward the punch bowl.

"Well, of the lieutenants, I see Henry Speedwell, Charles Harvey, Robert Nelsonhurst, umm, and Everard Smythe. Then amongst the majors, there's Edward Simley, St. John Graham, Harry Hart—"

"Enough," Lily said, laughing. "Goodness, Mary, have you memorized them all? I do not want to know if everyone is here, just whether 'tis the usual number."

Mary peered over the edge of her silver punch cup. "I really do think so, Lily. Alicia Chalmers and her family are not here, so perhaps that is why William is not. Oh, and there is someone new. A colonel, how distinguished."

Lily had not realized how much Mary longed for masculine attention until she heard the wistful recitation of names. "Look, Mary, he is coming over here," she said. "Perhaps your prayers will be answered."

"Shush," Mary replied, but she perked up and looked a little brighter. Mary's father saw him coming and moved in to make introductions.

"Colonel Ware," Philip Hardison said, "allow me to present my only daughter, Mary. Mary, Colonel Randolph Ware."

Mary blushed becomingly as the colonel gallantly bent to kiss her hand. He smiled at her, then turned to Lily. "And her charming companion?"

Mary's father looked a bit put out but introduced Lily politely enough. Lily saw a bald spot on the colonel's blond head as he bent to kiss her hand. All amused thoughts fled, however, when he raised his eyes. She felt like a butterfly caught in a collector's net. His eyes were pale blue, very intelligent, and cold as ice.

"Mistress Walters," he said in a clipped British accent, "how are you this evening?"

"I am well, sir," she replied warily. There was something about his penetrating look that put her on guard. As if realizing it, he relaxed the intensity of his gaze. "Have you seen our host this evening?" he queried the small group standing near him.

"No," Mary plunged in with none of her usual shyness. " 'Tis passing strange."

"Why is that?" he inquired, his eyes scanning the ballroom as if looking for someone.

"The squire is very fond of entertaining. Often he does not stay late, but he is always here at the beginning of the evening and he always urges everyone to stay after he retires. He has a bad stomach, you know."

"Does he?" the colonel asked absently.

"Perhaps he retired earlier than usual and greeted only the first few guests. Or he could have . . ." Mary chattered on, oblivious of Lily's discomfort and the colonel's inattention.

Upstairs, Adam locked his door and stripped off his gaudy clothes hastily. Sweet holy saints, he had almost walked into the ballroom and found his former commanding officer there. When he invited the whole British garrison, he had not expected Ware to accept.

He knew Ware was here, of course, since seeing him that day at Raleigh Tavern. But the colonel's profile had been so low since then, Adam unwisely assumed he had returned to Boston. Adam pulled on one leg of his breeches, glanced down, and saw they were vermilion. He swore. Wrong clothes.

He kicked the squire's silks aside. Yanking on black breeches and black cotton stockings, he pulled his dark cloak out of the back of his clothes press. Familiar with the way down, he lowered himself out the window, ready to jump to the kitchen roof beneath. From there he would walk over the roof until climbing down near the stables at the rear of the house.

He had no time to worry now what Ware's appearance at his soiree meant or why Dodgett had not shown himself. A yearning to see Lily flickered, along with guilt that she had been kept in the dark about the raid, then he set it aside. Later. Matters of the heart could wait; they always had.

He muffled his horse's hooves to avoid alerting the coachmen waiting outside for their employers. When he reached the grove outside town, he pulled off the horse's socks and rode the hunter hell-for-leather toward the rendezvous point.

Ten

In darkness, and with dangers compass'd round . . .
      —John Milton,
      Paradise Lost, 1667

Circulating around the ballroom, Lily searched for Adair, also looking for an excuse to escape the cold-eyed colonel. She wondered what Squire Sotheby's absence meant. Someone recounted the story of his digestive problems. She had not known about his delicate stomach because that was the night she had fled Alicia's fiancé. This was the first party the squire had held since then.

Concerned for him in spite of his peculiarities, she left the ballroom while the too-observant Colonel Ware was engaged in conversation with someone else, heading toward the kitchen and servants' area, where she hoped to find Will Evans.

Low sounds from the billiards room, the last room before the service area, diverted her. Could the squire have fallen ill in there alone?

The room was bereft of light. At the last moment before she crossed the threshold, she realized there was more than one man inside. "The game's afoot, George," a voice exulted from the shadowed interior. "This is the night the rebels are run to ground." A Tory, perhaps an officer.

Lily drew back cautiously, hoping her skirts had not rustled. "How d'ye know?" asked another man with a scratchy voice. "Ware is here."

"Aye, but 'tis only to preserve appearances. He wanted to meet this Squire Sotheby anyway, see if the man can be any help to him. 'Tis Dodgett who is in charge of the ambush."

"But some of his men are here," the scratchy voice said.

"Aye, 'tis all part of the colonel's plan, to allay suspicion. A group from my company was sent on ahead earlier this week to Yorktown. We swapped men, rather unorthodox I know, but Ware's keen to foil any word that we planned to ambush the Colonials."

"I thought the colonel was put out that nobody had infiltrated them."

"He was, fair blistered Dodgett's pink arse. The colonel's a smart one," the British officer said admiringly. "He took the chance, and I think he was right. One of my men tells me a quick check of the taverns shows hardly a man in them tonight. The colonel is convinced they will try to seize the stores when they arrive at Yorktown, not when leaving Williamsburg."

Lily waited to hear no more. A trap! Colonel Ware was in charge of the operation against the Sons of Liberty, not Lieutenant Dodgett. She moved quietly toward the back entrance to the large central hallway.

Fortunately, it had been left ajar to admit air to cool the heat from hundreds of candles. She slipped out the huge paneled door without a sound, grateful once again that her lamentable habit of eavesdropping had done some good.

But her temper quickly rose. She'd been left out again. Fear for Peter and Adam forced her to suppress her injured pride. The men were riding toward an ambush. Lily stumbled on the last step down to the garden, tearing her dress on the pebbled path and skinning her knee.

How was she to get out of here? Certainly she would not be allowed to commandeer the Hardisons' coach.

The stables. She would take one of the squire's horses.

Lily limped toward the stables, heedless of the stinging scrape on her knee. She took a lantern from its hook outside the stable door. Neighs and pawing greeted her entrance. The horses seemed agitated. She found a mare she had seen Will riding on his errands in town, a tall chestnut with clean lines and a good-natured disposition.

Throwing a saddle over the mare's back and cinching it tight, Lily blessed her father for teaching her and Peter to ride equally, without the confining convention of the lady's sidesaddle. "What your mother does not know cannot hurt her," she remembered him saying as he positioned her atop the pony's back.

Cloakless, bedraggled, and possessed of desperate haste, Lily nevertheless remembered to keep the well-trained mare at a walk until she reached the dirt road beyond the squire's raked gravel pathways. Then she urged the fleet horse onward, plunging onto the road toward town.

The crescent moon had already risen. She headed for the clearing where she had seen the Sons of Liberty train. "Please, let them still be there," she prayed aloud. There were too many paths to Yorktown. She had no certainty she could find them, especially if Adam knew Indian ways. If they were dressed in dark clothes and traveled silently, she might even pass them unaware. She could hardly ride the roads shouting "Ambush."

The mare took the bit with alacrity, her long strides eating up the ground between Oak Grove and the clearing. Lily slowed her to a trot, then a walk as they entered the dark pine-strewn confines of the woods. Not even a hint of banked firelight flared. Lily was in the clearing before she realized it was empty. She smelled no heat from recent fires, nor detected any trace that men had been there recently.

Dejected, she turned the mare toward town, allowing her to pick her own way out of the forest. Once back on the path, Lily urged the horse into another gallop, although she knew in her heart it was useless.

Where else to look? The Sons of Liberty would not be gathering at her house. Adam's sense of security had taken care of that after the first night. She did not know where else they met. One last, fleeting hope occurred to her.

Jack Cameron's farm lay near Williamsburg. She had long ago guessed he was the leader of the Sons of Liberty. Perhaps Amy or Mistress Cameron could tell her.

She pulled up at the farmhouse a few minutes later. Throwing the panting animal's reins over a low-hanging magnolia bough, she boldly pounded at the door.

Mistress Cameron peered out, her face apprehensive in the light of the candle she held aloft. "What is it?" she said. "Oh, 'tis you, Lily Walters. What do you here so late of an evening?"

"Mistress Cameron, I am looking for the Sons of Liberty. Have they been here this evening?"

A second circle of candlelight spilled out of the entrance to the farmhouse. Amy's flame-red hair gleamed. "Do not be telling her anything, mother."

"Mistress Cameron, Amy, this is a terrible situation," Lily pleaded. "The men are riding into a trap. The British know they plan to steal the ammunition before it is loaded onto the ship at Yorktown."

"How would you know that? From your British friends, I suppose." Lily watched with despair as Amy's bitter words had their intended effect on her mother.

"They are not my friends," she protested. "If they were, do you suppose I would be here now?"

" 'Tis only Peter you care about," Amy accused.

"Please, you must believe me. Everything I have done has been to further the Patriot cause. I would never betray my brother, or any of them. Please."

Mistress Cameron spoke at last. "I believe you, child. 'Tis not my place to judge. I fear 'tis too late though. They left an hour since."

"An hour?" Lily said in dismay. "They will have reached Yorktown by now. Do they mean to act so soon?"

"Aye." The older woman sighed heavily. "They were thinking that the sailors would have their grog with dinner, their reward for a smooth passage. Waiting until the dark o' the moon to strike would see the sailors sober by then."

"I see. Thank you, Mistress Cameron. You too, Amy. I . . . I shall go home now."

Margaret Cameron reached out a work-worn hand toward her, her Scots accent stronger in her compassionate voice. "Would ye be wanting to bide a wee with us, Lily? Ye need not stay alone this night."

A portion of Lily's despair lightened at the invitation. "You are very kind, mistress, but I had best go home. Peter would not know where to find me." She did not speak aloud her fear that Peter might not return at all, but Mistress Cameron nodded.

"I understand, lass. Go wi' God."

"Take care," Amy added grudgingly.

Lily mounted the mare and rode slowly away from the Cameron farm. Her urgency was no less, but the mare was winded. Besides, there was no one to warn now. The trap would be sprung long before she reached Yorktown. Only a night of waiting lay ahead of her now.

Adam knew the precise instant they rode into a trap. The party had been moving as quietly as possible, weapons wrapped in women's shawls or blankets to avoid the chink of metal against wood. Sound carried a long way in the dark.

The sound of owls hooting tipped him off. It was an old Indian trick, learned by the British at great cost. The Indians had used it to communicate with their French allies in the French and Indian War, ambushing the British successfully on numerous occasions.

"Cameron," he called softly to the man riding just ahead of him.

Jack slowed his gait to let Adam pull abreast. "Aye?"

"They are on to us. We must turn around," he said in an urgent voice.

"Why?" Cameron started to ask. Adam heard the modulated note in the bird call. Too late.

"Back!" he shouted. " 'Tis a trap! Retreat!"

The woods came alive suddenly with soldiers running toward them on foot, clad in clothing as dark as the night.

Adam allowed one fleeting moment of admiration for his foe. Ware, the man from whom he had learned unconventional tactics, had done it again. Left to himself, Dodgett undoubtedly would have kept the British in their scarlet uniforms and disdained the element of surprise.

Spooked by shouts and grabs at their bridles, most of the Patriots' horses unseated their riders. The British, it seemed, wanted the animals and the men alive, for he heard no gunfire. But Adam had taught the Patriots a few things, and their dark clothing helped them melt into the forest, once unhorsed. Adam had also taught them when to retreat. Without the ammunition there was nothing here worth loss of life. They were irregulars still, not yet at war with the British.

Adam yanked back his mount the moment he gave the order to retreat. He would not leave without accounting for every man, but he needed to keep his seat to see the terrain better.

Peering intently through the dark, he reckoned that enough shadows had passed to account for every man but two.

He prayed one of those was not Peter Walters. Muffled sounds of struggle to one side alerted Adam. He looped his horse's reins over a tree branch, then dismounted and ran forward, a knife clenched between his teeth Indian-style.

He heard a dull thump, then the unmistakable sound of a body hitting the ground heavily. In the dark he could not tell where his enemy was, then he heard a muttered curse.

"Damn. Did you 'ave to crown 'im? They are all supposed to stay alive."

"Fought like a right bastard, he did," came the other voice, justifying his actions. "C'mon."

Adam leapt in the direction of the sounds. He took one man down with him, but the other stood a little distance away. The pistol retort roared in the night, its powder flash briefly illuminating the night. In the flare of light Adam saw Peter Walters slumped against a tree.

That was all he saw before the ball caught him in the arm. Adam had just enough presence of mind to fall into a tangle of bushes. He crawled beneath it. Quiet descended on the woods except for the harsh sounds of labored breathing in his ears. His own.

"C'mon, colonial, give it up," a voice called into the still, dark night. "If I bring you in alive, the colonel will overlook that I shot you. Do not make me find you." Adam heard the soldier's half-wheedling, half-frightened voice through a dim haze of pain.

Using another Indian trick and the last of his strength, Adam levered off his boots and began to climb the nearest tree. He could not go very high, but he was sure the soldier would not think to look anywhere other than on the ground. Ware would have, had he been here, but he was in Adair's ballroom, Adam thought dizzily, holding on to consciousness with great difficulty.

Within moments he was glad he had climbed. The British soldier regained his wits. Adam heard the flint strike, then saw a branch light up. The soldier used the flaming brand to search the area where he thought Adam had fallen.

The night was too dark to see the trail of blood, Adam hoped. In the wavering yellow light, Adam also saw Peter. His face was pale and smudged, but thank God he appeared to be breathing.

The soldier spent little time searching. He had one prize already, Peter, and as he turned with the brand, Adam spotted a second body lying farther away.

The woods were eerily silent now. "Oy," the soldier called in the direction of Yorktown. "Over 'ere. Bill is wounded and I need 'elp with these two prisoners." Royal Navy marines from the docked ship pushed their way through the forest a few moments later.

Hefting the bodies of the fallen soldier and the two Sons of Liberty onto their shoulders, they departed, leaving Adam alone, cold, and bleeding. He knew he would pass out soon, that he had to get out of there while he still could. With only one working arm he could not climb back down. He dropped to the ground, rolling to one side to avoid falling on his injured arm. His black hunter, Mercury, bless him, remained obediently at his reins, nipping at nearby plants.

Adam no longer had the strength to mount the animal one-handed. He looped the reins over his good arm, starting to walk Mercury quietly in the direction of Williamsburg. When he came to a little-used path, he stumbled down it, hoping to remain conscious long enough to get on Mercury's back. He could rig the reins so that he would not fall out of the saddle. But if he passed out now, he would bleed to death in the forest.

The fallen tree trunk almost tripped him. It loomed across the path, visible only at close range, a darker shadow among many. Adam held Mercury's mane while he pulled himself up onto the trunk. Then he threw himself over the saddle as best he could. Mercury almost shook him off once he felt the unusual distribution of Adam's weight on his back.

The problem was that Adam lay sideways across the saddle, a position from which he could not control the horse and would certainly fall. "Hold, boy," he croaked hoarsely. Laboriously, he worked his way upright, using handfuls of mane to drag himself into the correct position.

"All right, Mercury," he whispered. "See if we can get to Williamsburg. To Lily."

The horse took off at a pace that an hour ago he would have called a trot. Now it was pure hell. Biting his lip savagely to keep from passing out, Adam leaned low, resting his head against Mercury's sleek, muscled neck. Keeping a proper seat at this point was a laughable idea. He prayed only that he would not fall off, because he knew he could not get back on Mercury again.

The wound was unimportant. He had to stay conscious long enough to tell Lily that Peter had been captured.

Eleven

*With how sad steps, O Moon, thou climb'st the
   skies!
How silently, and with how wan a face!*
                              —Sir Philip Sidney,
                                 Sonnet 31, 1591

Instinct made Lily douse the candles. Fear of attracting
unwelcome attention from redcoats, perhaps. Obscurity
for Peter to return unseen. If only her intuition could tell
her what was happening out there in the dark night.

Certainly she had no intention of going to bed. Terrible
dread assailed her, had followed her ever since she'd overheard the whispered words in Squire Sotheby's billiards
room.

She yielded to the late hour at last by undressing and
readying herself for bed. Then she returned to the kitchen
to pace in front of the fire, alternately cursing Peter and
praying for his safety. Adam came in for equal condem-
nation—and equal fervency in her prayers.

Near midnight she heard a faint sound from the garden.
Pushing open the door, she stepped uncertainly onto the
garden path. Suppose they were English soldiers come to
look for the perpetrators of the raid? Then she heard a

groan. The ball-and-chain mechanism at the back gate began to squeak.

Lily hurried forward. As she pulled open the gate from her side, something fell through it with a heavy thud. Hoofbeats thrummed on the dirt path, but the horse was already gone.

Lily looked down. A man lay there, wrapped in a dark cloak. The moon broke free from clouds, outlining the form.

"Adam? Are you all right?" Stupid girl, she chided herself. Would he be lying on the ground if he were all right? She bent down, trying to roll him onto one side. A sound of terrible pain issued from him.

She pitched forward to kneel in the dirt, frantic now to see what was wrong. Observing that Adam clutched one arm to his side, she parted his cloak. It was too dark to see, but she felt wetness.

Before lifting her damp hand to test the scent, she knew what it was. Adam's blood, seeping into the dirt at her feet.

"Adam, what happened?" she asked, afraid now as never before. "Oh God, where is Peter?"

Adam responded to the sound of his name, or perhaps to Peter's. He lifted his head. Lily dropped from her knees to sit, lifting the dark head to cradle it in her lap. She feared she would be unable to lift him, that he would bleed to death there in her garden.

"Lily," he rasped. "Peter . . . alive," he managed to get out before his head fell back. She stroked his hair as he had once stroked hers, but she could impart no comfort.

"You are hurt. Were you ambushed?"

"Yes. Need to get away . . . you . . . danger," he panted.

"You are not going anywhere. Just tell me where you are wounded. Do not try to talk! I will get you inside."

Whatever had happened to Peter, she had to help Adam now. If she could.

"Arm . . . rifle . . . ball through . . ."

"All right, 'tis all right, I will look at it inside," she soothed, worried he was wasting his strength on words.

"No . . . have to leave . . . they will look for me." His voice grew fainter.

"Adam, please, you must listen to me. I have to get you inside."

"No . . . away."

"No! Your horse, I assume that was your horse I heard, has gone to seek its stable, I suspect, and you are in no condition to ride." She was babbling, she knew. She must move Adam indoors before he passed out.

"Adam, listen to me." She spoke sharply on purpose. "You have to help me get you inside." Feeling his head move in her lap, she overrode his protest. "You are in no shape to leave. You must help me or I will not be able to get you into the house. Besides, you will not help me if you bleed to death in my garden," she said in a pathetically weak attempt at humor.

"All right. Stubborn . . . wench," he said. "I can . . . stand. Push." She pushed at his shoulder while he tried to get his feet under him. After a few abortive tries, they managed it.

"Put your good arm over my shoulders," Lily said. Stumbling at every step, they negotiated the garden path. Lily was afraid Adam would fall and never get up again. But they made it to the kitchen door. She told him to lean against the house while she opened it.

Adam stood, his face stark white, visible even in the poor moonlight. His eyes were closed against the pain. When she opened the door and took his hand, he lurched forward, lowering himself into one of the oak chairs.

Then he passed out, his head on the long table. Either his Indian skills or his military training accounted for his ability not to fall out of the chair while unconscious, Lily thought.

She pulled his cloak gently off his shoulders. Lighting a candle from the fire's coals, she stuck it in a tin lantern base to see his wound. The gash was large and ugly, and too bloody to tell whether the ball was still embedded. Adam had not been clear about that.

Should she clean the wound here or wait until she got him upstairs, into a bed? Treating him would be difficult as he was now. He would be better off lying down.

Lily found the fine aged brandy that had been her father's. Splashing some hastily into a glass, she brought the snifter under Adam's nose for the fumes to rise. He caught the scent, half lifting his head. Once he raised his head, she brought the glass to his lips, parting them none too gently to get the liquid in.

Crude, but successful. He choked, but in doing so, sat up. Once he was reasonably upright, Lily spoke urgently. "Adam, I am sorry, but I must tend your wound. Can you stand?"

"Whiskey . . ." he muttered.

" 'Tis brandy, but as long as it works . . ." Lily pressed the glass against his lips again. Adam grabbed it in his good hand. To her surprise, he threw it over his injured arm. He winced, a shudder passing visibly through his body as he stood up.

"Go . . . now," he said. "Pain helps."

Suddenly Lily understood. She knew alcohol helped cleanse a wound, but Adam had wanted the stinging effect. Apparently he meant the pain would keep him conscious, for now at least. He wavered on his feet. She draped his good arm over her shoulders once again.

"All right, then. Let's move along." She led him to the staircase. Her room was at the top of the staircase, Peter's farther down, the room that had been their parents' farther still. Lily was gasping as she reached the top of the stairs.

"In here." She pushed him toward the first room. Without ever opening his eyes so far as she could tell, Adam collapsed across the bed.

One last thing. "Turn over, Adam," she said in a deliberately severe voice, suspecting that once he passed out this time, she would have trouble reviving him. "Now."

He tried to turn, but it was in the direction of his wound. Groaning, he rolled back to his stomach, blood dripping onto the mattress. Lily bent over to push him in the right direction. She did most of it, knowing that Adam had surpassed even his own formidable limits. He was limp and exceedingly pale by the time she had him on his back.

All this effort and she had not even begun to cleanse the wound. One knee on the bed, she leaned over Adam to peel away the remnants of his shirt.

Then she started bolt upright in terror. Someone was pounding on her front door.

"Colonel Ware," Lily acknowledged moments later as she stood on her doorstep, trying to regulate her panicked breathing.

"Mistress Walters," the tall, spare man returned with a small bow in her direction. "May I come in?" Since there were two soldiers standing behind him, she was sure neither of them was in any doubt that he would do so.

" 'Tis most improper," Lily said as the colonel's glance traveled over her. There was nothing lecherous in it, merely keen observation that missed nothing of her mussed hair, wrapper, and night rail. She hoped none of Adam's blood was on her.

"Indeed," the colonel said without apologizing. "Without these unusual circumstances, I would not be here."

She did not move an inch from the doorway. "What might those be, sir?" she asked.

"Come, my dear, surely you know. Is that not why you left Oak Grove early tonight?"

"Is the squire ill?" she asked, hoping a suitable concern showed in her voice.

"The squire? He is abed."

She seized upon his statement. " 'Tis why I left, sir. I did not feel comfortable remaining in the house with our host incapacitated. I sought to learn if he was ill."

"Two of the squire's horses are missing," the colonel said.

"Are they?" Lily wondered what the man was getting at. She had taken only one. "I did not see the squire when I left."

"Where is your brother, Mistress Walters?" Ware had evidently tired of pleasantries, such as they were.

"He has not returned home tonight."

"Why is that?"

Lily's face flushed with anger. She willed herself not to display it. She tried for a lighter tone. "Colonel, my brother is not a child to come home at midnight, will he, nil he."

"Out with his rebel friends, is he?"

Lily was furious. Ware was trying to bait her. Surely he knew by now that Peter had been captured. "Colonel," she said, her voice cool, "my brother's activities are his own business, especially at night. Surely no maiden sister needs to be aware of such things? My brother and I are not as one over the present political situation, as you must know from my choice of friends. Therefore, I leave him to his."

"A pretty speech, young lady, but I think there is more to it than that. Stand aside, for I intend to search your house."

You have already arrested Peter, she wanted to shout, but that would be giving herself—and Adam—away. "On whose authority?" she forced herself to ask in an icy voice.

"On the authority of the Crown and of the Royal Governor." Lily could not think of any reason to stall him, except her original objection.

"My reputation would be ruined, sir, were you to enter my house this late and without any male relatives present."

"My dear gel," Ware said in a voice thin with repressed anger, "I would never compromise the reputation of a loyal subject of the Crown. These two gentlemen with me will assure that nothing untoward occurs." He gestured the men forward. "Now let us pass."

"Sir, I must protest. I have a sick friend here at the moment, and your presence will disturb her."

"Indeed?" Ware's light eyebrows rose until they were almost indistinguishable from the fair, thin hair at his crown. "And who might that be?"

"My friend Mary Hardison, whom you met at the squire's. She . . . she knew I was not comfortable alone and accompanied me home. She is spending the night with me. Mary then felt ill and is asleep."

As if such a simple lie would work. Not bothering to reply, Ware took a step forward. One step more and he would touch her.

As Lily stepped back reluctantly, Ware motioned the sergeants ahead of him. She had to stand back then, clutching her wrapper around her. The sergeants were not as disinterested in her dishabille as their leader.

Ware followed, his penetrating blue eyes sweeping every corner of her house as he walked behind the soldiers. In the kitchen he stopped at the sight of a bloody rag on the table.

Lily rushed over to it, coloring deeply. Ware moved toward her as if to take it from her, but she dropped it quickly into a bucket of water by the kitchen fireplace. "Colonel, I am so sorry, really, with just two women about and Mary's indisposition . . ." She hoped he would take her insinuation as she meant it.

He did. He stepped back quickly as if she were unclean, while the soldiers practically trampled each other in their eagerness to leave the kitchen. Lily was disgusted by her own subterfuge about Mary's monthly, then remembered the man upstairs. Adam had suffered far worse than embarrassment. Surely she could bear a little.

"Quietly, I beg you, gentlemen," she said as they returned to the front of the house. "Mary is feeling quite indisposed," she said in warning as their boots clattered up the stairs. Ware swept ahead of his soldiers. He strode quickly down the hallway to the farthest bedroom. He looked in each room, then came back to the closed door of her room.

"My friend is sleeping, sir," she said softly, praying that Adam was still unconscious. The soldiers remained halfway down the steps. The colonel made no move to urge them forward. He merely trained another astute glance on Lily, then quietly opened the door.

Lily bit her lip to keep from crying out in nervous anguish. Standing behind the colonel's lean frame, she peered around him, seeing what he saw: a dark head turned away from the door, the sheet almost obscuring it.

The covers reached the back of Adam's head. She caught herself before she sighed in relief. Thank God she had thrown the coverlet over him before she rushed downstairs. She saw no signs of blood on the linen that was visible, practically a miracle.

With Adam's hair unbound during the ordeal, and not all of it showing, it was just possible to think a woman lay in the bed. If the coverlet did not fall away and reveal those broad shoulders. If he did not roll over. If he did not groan in that deep voice.

Lily forced herself to unclench her fingers, to stop thinking of "ifs." She reached past Ware, terrified, but trying to show only concern about her friend. Slowly, quietly, she closed the door, daring Ware to stop her. He did not. No noise came from the still figure in the bed.

"You have seen quite enough, I believe, Colonel, and I will thank you and your men to stop harassing two ladies who are faithful servants of the Crown." Imagine herself calling on propriety! Oh Lord, was her voice shaking?

Lily started down the stairs in a haughty manner, not looking to see if Ware followed. She passed the two sergeants. They remained on the steps, looking uncertainly between her and Ware. She opened the front door in distinct dismissal.

Ware glanced once at the closed door, then descended the stairs, taking his time about it. He motioned to the men as he passed and they dutifully followed, floorboards creaking beneath their heavy boots.

"Give your brother my regards when he returns, Mistress Walters," he said, "unless you hear otherwise first." Although she heard and recognized the taunt, his voice remained coolly, irreproachably polite. She feared for a moment that he might even take her hand to bow over it in an exquisite mockery of courtesy, so she kept them both behind her back.

"Good night, Mistress Walters," he said. Then he and the soldiers were gone, their red-coated backs disappearing into the dark night.

Lily fought every instinct that screamed to run upstairs to Adam. It would be too obvious. The colonel was too smart to have left without looking back. The soldiers might be outside even now. In the kitchen she banked the fire, doused the candles, then slowly climbed the stairs with a single candle. She passed her own bedroom and headed to the last chamber, which had belonged to her parents.

Once there, she could keep up the pretense no longer. She left the candle near a window, then crept down the hallway until she stood in front of her own room. Opening the door slowly, fearing irrationally that Ware and his men could somehow still hear her, she looked into the room. Adam had pushed off the covers and rolled to his back. His broad chest was sheened with sweat. Bright red blood dripped from his shoulder onto her bed linens.

Twelve

. . . in darkness and in the shadow of death.
— Psalm 107

In the end Lily was grateful Adam remained unconscious. She did not think he could have borne her ministrations otherwise. As she gently probed the wound, she caught sight of the ball protruding from the flesh of his upper arm. Clenching her teeth against a wave of nausea, she removed it.

Warm, and slippery with Adam's blood, the dull metal object both fascinated and repelled her. It was intact, so that meant there were no fragments in the wound.

She poured more brandy over the site, holding his arm still with all her strength as his body jerked. Once he subsided, she stitched the wound closed with thread while tears poured down her face. "You smell like a drunken lord," she whispered, too sick at heart to smile at her own silly jest.

Hours later something woke her, but it certainly was not dawn. The candle guttered by Adam's bedside, the taper nearly spent. Even the curtains, still open, admitted only starlight.

Still open! Lily rose stiffly from the hard chair where she had slept, hastening to close them. She must not offer light for anyone who might be observing.

The candle's flame died. She lit another to see the condition of her patient. As the taper flared to life, she saw Adam's face no longer pale but flushed with high color along his cheekbones. Lily touched his cheek. He felt like fire.

"Oh, Adam, no," Lily whispered. Adam had already developed wound fever, which often killed the injured even when their wounds were not fatal.

She had to lower his temperature. She flung back the heavy coverlet. He needed to be sponged down, to cool his skin. Her maidenly modesty was useless now. She had cut his shirt away earlier to tend his arm, but now she had to divest him of everything.

Her fingers moved to the waistband of his breeches, hesitated. A line of dark hair ran past his navel and disappeared. It was difficult to draw the breeches down over his muscular thighs, then remove the linen underdrawers. Lily blushed furiously when she had to reach behind to pull the breeches down.

Everything she touched attested to the vigorous life Adam led. He was large and firmly muscled; Peter's sturdy frame seemed adolescent by comparison. But then, and Lily blushed again in the dim light, she had never seen a grown man fully naked before.

Despite her fear for his life and her timidity about looking at him, she could not fail to notice Adam's powerful masculine beauty. His broad shoulders and chest tapered to a narrow waist and hips. There was not an extra ounce of flesh anywhere on him, and his fine dark hair seemed even darker on those parts of his body that did not normally see the sun.

Lily looked at his manhood where it nestled in a dark cloud below his belly. As she lifted the damp cloth from the bucket of water and moved it down his powerful legs, she wondered why the whispered tales said a man's sex was such a fearsome thing. It did not look at all fearsome to her. In fact, it seemed quite small, really. She sighed, stilling the cloth momentarily on his knee. Here was a subject where eavesdropping might have done her some good for a change.

Once finished with the task, she feared Adam might catch a chill from the cool night air, although his skin still radiated heat. She needed to keep sponging him down at regular intervals. Lily pulled the sheet up to his waist, laid the cloth on his burning forehead, then sat back.

The discomfort of the wooden chair woke her from an exhausted doze. She looked around, momentarily disoriented. Glancing toward the bed and the man in it, she saw the cloth on the floor and memory of the night just past flooded her. Adam had somehow flung away the cloth from his forehead. It lay on the floor by the bed, dried out.

Lily rose wearily to check the dressing over his wound. The flesh was red and swollen around the site, but it did not look any worse than a few hours ago.

Adam was restless. "No . . . damn you . . ." He swore when she touched him. His good arm rose to fend her off.

"Adam, I must take care of your arm," Lily said firmly. He stopped fighting although he muttered unintelligibly now and again. She retrieved the cloth and dampened it, sponging him again to cool him.

Toward dawn he seemed calmer, a bit cooler. She was too exhausted to do any more. Returning to the chair was an intolerable thought, but she dared not leave him to seek another bed.

"Oh, heavens," she muttered to herself as much as to him. "If I can take your clothes off, I can certainly lie next to you. I will not sleep on the floor. So be it." Lily quickly unlaced the bodice of her dress and let it drop. Clad only in her chemise, she crawled into bed beside Adam.

Mourning doves cooing outside the window and a rooster's proud cackle over at Wetherburn's Tavern woke Lily much sooner than she liked. She had edged closer to Adam since she had fallen asleep. In fact, her head rested next to his right shoulder and his chin touched the top of her head.

Lily was startled to feel crisp hair rubbing pleasantly across her forearm. Her arm was draped across Adam's broad chest. It felt alive, warm, solid.

The curiosity that had always been her undoing surged to the fore. Experimentally, she traced her fingers through the light matting of dark hair. The texture was enjoyable, as was the feel beneath the hair of his smooth, hard planes of muscle. She stretched, reveling in the sensation, still half asleep.

Reality intruded quickly on the brief sensual fantasy. Adam's body emitted heat like an oven and sent her bolting out of bed. His fever was on the rise again. Lily scrambled out of bed and grabbed a wrap from the clothes press. The man might be dying and she was mooning over him like a lovesick calf!

She ran downstairs to fetch fresh water and more linen, snatched a quick bite of bread and cheese, then ran back upstairs again to tend her patient. Adam's lips were cracked with dryness from sustaining the high fever. She put salve on them and tried to lift up his head so he could drink. After a few sips of water, his head fell back. She could get no more liquid into him unless she wanted to risk his choking.

Trying to revive him with brandy as she had done last night would do him no good now that he was parched. "Come on, Adam, you're the resourceful one," she muttered. "Help me think of something." Lily had never been one to wring her hands with helplessness, but she did so now, twisting the cloth she'd used to sponge his body the previous night. No movement, no sound except harsh, shallow breaths came from the man in the bed.

She looked at the cloth she held, wondering why she hadn't thought of it before. Lily quickly snatched a clean chemise from the wardrobe. Tearing a strip off, she dipped it in water and held it to his lips. As she had hoped, he reacted, his lips parting faintly as if he wanted to drink.

She pressed the cloth over his lips, the memory of them on hers but a distant ache. She squeezed the fabric, releasing a trickle of liquid to run into his mouth. She repeated the act again and again. At least he had taken in some liquid.

All day his fever raged. He muttered words in his delirium that she could not understand. By midday her back ached and her eyes were gritty with fatigue. Yet every hour she continued to trace the damp cloth over his head, torso, and legs. She had long since forgotten any bashfulness. She no longer cared what he looked like. It was the precious life within that mattered. She prayed over and over for God to let him live.

As the afternoon shadows lengthened, Adam's fever seemed to abate. A good sign, Lily thought, remembering her mother had said that fevers were lowest during the day and tended to rise toward evening. If Adam's fever was dropping this late in the day, Lily reasoned, perhaps the crisis was past.

He seemed peaceful enough that Lily dared leave his side for the first time since she had fetched water that morning. She descended the narrow stairwell again, checked to be sure the CLOSED sign was still outside her shop, then went outside to fetch more material for a poultice from her herb garden.

Back in the sickroom, Lily frowned as she bent over the wound. Blood had seeped through the dressing, but the area around the injury seemed unchanged. She examined his arm closely for the red streaks that indicated poison in the blood but found none.

Lily sank back into the chair by the bed after changing Adam's dressing. He was still delirious and not very cooperative. With only one good arm he was still far more powerful than she and could easily frustrate her efforts. From his mutterings and curses, she wondered if he thought he was back in the French and Indian War, fighting off a military doctor. He must have been very young, for she did not think he was past thirty-five. Lily wondered what had driven him into the army at such a young age.

In the end, she found the only way to keep him still was to talk to him. Whether he understood her, she did not know; the sound of her voice seemed to be enough. Perhaps a female voice reminded him that he was not fighting out on the frontier.

After a while she began singing fragments of songs. It was less awkward to sing than to hold a one-sided conversation. Adam was least restless when she sang softly the melody of a tune she loved. With her energy flagging, she was hard pressed to remember more than a few lines.

My soul retains thee still in sight,
When thou art far away.
Thou art my vision in the night,
My waking dream by day.*

She smiled. She might have a private vision of Adam, but all she really knew was how he looked when ill. She would recognize his deep voice anywhere, but she still might pass him on the street and not know him. She didn't even know what color his eyes were.

At dusk Adam lay silently against the pillows. He looked less parched, but his skin was pale and drawn against his cheekbones. He appeared to be resting more easily, but it was not the true sleep of healing. Lily swallowed tightly against rising despair. He was not worse, true, but neither could she say he was better.

The second and third nights were much like the first. Lily climbed into bed beside him again when she could tolerate the chair no longer. Adam seemed to sense her presence, because he turned his head toward her, as if seeking reassurance from her head tucked beneath his chin. She slept lightly, awakening at every move he made. At dawn on the fourth day she rose to sponge him yet again, and he spoke aloud, in a clear voice.

"Lily . . . tell Lily . . . Peter taken. Ethan too . . . Captured, not . . . not dead . . ." His voice trailed off. Lily's heart slammed against her chest. Were those his dying words? She peered closely at him. His chest still rose and fell but he had not opened his eyes. He seemed to have passed a crisis, however, because when she finished sponging him, he was cooler than he had been during the past few nights.

*Williamsburg Songbook, J. A. Edmunds.

She sat watching him until morning, unwilling to close her eyes again for even a moment. Throwing open the shutters so she could see him better, Lily examined him closely. His forehead was almost cool. Even better, she saw his chest rising and falling at regular intervals instead of the shallow gasps that had accompanied the fever. Although still pale under his browned skin, his face seemed less haggard. She closed the shutters again so the morning sun would not wake him.

Lily took a deep, ragged breath. Some of the tension in her eased. Adam would live. Only when she went down to make herself something to eat did the full import of his words strike her. Peter had been captured and must be in jail for his part in the ammunition seizure.

By the Crown's laws he was a traitor. Redcoats had been here once already. They might be watching the house even now. Until she found a way to do something for Peter, she had to keep Adam safe from the same fate.

But why had no one come to tell her? Did they distrust her that much? Remembering the look on Amy Cameron's face, Lily wondered.

After picking listlessly at her bowl of porridge, Lily went upstairs to find her patient sleeping peacefully. The hectic flush of fever had left his face and the earlier pallor had not returned.

Lily glanced down at herself and realized she was as filthy as Adam had been the night he arrived. She broke off her contemplation of him with some reluctance. Leaving Adam alone in his first healing sleep, she went out to the garden to draw well water, this time for herself.

After dragging the heavy buckets into the kitchen to hang over the fire to heat, she drew the curtains. Once the water in the kettle was hot enough to use to bathe, Lily decided she was too exhausted to bother with the hip tub. Instead, she stripped off her dirty dress and shift and scrubbed herself while standing on the kitchen floor.

Donning a clean wrap, Lily brought bread, cheese, and cider upstairs with her on a tray. She entered her room and bent over Adam to check his wound. It looked the same as it had two hours ago when she had wrapped it. But his color had returned to normal, and strength seemed to be flowing back into him.

Lily began to straighten the bed linens around Adam. Strands of her loose, freshly washed hair trailed across his broad chest.

Just as she turned to leave, his good arm came up suddenly to catch the locks. He tugged gently so that she had to bend over him again. The movement released the scent of lavender from her hair.

His eyes opened. Large and deep set under perfectly winged dark brows and dark lashes, their blue-green color was so unusual and so intriguing that all Lily could do was stare, her wits having fled.

Wrapping his hand in her hair, Adam brought her closer to him, until she saw only his magnificent eyes. "Stay," he said, his voice husky, his eyes closing again even as he said the word.

Thirteen

I wonder by my troth, what thou, and I
Did, till we lov'd?

—John Donne,
The Good Morrow, 1633

Lily was too tired to resist. Part of her exhausted brain knew she shouldn't lie down near him, that he was no longer so ill. Yet Lily wanted his comforting presence as much as it seemed he wanted hers, so she slipped in next to him.

He stayed awake no longer than the few moments it took to adjust their positions. With her damp hair spread out behind her like a fan, she lay with her face toward Adam. He turned blindly in her direction, moving awkwardly until his fingers met hers.

At first Lily slept the dreamless sleep of fatigue, heavy and unmoving. Then fragments of the past few days began to swirl in and out of her mind and nightmare took hold.

Through a fog she saw Adam stride toward her, his cloak flaring about his broad shoulders. As she ran to welcome him, he stumbled, then slumped to the ground just before she reached him. Horror-stricken, she saw blood flow from him, spreading everywhere. It rushed through the gazebo, flooding it, engulfing her flowers in a slick, warm tide.

In her dream she tried to lift him, to get him into the house. He was a dead weight; she could not move him. She pushed and pushed, increasingly frantic that he was bleeding to death in front of her eyes.

Suddenly, his deep voice broke into her dream, hushing her, soothing her with murmured words, then with gentle caresses along her face and hair. She quieted, surrendering herself to his comfort, his strength, the reality of him beside her. The dream faded. She slept.

Hours later Lily rose to the surface of consciousness again. She was snuggled up tight against Adam now, and the warmth she felt was not merely physical. The sensations rippling through her were myriad, unexplored, delightful . . . and confusing.

Was she dreaming? Was it the dream-Adam who had drawn her closer into his embrace? Yet she seemed to be lying in her own bed, with Adam's face inches from her own. Whether dreaming or not, his warm mouth had to span the merest distance before it claimed hers. With a ferocity that surprised her, Lily hoped that he would . . . and that this was no dream.

Then, with great care and tenderness, he joined her lips to his, and Lily thought nothing in her life had ever felt so wonderful. She remembered the last embrace they'd shared, and her lips parted of their own accord. The kiss deepened. Pressing her body shamelessly to his where they lay on their sides facing each other, she raised her arm to bring his head closer. She curled her fingers in his thick, dark hair.

Any warning bells in the back of her mind were too faint for her to heed. Lily was alive as she'd never been before. She did not want the wonderful sensations swirling through her to stop.

Her wrap had fallen open while she slept. Her chest felt the faint chill of the evening air, but that was not what made Lily shiver. She realized that her breasts were revealed to Adam and that she wanted his touch. The slow descent of his hands caressing her shoulders was the reason she trembled—it was anticipation.

Adam's awareness of Lily had steadily grown since his fever had begun to ease. He'd floated in and out of lucidity a dozen times these past few days. She had been there, in his delirium and pain, and he was not certain whether her constant presence was real or fever-induced. Perhaps she had, in truth, always been there. Perhaps this warm, seductive woman sleeping beside him was not a product of his fevered imagination.

As the life force surged back into Adam, his senses awakened with a vengeance. His need for Lily was fierce after so many weeks of self-denial, heightened tenfold by his brush with death. When Lily cried out in her nightmare, Adam lost his hard-won control. He'd drawn her up against him until not an inch separated their bodies. Although she slept again, comforted, Adam had not.

He could no more stop his reaction to Lily now than he could stop the tide. Disguise was the last thing on his mind. The kiss deepened quickly as she met him action for action. She opened her mouth to him in a gracefully seductive gesture that nearly made him groan aloud. He stiffened in the most ecstatically painful arousal he'd ever experienced.

"Lily, Lily love," he murmured as his hand traced a passage down her slim throat to her breasts. "Come, open to me." With his good hand he parted what little was left of the wrap covering her. Her breasts gleamed in the lengthening shadows of evening.

He circled one with his thumb, moving slowly in contracting spirals that grew ever closer to the rosy tip. He brushed it lightly, gratified to feel the nipple harden instantly under his caress.

Adam affirmed his return to life with all the intensity of a passionate man who had held himself in check too long. He had not escaped his nature, not buried it deep enough within him. For the first time in years, he gave it cautious rein.

A low moan escaped Lily. Attuned to her need, Adam moved one leg to press her closer to him, his arousal brushing her thigh. Between kisses Adam murmured to Lily all the things he wanted to do. He knew from the spark in her golden eyes that she shared his passion. Much of what he planned, unfortunately, would have to wait until his arm healed.

The deep voice whispering huskily to her brought Lily back to full awareness. Shamed by her forgetfulness of his condition, she tried to break their embrace. His good arm shot out to clasp her waist.

"Nay, sweetheart, I said only certain things would have to wait." There was humor in his voice. "Not all." He placed his hand and hers near the junction of her thighs, where the strange heat flowing through her centered. She felt his sex near her femininity and dared to touch it.

Lily drew back in surprise. Adam's arousal was a far cry from the calmly nestled manhood she had seen before. The hard, heated length of him was a bit intimidating, and she knew a moment of panic. She looked up into his eyes, losing herself in the ocean blue of his gaze even as she did so.

His rich chuckle flowed between them. " 'Tis all right,

sweetheart. 'Twill fit when you are ready. Or, unfortunately for me, when I am ready."

As his hand caressed her, she relaxed, parting her legs unconsciously to allow him better access. Her whole being focused on the anticipation building within her.

Adam's hand passed over her belly, his big hand cupping her below. Lily felt the damp heat between her legs against his palm. Adam pressed lightly downward and his fingers slipped inside her cleft.

He sucked in his breath. "Ah, love, you are ready for me, but I can't manage with this arm." He leaned his head against the top of her head, breathing hard. "But I can give you this." Before she knew what he meant, his supple fingers pressed against her and there were no more words.

Lily began to move her hips in natural accompaniment to the rhythm he was building as his fingers stroked her. She could barely breathe. Small, soft cries came from her throat as he built her toward an unknown peak. Lily pressed herself against his hand and threw her head back. She kneaded the muscles of his shoulder in unconscious tempo to the rhythm he had created, pleading wordlessly for something that was just out of reach.

Adam kept up the rhythm, encouraging her with the deep voice that seemed lodged inside her innermost being. Then, with one sure motion, he placed his thumb directly onto the sensitive button of flesh and massaged it while his fingers slid down until they penetrated her. It was more than enough. Lily moaned and tightened convulsively around him, surrendering to a fierce, intense pleasure she had never known.

Adam was stunned at the force of her climax. He lay watching her face with a tenderness he had never felt before for any woman. Damning the wound that prevented him from doing more, he guided her hand back to him again. He would have to remain on his side until he regained strength in his arm. He wanted nothing more at that moment than to open her beautiful white legs and plunge into her depths.

He thought he might die if he couldn't enter her and was shocked at the intensity of his own longing. As Lily closed her small hand around him, he was momentarily grateful for the weakness caused by his illness. Otherwise he would have lost all his control that very instant.

"No more, sweetheart," he murmured, "unless you want to kill me." He brought her hand up to his mouth and kissed the tip of each finger while he remained perfectly still, attempting to gather the shreds of his self-control.

She reached across him to check his dressing. "Oh, Adam, have I hurt you?" she asked anxiously.

His laughter, rich and rueful, cascaded over her. "I believe that is normally the man's question." Pulling away from her, he hauled himself up on the pillows with difficulty. "In fact, little flower, it is my turn to take care of you."

He reached for the pitcher and clean cloths she kept at the bedside table. Then slowly, tenderly, he stroked a damp cloth over her breasts and between her legs, cleansing her with his good arm, tending her as she had tended him.

Though a haze of sleepiness enveloped her, Lily remembered vaguely that he was her patient, not the other way around. "There is . . . food. Ummm . . . are you hungry?" she asked, not certain she would be able to rise and fetch him some.

Adam felt her body's limpness, knew she was sliding into well-deserved slumber. "Far more than you know, Lily," he said so softly that her eyes closed as if she had not heard him. "Far more, I fear, than is good for either of us."

She made no answer. Lily fell asleep, cradled in his good arm with his hand lightly caressing her silky hair. Adam had trouble thinking calmly, knew his body was screaming for a release he would not allow. He had not experienced such an onslaught of desire since he had first tamed his body's urges to his will years ago. Yet he had to think, to bring some reason to this tangled situation.

His first task was to leave here and rescue Peter and Ethan, if he could. His second task was to exit the life of Mistress Lily Walters. The hole in his life he'd tried to suppress, the existence of which he'd tried to deny, even to himself, was now glaringly apparent. She'd slipped under his guard, his long-cultivated barrier. His dangerous occupation and the series of lies he was living left him without anything to give her. Not even—most especially not now—the protection of his name. And for that he cursed himself late into the remnants of the night.

Lily arose soon after hearing the cock crow, refreshed and feeling alive as she had not been in days. She glanced at Adam, her gaze resting approvingly on the healthier color of his skin. Then she looked at the broad planes of his chest and the stark white bandaging against his shoulder.

The shadows under his eyes betrayed the difficult nights he had passed since his injury. Augmented by fatigue . . . perhaps from last night . . . Her cheeks burning, Lily quickly fled the room, away from the powerful masculine chest rising and falling with regularity.

Now that his health seemed assured, Lily surveyed her

pitifully small food supply. She hadn't been out since the raid four nights ago. She must open her shop again and quickly. She might have already attracted attention by closing, but that couldn't be helped. Preoccupied, Lily didn't hear the tapping at her door at first. It was early, after all, and the sign proclaimed her shop closed. The tapping, respectful at first, became more insistent.

Moving toward the front door, she suddenly realized she wore only a wrapper. Another blush stained her cheeks. She stepped into the hallway leading to the front door and called, "Come back later. The hour is early yet."

"Mistress Lily, 'tis Will," a voice answered. Lily relaxed. She hadn't realized she was holding her breath.

"Will Evans? Is that you?" she called.

Fourteen

Show his eyes, and grieve his heart;
Come like shadows, so depart.
                    —William Shakespeare,
                    A Midsummer Night's Dream, 1596

The knock at Lily's front door brought Adam instantly awake. His soldier's instincts, honed by the deceptions he had been living, rose to his service. He swung his legs over the bed, realized he was naked, and peered through the shutter out the dormer window.

What he saw made him suck in his breath and step back at once, reaching automatically for his breeches with his good arm while he experimentally flexed the muscles of his wounded arm.

Will Evans stood at Lily's door. Recalling his role as Squire Adair Sotheby, Adam tried to remember how long he'd been there. He did not know, but he realized he had to get home at once with a story to account for the missing days.

His brain was tired of deception, his body weakened from the wound and fever. It was not easy to think logically this morning. He looked around and found his clothes clean and draped over a chair along with his cloak. But he did not see his shirt, it must have been ruined.

Blast it, if Will was looking for him, he must have been gone quite a while. As a rich gentleman planter, he was used to a degree of service that made it unlikely he would go without his manservant for several days. Will was undoubtedly checking the places he patronized to find out if he should be concerned about his missing master. He heard Lily let the lad into the hall as he looked around the room for a means of escape.

There could be no explanations for Lily, no good-byes. Nor must there be anything to connect him to Adair. For her sake as well as his, she could not afford suspicion. He had to leave her house with no clue that he'd ever been here.

Adam raked his fingers through his hair. Across the room he spied a closed set of shutters. These opened to high windows that looked out onto the garden. Adam realized he could let himself out the dormer and drop to the ground. The upstairs of the house was not large and had low ceilings. In his normal condition the drop to the soft flower bed below would have been a simple matter. But now? He was not so sure.

If he could drop and roll onto his uninjured side, he would be fine. Pray God he did not miscalculate. He smiled grimly. He'd taken worse wounds in the French and Indian War. He could handle this.

Halfway to the window, regret for his sudden departure assailed him. He hated to leave Lily this way, especially since he didn't know when he could contact her again. The redcoats would question her, if they hadn't already. In that case it could be dangerous to see Lily again anytime soon.

His urgent gaze lit on a pitcher filled with blooms, sitting on a table near the wall. Even while she tended him—

or perhaps because of it—she had kept the room from a grim demeanor by adding a few flowers from her garden.

Adam strode over to the oval table, taking care that his boots made no noise on the wooden floor. He drank in the scent so reminiscent of Lily for a dangerous moment, then with care extracted a flower that he vaguely remembered from the vocabulary. It was not one they normally used, but he thought it would serve.

Swiftly, he laid the blossom on the pillow where Lily's head had rested beside his. He could do no more. Voices were still wafting up the stairwell from downstairs. Perhaps Lily was giving Will breakfast.

Despite his haste, Adam did not like the thought, remembering the puppy fancy that Will had for Lily. He swore silently to himself. What a fool he was. He had no time for jealousy. At any moment Will might leave the house and Adam must make his way to the town house. Without further ado he swung himself onto the window ledge, paused to see that no other neighbors were within sight, then jumped.

He prayed that the flowers below him were not roses.

Lily heard a faint thump behind the house but could not investigate now. She wanted to be certain Will sought only Sotheby and wasn't here as some kind of advance search party. His master was a well-known Tory after all.

"Will, I've not seen your master," she said. "In truth, I have been very busy these last few days. I confess that I've not even delivered flowers to the town house."

Will set her mind at ease about his motives. "Mistress Lily," he said earnestly, squeezing her hand for a moment before she gently removed it. "I may work for a Tory fop, but never think I would be one of them! Word is out about the raid at Yorktown. But the British will not say who they captured, or how many."

He looked around. "Is Peter . . . ?"

"I know absolutely nothing about what went on that night." She stared intently at Will. "Do you understand?"

"I knew what Amy said about you wasn't true," Will said triumphantly. "You've probably been hiding some of them here and 'tis why your shop has been closed. . . ."

"Will! The redcoats have already been here. There is no one here. No one." Regretting her sharp tone and blushing at the thought of facing Adam after last night, Lily postponed the moment by offering Will breakfast. Unknowingly, she gave Adam the time he needed to make his way back to the town house.

The fall from the window hadn't been pleasant, but when no one came running, Adam reckoned he'd been quiet enough. He now had a sore right shoulder where he had taken the brunt of the fall, and possibly a sprained ankle. Not bad, given the circumstances. He checked the dressing and saw no bleeding. Lily had tended him well. After he dusted off his breeches, he bent low and carefully made his way to the rear of the garden.

Easing himself out the back gate, he straightened. In the crisp morning he limped toward the town house. Only when he was halfway there did he realize why he felt so odd. It was not his ankle, not the wound, not even leaving Lily. It was the fact that he was walking down a Williamsburg street in broad daylight—as himself. Whoever that was.

Had the situation been different, Adam would have laughed at the irony, but his thoughts were for Lily. He had left her with her brother captured and naught but a flower on her pillow. It could not be much consolation against an uncertain future.

Nearing the town house, Adam slowed his pace. He looked around, seeing no one nearby as he slipped through the small garden and into the back door of the house. He scratched irritably at his face as he walked into the front parlor. Several days' worth of stubble on his chin would actually help him in his next action.

Adam unlocked the cabinet that held the whiskey. He quickly slugged down a goodly portion, appreciating the warmth that spread to his belly, then slopped some onto his face and shoulders. He grimaced in distaste, but there was no help for it. His excuse needed to be good or he would not fool Will.

Adam went upstairs and removed his dark clothes. He found a linen shirt and a neckcloth, then crushed them in his fists until he created enough wrinkles to look as if he'd been wearing the same clothes for days. He dragged one of his more bilious frock coats out of the armoire, donning it only after he had deliberately spilled more whiskey on it and dropped it on the floor a few times.

He did the same thing to the canary-yellow breeches he donned next. He covered his hair with a powdered white wig, yanking out some of the strands to trail messily from the queue, then grabbed a pair of yellow-tinted spectacles and plopped them on the bridge of his nose. When they slipped, he did not bother trying to straighten them.

Then he sat down in a wing chair in the library to await his manservant. With no feigned effort he drifted off quickly into a half-stupor, the recently consumed alcohol on his empty stomach making the task easier. Half suffocating under the heavy clothing and wig, the resumption of his identity only reminded him of how good it had felt to lie beside Lily with nothing between them.

Nothing between them, that is, except his lies. Lily knew no more about who he really was than when he had stumbled into her house half dead. Then he'd left her with neither farewell nor thanks, much less assurances that he would rescue her brother. He could at least rescue her brother, and so he would, or die trying. He owed her that and more.

Sliding down in the chair, Adam willed the alcohol to spare him the pain of an introspection he hadn't endured in years. The jealousy he'd felt when he heard Will in Lily's hallway had surprised him, as did the fierce protectiveness for her that he now felt. His thoughts bleak, he found it easy to snarl at Will when the young man arrived a few minutes later.

"Your worthiness, uh, sir, I've looked for you everywhere," the lad exclaimed.

"Well, here I am, boy. You must not have looked very hard."

"I . . . you weren't at Oak Grove, and I was already here once this morning," Will said, goggle-eyed at Adam's condition.

"A friend dropped me off here in town. Even he got tired of my losing at cards." Adam looked at Will from under lowered lids, hoping the boy would buy the story that he had been upriver drinking at another Tory's plantation. "What day is today anyway?"

He watched Will take in his disheveled appearance, saw him surreptitiously sniff the air and correctly identify the scent.

"Er . . . 'tis Monday, your sireness," Will said.

Adam barely controlled a start. Monday? Good God,

he'd been at Lily's house since last Thursday night. Anything could have happened to Peter and Ethan since then.

To cover his concern and to keep Will from tending him, he gave vent to a series of petulant complaints designed to distract Will from noticing his injured arm. Adam had never undressed in Will's presence anyway, because of his padding, so there was nothing unusual in that.

"Bathwater, boy," he whined, "can't you tell I stink? No wonder I lost, with all the whiskey they poured down my throat." He figured by the time Will brought up hot water, he would be more than happy to stay a good distance away from his foul-humored employer.

Adam was able to dress himself and check his bandaging without Will being any the wiser. Although he had an attack of conscience at his rude behavior, he was not particularly sorry. Will had seen more of Lily in daylight this morning than he had, dammit.

After bidding Will good morning, Lily worried briefly about where Squire Sotheby might be. Then her concern for Peter and Adam overwhelmed her again. The squire was no lad. He was a grown man, and a rich one. He could take care of himself.

She set the breakfast dishes in a bucket. Carefully drying her hands, she removed the homespun apron and smoothed the wrinkles nervously from the dress she had donned so hastily. She had grabbed it from the clothes press in her mother's room, since she had not wanted to wake Adam.

Thoughts of her mother made her blush. How would her mother have felt about Lily and her involvement with Adam? Lily had always watched her parents with love tempered with confusion, knowing that although she adored her children, their mother had had eyes only for their father.

Amanda Walters had not wanted to live after word arrived of the storm that wrecked her husband's ship on its journey back from England. He'd been on another journey to take the plants of the New World to satisfy the passion of the Old. The Royal Society had paid well for the treasures for which so many of its noblemen vied.

Lily refused to continue the exportation after her father's death, and her mother, sick at heart, had agreed. But Amanda had followed her Robert the next winter, too weak to summon the will to go on living. A young Lily had been left with an even younger brother and the necessity of earning a livelihood. She'd chosen the plants that had meant so much to her parents.

Lily found she was clutching the banister as if she feared falling from some height. What had made her think of her parents? Love. She had never thought to find it. She was too unconventional, neither biddable nor beautiful, and now she was an old maid.

She forced herself to let go of the wood. Did Adam love her? Did she love him? Lily was worried about coming face-to-face with the man she had just . . . the man with whom she . . .

She could not complete the thought. She touched her lips, which remained tender from Adam's thorough kissing and his raspy beard. She grabbed at the distraction gratefully. Shave . . . now, that was something he was probably ready to do, she thought.

Lily went to fetch Peter's strop and a basin. She could help Adam if he needed assistance, but she doubted he'd remain abed much longer. The vitality that blazed from the man, even though he was just recovering from a wound and fever, amazed her. Lily smiled as she headed for the stairs.

Lily opened the door with a trembling hand, stopping at the threshold. Her eyes scanned the room once, then again. Adam was gone. His freshly laundered clothes had been removed from the chair where she had placed them. But for that and the tangled sheets, there was nothing to indicate he had ever been there.

Lily experienced profound disappointment. In just a few days she'd begun to take for granted his presence in her house. Even the exhausting work of caring for an injured man hadn't been so bad because it was Adam.

Suppressing her sorrow, Lily gathered up the bed linens to wash. Then her eye caught sight of the flower on her pillow and her heart skipped a beat. There was no note, but perhaps Adam had heard the knock at the door and thought there might be redcoats in pursuit. He'd have had no time to leave a message.

Or was this a message? As Lily picked up the apple blossom, its pinkish-white petals softly brushed her skin. Apple blossom was one of the first flowering trees of spring. She'd placed it in a pewter pitcher to freshen the air once Adam seemed better.

Slowly, the meaning of the flower dawned on her. Adam had the vocabulary she had written. Surely he knew its meaning, which was temptation. Eve had tempted another Adam long ago in the garden with the fruit from this tree. They had indulged in the sin of the flesh and been forced to leave the garden.

Surely Adam did not mean this? She had not tempted him! Except that he had woken from a fever to find a mostly naked woman in bed with him. Her cheeks flamed.

Perhaps she was reading too much meaning into a simple flower. Perhaps he just wished to acknowledge that she had helped him. If not for the flower vocabulary, she would have seen the token as just that, a man giving a flower to a lady.

She had helped weave the web of deception. Now she was ensnared by it. Laying the stem on the bedside table, she gathered up the linens and slowly left the chamber.

Fifteen

But in deed,
A friend is never known
till a man have need.

—John Heywood,
Proverbs, 1546

Lily tried to go about her business that day, but it proved impossible. She was filled with worry about Peter and uncertain how to proceed. No one came into the shop whom she knew well enough to question.

That night was even worse. Although to another eye Adam had disappeared without a trace, Lily knew better. Reminders of him were everywhere.

At the well, where she had drawn the water to bathe him. In the kitchen, where she had prepared the broth that nourished Adam through his fever. And her clothes press, from which she'd drawn linen and muslin cloths for his bandages.

Worst of all was her bedroom. Everything in it spoke to her in some way of Adam. She pressed the apple blossom between the pages of a book of essays by Thomas Jefferson, and barely slept.

The next day she knew she had to take action. She

would not wait meekly. While pondering what to do, Mary Hardison rushed into the shop mid-morning.

"Lily! Are you all right?" she gasped, out of breath as if she had been running. Fortunately, no one else was there to see her odd behavior.

"Why, yes, Mary. What in heaven's name is the matter with you?"

"One of us is in terrible trouble."

"What?"

"Colonel Ware turned up at our house the other day to see Papa. He went into the library with him, and when he came out, Papa looked ever so angry. He called me in and asked me . . ."

"Colonel Ware came to your house?" Lily asked.

"I didn't have to talk to him. He didn't seem at all pleasant, as he had the other night at Squire Sotheby's."

"Mary, for pity's sake, what happened?"

"Papa asked me if I'd been with you the night of the revel at the squire's." Lily's heart sank, but her fingers moved of themselves to coax a tulip's petals to curve outward.

"And?"

"Well, of course we were there, but then Papa asked me the strangest thing. He wanted to know if I had left when you did, or come to see you later, or some such. I came home with Mama. But Colonel Ware seemed to think I had been ill and spent the night with you." Mary's earnest brown eyes were dark with worry. "Was I supposed to tell him I had been here?"

Lily pinched the tulip too hard and a red petal fell off. She had been too busy tending Adam to see Mary and ask her to lie about her presence.

"Mary, I'm sorry. I wanted to ask you if I might put that about because . . . because . . ." Lily could not think of a decent reason why she might have asked Mary to say she'd spent the night here.

"Lily, you know I love you and would do anything for you, but I didn't know what to say," Mary said in a reproachful tone. " 'Twas all such a surprise. Then, when Amy Cameron said Colonel Ware had been seen coming from your house very late that night, I didn't know what to think."

Mary bit her lip. "But I cannot believe 'twas Colonel Ware, because if he was the man who spent the night here, then why would he be asking Papa if I had been here?"

The head of the tulip snapped. Lily threw the stem down onto the table with more force than necessary. "Who is saying a man spent the night here?"

"No, no," Mary said hastily. "Amy Cameron said only that she had heard that Colonel Ware was seen at your house the night of the raid, not that she had seen him herself. Oh, Lily, does this have to do with Peter being arrested?"

"Peter arrested?" Lily could barely think, only stupidly echo Mary's words. She thought the British were keeping that information secret, although it could hardly be a secret for long.

"Well, 'tis all around town that Peter and Ethan Holt are missing. I thought your shop was closed because you were trying to hide Peter or protect him. But then I heard whispers about an attack or a raid. The British are so nervous about the state of Williamsburg that they don't want rebels possibly storming the jail and—"

"Mary, slow down and tell me what you know. Or think," she added, wondering if Mary would repeat the worst gossip or refuse from loyalty.

"This is what I've heard: Last Thursday night the Sons of Liberty carried out some action against the Crown. Your brother and Ethan Holt were arrested. The others got away.

Colonel Ware was seen leaving your house late that night. Some say he was questioning you about your brother's activities. Others say he was . . ." Mary clasped her hands together nervously, looking anywhere but at Lily.

"Are saying what?" Lily asked.

"Others say he came here to thank you for your assistance . . . that the attack was a trap and the British knew about the raid. Some people think Peter must have told you and that . . . that you were the source of the information."

Lily laid her hands on the counter, knowing she would shred any flower she touched just then. "Why would they think that?"

"Because you've spent so much time of late with the Br-British and . . . and Loyalists. But I do not believe that," Mary rushed on, "because you would never betray your brother, even if you are 'coming around to the right of things,' as Papa says."

"Thank you for coming to tell me this, Mary." Lily reached over to pat Mary's hand. "You really are a true friend. I'm sorry I said you were here. . . . I was trying to protect someone."

"Have I made things worse?" Mary asked, her brow puckered with concern.

"It matters little now," Lily said. Her reputation could hardly get worse, but that wasn't her most pressing concern. Colonel Ware knew she had lied. Why hadn't he come to question her again once he found out she'd lied about Mary?

Suddenly, she knew what she had to do. Adam was gone, his secrets with him. He was safe. But Peter was under arrest and she intended to find him. Even if she had to knock on Ware's door herself.

* * *

Which was just where she found herself an hour later. Mary had wanted to accompany her, but Lily thought Mary was in enough trouble as it was and declined firmly. Lily stood in front of the fine brass knocker at the house Ware occupied, her heart pounding. Two women walked by. She heard their comments clearly from behind her.

"Look at her, knocking on the redcoats' door as bold as you please. Do you think she's come to claim a reward for turning in her brother?" That was Sarah Braxton, a thin, stooped woman.

The other woman was slightly more generous. Lily recognized the buxom Mistress Thornton. "I never would have thought it myself, not of Robert and sweet Amanda's daughter. But they have been on their own a long time, those children, and you never know how they might turn out. Still, I can't believe she would turn in her own brother."

Lily whirled to face the two middle-aged women. "I have not betrayed my brother." She marched down the sidewalk toward them. "I came to find out where my brother and Ethan Holt were taken. Do you know?"

Mistress Thornton stared, her round face looking uncertain. Mistress Braxton, her worn, wrinkled face suspicious, found her tongue more quickly. "Why should we tell you?" she asked.

Mistress Thornton put her hand on her friend's arm. "No reason why we should not," she said. "He is her brother after all, and if she really had betrayed him, she would already know. So where's the harm in it, I say? He is in jail here in Williamsburg," she said, turning to Lily.

"Not Yorktown?" Lily asked, surprised.

"I heard they were to be transported," Mistress Braxton sniffed, glaring at Lily.

"There's been no time. Justice still exists, whether or not you support the Crown," Mistress Thornton said.

"I thank you," Lily said, eager to be away. Thank God she needn't confront Ware, for now she must contact Adam. If he didn't know already, she'd tell him the prisoners were still in town.

Could they be rescued? Lily vowed she would do it herself if she had to. She ran the rest of the way back to Francis Street, ladylike behavior absolutely the last thing on her mind.

Adam stared at the flowers Will was bringing in to him. He had affected a terrible hangover to account for his sluggishness in rising from bed. Although his arm was healing, he'd had to stay off the twisted ankle. Cursing his weakness, he knew he had to meet with the Sons of Liberty to see if a rescue attempt was possible, but he'd not yet mustered the strength.

His blasted horse was in better shape than he. Mercury had found his way back to the stables and after a good rubdown was good as new. His servants were curious as to where the horse had been and how it had come back, winded and blown, but Adam pretended not to care. "Horseflesh is horseflesh," he had snapped in his petulant Adair voice. "As long as he is back, I don't care who took him out for a ride." Still, he'd made certain his grooms took good care of Mercury.

He looked carefully at the colorful flowers in the huge round bowl bobbing in front of the boy's face. "Will, what in blazes are you doing with those?" he asked peevishly.

"Your squireness, ah, your worthy, I thought you might like a bit of color in the room, what with your feeling poorly and all."

"Harrumph," Adam snorted. "Very well, leave them there. Get me some broth, would you? My stomach does not fancy anything stronger." Will obediently went to do his bidding, leaving Adam to confirm what he had suspected the minute he spotted the tall signal waving from the center of the arrangement.

Message. He gazed at the iris. Lily had to be frantic, of course—about Peter, he reminded himself. Could he go to her tonight? He had to.

Suppressing the mad urge to drag his battered body immediately off on yet another foolish quest, he forced himself back against the pillows. Rest was the only thing that would help Peter and Lily now. He had to be in better condition or he would be of no use to anyone.

Lily sat in the gazebo, wondering where Adam had gone the day he left her. Was he safe? Was he healed? She would not think about what had passed between them, but her traitor heart was already beating too fast with anticipation.

She knew he was there the barest moment before he spoke. The clean masculine scent she associated with Adam was her clue. He was as silent as ever in the dark, but then, her senses were heightened where he was concerned.

"Are you well?" he asked from behind her, his voice deeper and a bit slower than usual. She thought he sounded terribly tired, feeling the pain in his voice settle inside her too.

"I believe I should be asking you that," she said, remembering when those words had been last spoken.

He was too tired to acknowledge her faint jest, or perhaps he did not wish to. "I am better," he said. "Thank you," he added with a light brush of his hand against the back of her head. She turned into his arms. He gathered her against him after an initial moment of hesitation.

Adam held Lily only an instant. The awareness that flowed between them was too revealing. He could not let her know how much he cared. It would do neither of them any good.

"I have learned that Peter and Ethan are being held in the Williamsburg jail," she said after a moment.

"Yes," he said neutrally, not giving away whether he had already known.

"They are to be transported." This he had not heard.

"When?"

"I don't know. Adam, can't something be done?"

"I don't know, Lily."

"You do not know or you will not tell me?" she asked. "You would not tell me your plans before, and I could not help you. Why won't you tell me now?"

Tell? What was there to tell? He was having trouble standing up, and she wanted him to play the hero.

"Even had you known our plans, you could not have warned us in time. You learned only that same night at the squire's, did you not?"

Lily's heart skipped a beat. So he had heard some of the one-sided conversations she had conducted during the endless hours of his illness. "Yes, but if I'd known where you were gathering, perhaps I could have reached you in time." She knew she grasped at straws but was unwilling to concede his point.

"You never give up, do you?" he said in reluctant admiration. As he'd said that first night, she had spirit, more than most men. The thought shored up his flagging energy. He could not keep from touching her again. This time it was for his own selfish pleasure, because he needed her strength now more than he had ever needed anything in his life.

Lily did not want to soften at the feel of his arms around her, at the simple gesture of smoothing a wayward curl. "Will you let me help with this?" she asked.

"No," he said in a set voice, his hold tightening.

"I did not expect you would," she admitted.

"You can assemble the Sons of Liberty for me though, little flower. Without Peter to tell the others, I have no way to get in touch with them directly."

This was what she wanted, Adam thought, to be involved. Why then did he feel her hesitate?

"I'm not sure they will listen to me," she said softly.

"Why?"

" 'Tis being said that I betrayed Peter and the Patriots." Anger burned through Adam in a fierce wave, giving him a strength he had not felt in days.

"Who says so?"

"There are many who say so. But 'tis all right," she said.

"Never," he breathed. "There is no treachery in you." His mouth descended on hers, intent only to comfort and reassure, but he quickly found himself far exceeding those simple bounds. He kissed her as if she anchored him to the world, as if it had been years since they touched, as if she held his heart in her small, lightly callused hands.

Lily knew there was more in the kiss than simple physical contact, although she craved that as well. Her hands slid up to encircle his neck. She spread her fingers through his thick hair, reveling in the feel of him, so alive, beneath her hands.

His lips, which had moved gently against hers at first, became demanding. She had no reserve about giving him everything he wanted from her and more. Certainty, comfort, passion, warmth.

He wanted it all, Lily sensed, even if he could not, or would not, name what he felt. Love. Home. Family. The things she somehow knew had not been his in a very long time, if ever. In return, she forgot her doubts and gave him all her love and longing, holding nothing back.

He was the one who stopped the kiss, as she had known he would. But as he continued to hold her, she wished she could see into the ocean depths of his eyes so he would know she had every confidence in him.

"Very well," he said against her cheek, continuing the thread of their conversation as if he could not acknowledge what he had revealed to her in his embrace. "If you cannot call the Sons of Liberty, I will ride alone."

She pulled away, her certainty tinged with apprehension. "No, I would never ask that of you," she said.

"I know, little flower. But we have few choices, you and I. Do this for me," he said, cutting her off when she would have continued to protest.

"Do this," he said again more firmly. "Take Peter flowers. 'Tis common knowledge now, even if not officially confirmed, where the prisoners are."

Flowers? He wanted to limit her to taking flowers? Sensing her outrage, he continued, holding her gently by the shoulders. "Listen to me. The bouquet should contain the flowers that will warn Peter."

"Pennyroyal," she said reflexively. It meant flee away. "Aye. Add two . . ."

"Roses." That would indicate both prisoners were to be freed.

"Yes, and also . . . also . . ." Presentiment raced up her spine, chilling her to the core.

"You want me to add rhododendron," she said in a flat voice. "Of course." Rhododendron meant danger.

Lily was not aware she trembled until Adam wrapped her in his embrace again. She bumped into the bandage at his shoulder and pulled back. "Adam, what of your wound? You are not recovered enough for such a mission."

"As I said, there are few choices. If I wait any longer, they will be gone."

"What about a trial?"

"I do not believe one is necessary in this case."

"What do you mean?" she said, alarmed.

"Lily," he said roughly, "they have committed treason. They could be hung. Believe me, I know. Transporting is considered a lenient sentence, a decision probably made only to quiet the townspeople."

So Mistress Braxton had been wrong. "When is this to be, Adam?" she asked.

"Put three yellow flowers in your bouquet. Three yellow but also two white, in case time is short."

"Yes." Daisies would indicate the days. That meant the rescue attempt would take place in three days, possibly in two.

Sixteen

*For many men that stumble at the threshold
Are well foretold that danger lurks within.*
—William Shakespeare,
King Henry VI, Part 3,
1590

Two days later Lily stood in the entrance hall of Squire Sotheby's town house. Will Evans shook his head regretfully. "If I could help you, Mistress Walters, you know I would. I have tried to tell people they are wrong about you, but the Camerons carry a lot of weight in, ah, certain circles."

"Master Cameron, or his opinionated daughter?" Lily asked more sharply than she intended. She stretched out her hand to Will immediately. "I am sorry, Will. 'Tis just that I am not used to being viewed so . . . so suspiciously."

A clattering sound warned her. She jumped back, almost spilling the vase of flowers she was holding. The squire, leaning heavily on his elaborately carved walking stick, half stumbled down the stairs.

He looked rather paler than usual, although between his wig and his blue-tinted lenses, she never could see much of his face. His reliance on the walking stick seemed no affectation this time. "Well, Mistress Walters, how do you do today?" No elaborate compliments, none of his usual extravagant good cheer, Lily noted.

"I do hope you are well, Squire," Lily said with a small curtsy in the squire's direction. She had not seen him since before the night of the raid. Although Will had told her the squire had been upriver drinking and gaming, and his complaint this time had not been his stomach, she wondered. He seemed more unwell than someone merely suffering the aftermath of strong drink.

"Ah, well, we old men do what we can, you know, my dear." He looked at Will, the sharp glance belying his protestations of feeble old age. "Do you not have some work to do, young man?" he asked in a querulous tone.

In truth, although Adam felt the usual annoyance at seeing Lily with Will when he was disguised as his foppish alter ego, he wanted to be rid of Lily. He knew what she was trying to do, knew also what he planned to do that night, and the last thing he needed was her interference.

Will scurried off. Adam could have sworn Lily shot a reproachful glance at him for his rudeness, but he could see she did her best to maintain a professional demeanor. Probably cursed him inwardly though. The thought warmed him, and he had to smile.

"I mustn't keep you here, m'dear, much as you grace my hall more beautifully than do your flowers. I trust I shall see you soon," he said. He had to get ready for the solo raid he planned that night. He was not yet sure how—or if—he would pull it off, but he knew he had no time to waste. He could sense Ware getting closer to him by the minute. After rescuing the prisoners, Adam Pearson could fade away, his job here done. Arrogant British behavior and the anger of the townsfolk would lead to the war no one could avoid.

Glancing at Lily, Adam knew he had irritated her. Fine. Whatever it took to get her away from him.

"Good day, Squire," she said coolly, and departed without a word of farewell or her usual wish for his health. He found himself particularly wishing for the latter. His arm was still weak, and for once he had actually needed the damned cane.

Lily wasted little time fretting about the squire's peculiarities. Her plan was working as she'd intended. After her futile efforts the previous day, she knew no one would come to a meeting at her summons, so she had started a rumor. One she hoped would help Adam, even if indirectly.

The rumor was not new. Everyone knew Governor Dunmore was increasingly leery of the colonists' intentions. She doubted that Adam would thank her for her interference, but with any luck he would never find out.

Walking from the squire's house toward her own, Lily remembered the hope in Peter's eyes when she'd handed him the flowers yesterday at the jail. He'd looked at the bouquet carefully, so she was certain he'd absorbed its message.

But there had been so little time. Even the officer at the jail—a sympathetic redheaded young man with whom she'd danced at the squire's—had not trusted her to be with Peter for long. He had not denied Peter was there, and had let her in to see her brother briefly, but that was all.

The lieutenant had taken the flowers and scattered them to check for a hidden weapon. But Peter had seen them, and she would not let him down. She had to trust Adam would not either.

"Thank you, Lieutenant Thomas." She had forced herself to speak politely. "I am glad to see you've treated my brother well." Peter looked the worse for wear but had sustained only scrapes and a bruise on the head, which he insisted did not pain him. Ethan had a broken arm, but it had been properly set.

" 'Tis the least I could do for a loyal citizen such as yourself, Mistress Walters," the lieutenant responded gallantly as Peter stared at her. "I hope to dance with you again soon."

"Yes, well," she said, letting the phrase trail off, hoping Peter hadn't heard every word, very much afraid that he had. "Good day to you, sir." She smiled the way she did when a particularly trying client taxed her patience with impossible requests.

Lily stood at the edge of the crowd, her shawl pulled over her hair, a shadow in the darkness that was punctuated by leaping flames of torchlight. In the chaos, she doubted anyone would recognize her, but why take chances? That she alone was responsible for the anger of the townspeople, she doubted, but at least she had helped provoke the desired diversion.

Outraged by the rumor that the royal governor intended to remove the gunpowder from the magazine again—it had been returned for safekeeping after the incident at Yorktown—hundreds of townspeople had turned out and so had dozens of British soldiers. Dunmore had used the excuse this time of an imminent slave rebellion to call on the redcoats.

The angry citizens demanded to know how they were

to protect themselves in case of a slave revolt, knowing he distrusted them, not the slaves. That was an excuse. Moreover, they had reminded the governor earlier that day, in a strained meeting at the governor's palace, that the citizens of Williamsburg had paid for that gunpowder. It belonged to the colony, not the Crown.

So tonight hundreds had gathered in protest to drive home their point. As far as Lily's plan was concerned, she was pleased to see that practically every British soldier in town was here, guarding the ammunition in the magazine from the enraged citizens of Williamsburg. Lily hoped fiercely the guard at the jail had also been lightened enough to help Adam.

Although every fiber of her being ached to be at the jail, she knew she could render no useful assistance. She would only be a hindrance. Despite her fierce desire to help, she would not take chances with Peter's life, or that of any Son of Liberty.

Hard as it was, she turned her back on the crowd and headed home. No doubt she had another long night of waiting in store.

Pray God it did not end as it had that other, recent night.

Adam was certain luck was with him when he came up behind the jail and saw no guards. He'd been aware of the crowd gathering at the Palace Green, but not why. Since the coincidence favored Adam's own ability to move about tonight, he had acquiesced easily to Will's request for the night off.

Now he wondered if he should have asked where Will was off to. The crowd sounded loud and angry. He briefly considered, then dismissed, the unlikely possibility that Lily had somehow gathered the Patriots openly. No, she had damaged her Patriot ties by attendance at his and other Royalist soirees. He doubted she could call together half a dozen Sons of Liberty without Peter's active assistance.

Someone needed to make her stop trying so hard to help the Patriots. She could very well get run out of town with Peter unable to protect her. If someone like that bastard Dodgett made another pass at her, her social reputation would be in shreds.

Although the information she gathered was useful, it probably harmed her more than it helped him. Yet he could not refuse the aid she provided, even assuming she would ever agree to stop. Behind the quiet jail, he ground his teeth. He'd exploited her aid from the moment she'd offered it so generously but he'd be damned if he'd exploit her feelings for him.

Remembering the night in her bed, he cursed silently. Had he not already taken advantage of her, her vulnerability, her loneliness? He wanted to again, aching to make love to her until he had buried himself inside her deeply enough to gather her body and heart together and fuse them to the emptiness inside him.

Enough, he told himself. He risked jeopardizing his own mission through inattention. Adam caught a glimpse of white ahead of him, probably the flowers Lily had brought. Pushing thoughts of Lily behind his mask of rigid discipline, he let his senses absorb the stillness of the night.

Moving closer, he saw two white tulips lying on the ground beneath the window, their stems snapped in half. Two for the prisoners he intended to rescue? Gleaming faintly in the moonlight also lay a stem of rhododendron, its luxuriant blossoms crushed.

Danger.

Hard on the heels of that thought came the realization that it was far too quiet here.

Adam turned and ran for Mercury, mounting in a flying leap from the rear that jarred his shoulder when he landed on the animal's back. With his knees he urged Mercury into a gallop, bending low over the horse's neck, his black cloak streaming from his shoulders.

Behind him half a dozen soldiers poured from the jail, rifles firing. "After him!" Ware shouted.

Damn, he had cut it too close, the colonel thought. There had been a mere half dozen men at his disposition because the governor feared the dratted townspeople were about to revolt.

His men's mounts had been hidden down the road, an important precaution so the jingle of tack would not give them away before the trap was sprung. But the clever bastard had somehow been alerted before he got close enough for Ware's men to seize him.

Ware ran for the horses with the rest of his men, mounting in quick, efficient motions, but he knew he was too late. The unknown rescuer had already seized too great a lead.

Ware slowed his mount while his men rode on in futile pursuit. The rebel leader could not possibly know where the prisoners were being taken, he told himself.

But tonight's rescue attempt . . . was it a lucky guess, like Ware's hunch that there would be such an effort? The tactics of the unknown Patriot leader ran so close to his own thinking that he had to wonder again if his mysterious opponent wasn't his former second-in-command.

Three days. Three days in which Lily had barely slept, scarcely eaten. Three days lying awake at night, sleeping only when exhaustion overcame her agitation. Three days pretending all was well while Loyalists in her shop complained of surly Patriots, and Patriots gave her looks fit to kill.

Yet no word came. She had not dared approach the jail again. Why had she heard nothing? Surely the Tories would talk if there had been a rescue attempt—especially a failed one. Unless they had clamped tightly down on such knowledge in the aftermath of the near riot outside the magazine.

Mary had dropped by, but she knew nothing as best Lily could tell, since she dared not ask leading questions. All the talk in town was of the brave citizens who had defied the soldiers. Ultimately, the ammunition stayed—at least until Governor Dunmore changed his mind again. Tensions in town grew ever higher.

And still no word.

On the fourth day Lily sent a flower message with Will out to Oak Grove. Nasturtium for the patriots, pennyroyal in symbolic recognition of the raid. Zinnia, because it represented thoughts of absent friends. *What happened to the plan to free the prisoners?* her flowers asked.

There was no answer.

The next night Lily sat in the gazebo after supper. May's flowers had begun to bloom, although a few days early. Azaleas had burst into color, and dogwoods waved delicately above her head. But for once Lily found little comfort in her garden. Memories of Adam were too strong.

Suddenly, as if her thoughts had conjured him, she felt a hand on her shoulder. Lily turned and threw herself into his arms. He did not speak, but his arms came around her in a tight embrace. She lifted her face for his kiss, forgetting everything for a moment but the longed-for, long-denied taste of him. Adam's lips were hard and possessive.

Lily pulled back first, her hands pressed to his broad chest. "Peter?" she gasped, the single word a tonic strong enough to quench her desire.

Adam kept her in his embrace, his hands curving her against his body. "Safe. Peter and Ethan are both safe, Lily."

She pulled back still more, half seeking Peter in the shadows behind Adam. Adam caught her hair between his hands, deftly unwound it. As he plunged his hands into the heavy mass, he bent down to speak softly into her ear. "Think, little flower. He can't stay here any longer. I took them to shelter."

That fact barely registered on her consciousness. For now, all she could think of was that Peter was safe. Safe, Adam had said. Safe.

"Oh, Adam, thank you." Her words were pitifully inadequate, and exhilaration overwhelmed her. She gave herself up to his touch, tugging on his queue to bring his mouth back toward hers. "Adam, how can I thank you? I've been so worried. . . ."

He silenced her with a single kiss pressed to her throat. "Don't ask that unless you really want to hear the answer."

"Then, will you finish making . . . amends?" she asked softly, wondering how the bold words had slipped out. Had he forgotten? For a second, long enough for the heat of embarrassment, she thought he had. She pressed her hands against his chest, struggling now to escape his grasp.

"Amends, Lily?" he asked, amusement in his deep voice. He swept her up into his arms. "All the amends you want, little flower."

There was joy and life here to be shared, and it would

not be denied. His mouth came down on hers as he strode through the garden. He didn't break the embrace until they were in the house, in a room he remembered only too well.

Seventeen

Love which in spite of darkness brought us hither,
Should in despite of light keep us together.
                                        —John Donne,
                                        Break of Day, 1610

Adam deposited Lily gently on the bed, throwing off his cloak as he eased his arms from around her. His hands were on her shoulders to push away her shawl when he realized he had not come to her in the best condition. He was dirty and unshaven, not to put too fine a point on it.

"Lily," he said, bending over her, "I have ridden hard and long this night. Do you want me to . . ."

She sat up, catching what was left of his neckcloth in one hand, which she swiftly unwound. "Adam, you were in worse condition when you were ill. Do you think I care?"

"Thank God, for I was not sure I could leave you." He followed her onto the bed, relishing the feel of her warm hands against his neck. She pulled off his queue ribbon, then began to unbutton his shirt.

Shuddering with pure pleasure at her touch, Adam did not realize for a moment that her interest was not purely sensual. Then he felt her small fingers probing at his bandage.

"Are you all right?" she whispered. He could feel her hesitation.

"No, for God's sake," he muttered, "not now." Lily started to move away at his answer. Adam realized he'd spoken aloud and that she thought he didn't want her. "No," he groaned. Then he reached for her, rolling her under him so that his lower body was in intimate contact with hers.

He moved his hips against her. "There is your answer, love." She gave a faint start, then relaxed, letting her hips cradle him as he rocked slowly against her. Adam twined his fingers through her hair, turning her face up to his for his kiss. "Forget I was your patient. Bloom for me, little flower," he murmured.

The dark, rich voice flowed through Lily, erasing thought, erasing fear. Her concern for his wound faded as his warm skin made her fingertips tingle where she touched him. As he kissed her, she pulled off his shirt, trailing her fingertips through the light matting of hair she remembered so well. She let her fingertips wander down to the waistband of his breeches, then danced them around to finish untucking his shirt.

He sucked in his breath, and her concern for his condition returned. "Adam, are you all right?"

"Stop asking me that." His voice was low but commanding. "What do I have to do to make you forget?"

"It was your . . . the sound you made," she said. "I thought I had hurt you."

At that, Adam chuckled. He rolled off her to his back, using his uninjured arm to bring her on top of him in one easy move. "That sound, my love, was an ache." He swept the shawl off her shoulders, his hands going to the neck-

Introducing Ballad,
A New Line of Historical Romances

As a lover of historical romance, you'll adore Ballad Romances. Written by today's most popular romance authors, every book in the Ballad line is not only an individual story, but part of a two to six book series as well. You can look forward to 4 new titles each month – each taking place at a different time and place in history.

But don't take our word for how wonderful these stories are! Accept our introductory shipment of 4 Ballad Romance novels – a $22.00 value – ABSOLUTELY FREE – and see for yourself!

Once you've experienced your first 4 Ballad Romances, we're sure you'll want to continue receiving these wonderful historical romance novels each month – without ever having to leave your home – using our convenient and inexpensive home subscription service. Here's what you get for joining:

- **4 BRAND NEW Ballad Romances delivered to your door each month**

- **25% off the cover price of $5.50 with your home subscription.**

- **A FREE monthly newsletter filled with author interviews, book previews, special offers, and more!**

- **No risk or obligation...you're free to cancel whenever you wish... no questions asked.**

To start your membership, simply complete and return the card provided. You'll receive your Introductory Shipment of 4 FREE Ballad Romances. Then, each month, as long as your account is in good standing, you will receive the 4 newest Ballad Romances. Each shipment will be yours to examine for 10 days. If you decide to keep the books, you'll pay the preferred home subscriber's price of $16.50 – a savings of 25% off the cover price! (plus $1.50 shipping & handling) If you want us to stop sending books, just say the word...it's that simple.

Passion-
Adventure-
Excitement-
Romance-
Ballad!

4 FREE BOOKS are waiting for you! Just mail in the certificate below!

BOOK CERTIFICATE

Yes! Please send me 4 Ballad Romances ABSOLUTELY FREE! After my introductory shipment, I will receive 4 new Ballad Romances each month to preview FREE for 10 days (as long as my account is in good standing). If I decide to keep the books, I will pay the money-saving preferred publisher's price of $16.50 plus $1.50 shipping and handling. That's 25% off the cover price. I may return the shipment within 10 days and owe nothing, and I may cancel my subscription at any time. The 4 FREE books will be mine to keep in any case.

Name _____

Address_____ Apt. _____

City_____ State _____ Zip _____

Telephone (____) _____

Signature _____

(If under 18, parent or guardian must sign)

All orders subject to approval by Zebra Home Subscription Service.
Terms and prices subject to change. Offer valid only in the U.S.

DN021A

If the certificate is
missing below, write to:

Ballad Romances,
c/o Zebra Home
Subscription Service Inc.

P.O. Box 5214,
Clifton, New Jersey
07015-5214

OR call TOLL FREE
1-888-345-BOOK (2665)

Passion...
Adventure...
Excitement...
Romance...

Get 4
Ballad
Historical
Romance
Novels
FREE!

lll..l..lll....lll.l.l.l.l..l..ll.l.l..l..lll..lll..l

BALLAD ROMANCES
Zebra Home Subscription Service, Inc.
P.O. Box 5214
Clifton NJ 07015-5214

line of her gown. "The ache of wanting, little flower. Not pain."

Adam unlaced her gown, pushing it down to her waist along with her chemise. His hands—both hands, some small part of her, still watchful, noticed—stroked around the sides of her breasts before he cupped them, filling his hands with her.

"Oh," she exclaimed, startled at the unexpected jolt that went through her at his touch. He chuckled. "Did that hurt?" he inquired, his voice richly amused.

"No. Oh, no." She could barely speak with her breasts his playthings, with the heat streaking inside her.

"Well, 'twas the same kind of sound I made," he pointed out, his laughing mouth close enough for her to feel his breath where he held her with his hands, rubbing, stroking.

"I . . . I see," she said, breathless.

The stubble on Adam's cheek grazed her breast just before his mouth did. "I do not want you to *see*," he murmured, teasingly displeased. "I want you to *feel*."

Then Adam renewed his sensual assault. He took her nipple into his mouth, his hands molding the curves of her breast as he sucked. The slight scraping of his beard heightened the sensation. She squirmed on him, finding the bulge beneath his breeches and positioning herself over it, yearning to feel pressure against her softness.

She ached sweetly, painfully. "Now I know what you meant," she said, still trying to find a better fit for him between her legs.

"No, you do not." The dark promise in his voice made her shiver. "Not yet."

Adam sat up, keeping Lily on his lap. He kissed her, his hands moving over her as if he could not touch her enough. Lily loved the feel of his hands, his caresses gentle, then more passionate. Her skin felt hot everywhere he touched her, and she thought he felt the same. His arms moved easily, although the injured one was still bandaged. But the bandage was much smaller than the one she had last wrapped around him.

He lifted her chemise and dress off over her head. Adam shrugged out of his shirt but did not unfasten his breeches. His hands remained on her possessively.

"You'll never get out of your clothes that way," she said.

"I know. But I find I do not want to let go of you." This time his voice held no trace of humor.

She moved back onto his thighs, feeling the strength in them. "Then let me help you," she said. Adam allowed her to unfasten his breeches, but when her hand brushed his arousal, he jerked. "Oh, God, Lily," he said. Holding her still with one hand, he levered off his boots, then lifted his hips to pull off his breeches.

There was something fierce about him now, although he remained in control. His teeth closed lightly over one nipple as his hand slipped between her legs, finding her soft and damp. She allowed her legs to part, feeling the sweet ache intensify. She was on fire, shuddering with the waves of heat that swept her head to toe. "Is this the ache you meant?" she asked in a small voice.

"Yes," he said. "Do you want more, Lily?" He took a deep breath. "Do you want me?"

She knew it had been hard for him to ask. In answer she reached down and closed her hand around him. "Oh, yes."

Spreading her legs across his thighs, Adam started to open her for his possession. Lily tensed as he began to surge inside her.

"I cannot promise that there will not be pain this first

time, love," he said in a strained voice. "But it will not last." Then Lily looked down and forgot the pain in the wonder of seeing him become one with her.

Adam looked down as well, kissing her forehead before moving his mouth softly over her cheeks and the bridge of his nose. "We are joined, Lily. Does it hurt now?" he whispered against her lips.

"N-no," she said uncertainly, wondering if she had been too bold again.

Adam brought her closer, slipping deeper inside her. " 'Tis all right, little flower. You were made for this." Fully seated in her, he thrust, and the incredible feel of him so deep and solid in her soft, unexplored center took Lily's breath.

He started to move in her then. Lily ran her hands up and down the smooth muscles of his back. He leaned forward and caught the peak of one breast between his lips, suckling as his body taught her a rhythm without words.

Nudging her legs wider apart, his hands cupping her buttocks, Adam leaned backward in a slow, controlled fall onto the bed that left him more deeply embedded in her, her knees to either side of his lean flanks.

"Ohhh," she murmured, experimenting with the ability to change the depth of him inside her.

"All amends are made, little flower. I yield to you," he said. She could feel his hands clenched at his sides as he strove to allow her to take control.

For a few delightful minutes Lily did just that, glorying in the power to make him groan by her slightest move. Then she leaned forward, her hair a scented cloud that enclosed the two of them even more intimately. "Show me," she whispered.

Released from his self-imposed restraint, Adam surged

upward, taking the rhythm they had built to a deeper, faster plane. Just when she was sure she could not stand it any longer, Adam reached down to where their bodies were joined and found the bud that he had taught to bloom. Lily cried out, her muscles contracting exquisitely as she found her release.

"Lily, Lily," exploded hoarsely from Adam as his body erupted inside her, his powerful thighs stiffening beneath her. His hands gripped her hips, holding her to him until she fell forward onto his chest, while he groaned her name into her hair as his body slowly lost its tautness.

Draped across his chest, her head resting on the shoulder of his uninjured arm, Lily dozed. She thought Adam did too, for his breathing slowed, as hers did, his body relaxing beneath hers.

He turned onto his side, bringing her with him, keeping her snug against his side. Having his solid, warm body along the length of hers made her sleepily content. Not so content that she forgot to ask about her brother, however.

"Where did you take them, Adam? Why were you gone so long?"

"One question at a time," Adam responded. "The prisoners had been taken from the jail. I had to find them before I could rescue them."

"Where were they?" Diverted by the rescue itself, she barely noticed that he had not told her where he had taken them.

"On the road to the river. They were supposed to meet a ship that had put in secretly. With the townspeople up in arms, I suspect the redcoats were afraid there would be a march on the jail."

He brushed strands of hair away from her face. "Did you create a disturbance near the Palace Green?"

" 'Twas not hard to do, after the Governor had threatened to take the ammunition out of the magazine again," she confessed.

"You did me an enormous service, little flower," he said. "Although there were redcoats at the jail waiting just in case something happened, they were far fewer than they might have been."

He thought meeting with "only" half a dozen armed men had given him good odds? Lily was impressed. Yet her principal concern resurfaced quickly. "Peter was uninjured?"

"Aye, neither he nor Ethan was hurt. Peter had a few bruises left over from the capture, but he is fine."

He did not laugh, but Lily felt, suddenly, the humor in him. "What are you finding so amusing?" she asked.

"I cannot say I have ever had this sort of conversation in, ah, this particular situation."

Lily stiffened and scooted away from him. "I am sure I would not know what conversation would be appropriate at this point, never having been in this situation."

He tugged her back toward him, laughter escaping him overtly this time. "I am sorry, love, I did not mean to mock you. I know your deepest concern is for your brother." That half-wistful note was in his voice again, as if he did not know what it was like to be loved and missed and worried over.

Lily allowed herself to be drawn back to his side. "I know you have never been in this situation before," he whispered. "The gift you gave me is beyond price, and I have no means adequate to thank you."

She did not especially like the formal tone of his voice, but she did not know what to say either. "You have given my brother back his freedom. 'Tis enough."

No, Adam thought. Not even close. But he said nothing aloud.

Lily relaxed against him, too tired for any more discussion. Her last thought was *This time I will see him in the morning.* If he had felt half of what she had, she did not see how he could move before daybreak. She was sure she could not move a muscle.

In the hour before dawn, a masculine cheek, shaved and clean smelling, pressed against hers. Before she could wake from her slumber, the deep, soft voice filled her, soothing her.

Lulled, Lily started to drift back into the embrace of sleep, but she refused to go alone. Her hand pressed to his freshly shaven face, she whispered, "Stay."

Adam looked down at her shadowed, sleeping form. The moon was long past its peak, yet enough remained to outline her lovely body in cool white light, to tint her tawny hair silver. He was tired from the long days just past and knew he should go.

He had ridden directly to her, intending to tell her only of Peter's safety but had been caught off guard by her passionate thanks. Like the selfish son of a bitch he was, he had taken her thanks, channeled it into sensual awareness, and stolen her innocence.

No, he thought as he lifted her delicate, callused hand to his face, he had not taken from her anything she did not wish to give. He was fiercely glad he had made her his, but this could not continue. His situation was no different from the last time he had lain in this bed.

Now that he had washed and shaved and steeled himself to leave, she had undone him with her simple plea, the same he had once whispered to her.

His hand stayed within hers as he lifted the sheet and slipped in beside her. She smiled sleepily, nestled against his side. The scent of her and of their lovemaking sent a sharp stab of desire through him. Adam smiled ironically at himself. He had not been *that* ready to go, or he would have dressed before approaching the bed.

As it was, he knew his erection tented the sheet. One more touch, however sleepy, however innocent, from Lily's hands and he would turn to her again. He lay tensed, torn between determination to resist and the certain knowledge that he would not be able to.

He did not have long to wait. Lily draped one arm over his waist, the other pressing lightly against his chest. He groaned, thinking of the short distance her hand would have to travel to find him ready for her. Her soft breath touched his throat.

Every muscle in his body was tensed. Ache, indeed. He snorted. This was pain, pure and simple.

Adam gave in to the absolute need to touch her. His hand slipped down her soft cheek, tracing the contour of her jaw, her neck, her throat. He touched her shoulder, willing himself to move his hand only down her arm, when she shifted slightly.

His hand dropped, his fingers trailing across her breast before he could snatch them back. Once he felt the velvety aureole contract, however, he was lost. Her creamy breast fit so perfectly into his palm that he was reluctant to let it go. But her other curves beckoned, and he traced his hand between the valley of her breasts, down her flat belly to the indentation of her navel.

Bending to kiss it, he used his tongue to outline the small circle. She moved again. He kissed his way past her navel, heading toward the soft curls. This was a temptation he simply could not resist.

"Adam!" Lily clutched at his thick hair, suddenly awake. "What are you doing?"

I cannot leave you. "Do not ask," he murmured, "just feel."

Despite her inexperience, Lily knew his passion and his attention to her were extraordinary. She reveled in a sensual haze. Adam gently opened her legs, tracing his thumbs around the sensitive insides of her thighs before parting the soft folds of her femininity.

His tongue followed. Lily could not express the intensity of her pleasure, for her voice was caught in her throat somewhere between wonder and surprise. Adam's mouth was warm, his tongue exquisitely caressing. Then he closed his lips over the bud that had bloomed earlier beneath his hands.

Lily caught fire. The dreamy quality of their loving vanished as heat flared within her. Her hands gripped Adam's shoulders as his fingers slipped inside her. Just as her tightening muscles signaled imminent climax, Adam slid up her body to enter her in one smooth, deep, liquid plunge.

Her aching center filled at last, the bud of pleasure at its utmost sensitivity, Lily contracted in a release so powerful, it was almost painful. She called Adam's name softly over and over, scarcely aware she was doing so.

Adam filled her so deeply that she could not distinguish her own shudders of pleasure from his as his climax seized him. He called her name in an anguished gasp. Lily, her senses stunned, was awed by the force they had created together, by the passion he had displayed, this man who so prized self-control.

Spent, he buried his face in her hair. But as she held him, she thought she heard, like echoes of the pleasure that still made their bodies tremble, the sound of her name faintly repeated, in wonder, in sadness, in joy.

Their bodies sheened with sweat, their breaths fast and shallow still, neither of them spoke as gray-splintered shards of predawn light trickled into the room. Lily shivered, this time from cold. Adam pulled the sheet up around them.

"All my best intentions . . ." he murmured, breathing as if he'd run hard. He did not lift his head to look at her.

Lily was in too advanced a state of languor to speak. Slipping into sleep again, she did not protest when Adam left the bed. She thought it only temporary, because he picked up the coverlet from the floor where it had been pushed off earlier.

He tucked it around her, murmuring quiet admonitions to sleep. As always, his voice settled inside her, taking her in its wake. She was asleep before she knew whether he returned to bed or not.

The pounding at the door some time later woke her effectively and unpleasantly. As she struggled out of the sweet cocoon of sleep, Lily became painfully aware of the scene's dreadful familiarity.

Morning . . . A knock on her door . . . The bed, empty. And a single flower on her pillow.

Eighteen

And resolv'd to live a fool . . .
—Francis Beaumont,
Letter to Ben Jonson,
1640

"Oh, no," Lily gasped. The only thing different about her situation this time was that she found herself completely naked.

The knocking came again, louder, more imperious. That was not Will Evans down there, she was certain. Lily looked for her clothes, remembering how they had fallen to the floor when Adam—

Heat flooded through her body in a rush.

"Mistress Walters, open this door!" She heard a muffled thump, as if rifle butts were being pounded against the wood.

Fear swept through her, clashing with the rush of desire in an unpleasant mix that left her shaky and lightheaded.

Another thump. Calling out would do no good. Whoever was knocking could not hear her from the second floor.

She looked around. Her clothes were spread out over the back of a chair. Lily had no time to be grateful for

Adam's thoughtfulness. She hauled on her chemise, then struggled into her dress as quickly as she could.

She spared one glance at the pillow to see what flower lay there. "Pray do not destroy my door. I'm coming," she called, tying the laces of her bodice as she went.

Lily yanked open the door, glaring. Colonel Ware actually took a step back.

"What do you want?" she snapped, too angry to be frightened. Ware took a quick glance back at his sergeants, who were staring openmouthed at Lily's tangled hair and bare feet. She suspected she hadn't tied up her bodice particularly well either, but she refused to look.

Ware's reflexes were swift, she had to grant him that. He stepped into the house, grabbed Lily's arm, and closed the door behind him.

"What are you doing?" Lily said, outraged.

"Protecting you, believe it or not," Ware snapped back.

Oh, so she had offended the colonel's sense of order, had she? In spite of her fear, Lily sensed she had unsettled the formidable colonel, a small victory in her favor. She wrestled free from his grasp.

She had no time to savor it. "Where is your brother, Mistress Walters?" Ware asked in his precise way.

"We have already had this conversation, Colonel," Lily said wearily, trying to comb through her hair surreptitiously with her fingers. "You knew where he was the first time you asked, Colonel. I did not. Why should now be different?" She dropped her hands to her hips, angry once more.

"You knew also, or why would you have visited him?"

" 'Twas no thanks to you that I did find out."

"What else did you find out, Mistress Walters? Where is he now?"

Lily's heart lurched suddenly. He knew Peter and Ethan had been freed.

"I grow tired of asking you this question, mistress."

"I grow tired of you asking it, Colonel." His icy politeness snapped then. He seized her arm again, dragging her toward the stairs.

"I will not suffer such insubordination. Not from you, not from Pearson. Not from anyone." Except for the death grip he had on her arm, Ware might have been talking to himself.

Another of Lily's internal organs shifted unpleasantly. He could not mean Adam. How could he?

The colonel's unyielding grip on her arm distracted Lily's attention from thoughts of Adam and the rearrangement of her heart and lungs. He kept dragging her deeper into her own house.

She dug in her heels. "What are you doing?"

"Where is your room?" he said. Lily started to fight him in earnest then.

All at once he let go of her arm, staring down his long, patrician nose at her. "I am not after your virtue, gel. Find your shoes, put up your hair, and get a shawl."

Lily was not relieved. In fact, she felt more apprehensive. "Why?" She managed to say the single word, hoping she still sounded brave and defiant.

"You are coming with me. I am placing you under detention."

Adam was still asleep in the Williamsburg town house when Will woke him. "What is it?" he asked none too kindly.

"Your squireness, 'tis Mistress Walters, she . . .
she . . ."

Adam had little need to feign irritation. He was exhausted from the rescue, from the ride, and from the
night with Lily. "I appreciate her flowers as much as
anyone, but you need not have woken me for that," he
said waspishly, praying nothing was wrong.

"Sir, but, your worthiness, you gave express orders to
wake you before noon, since you wanted to go back to
Oak Grove and—"

"And is it noon?" Adam asked, already knowing the
answer from the position of the sun that had not yet entered the bedchamber of his Williamsburg town house.

"No, sir, but . . ."

"Then off with you until then." Adam, always careful
to keep his body from view when he was not wearing
the squire's full regalia, pulled the covers up to his chin.
He grabbed a pair of spectacles from the night table,
shoving them abruptly onto his nose.

Will had not budged. Adam forced himself not to sit
up, to remain in bed as if lounging. The yawn he did not
have to feign. "Well?" he inquired in a bored voice. "Are
you leaving?"

"Sir, Squire," exploded young Will, "Mistress Walters,
sir, she has been arrested."

Adam sat up, the covers falling to his waist. "What?"

"She was seen with Colonel Ware this morning, sir,
and 'twas not like that other time, no one can say she
went with him willingly, sir, because there were two soldiers with rifles to either side of her."

That other time? Adam could not spare a moment to
inquire. Nor did he want to appear to be too interested,
which would be uncharacteristic of the indolent squire.

"Will, go fetch water to shave me, and lay out my vermilion frock coat."

God, it was hard to pretend all he cared about was his wardrobe, when he wanted to throw on a shirt and a pair of breeches and get out of there as fast as possible. He struggled against the urge to bark orders like the major he had so recently been.

He hoped Will was not staring at the evidence of his very unflabby chest. "Out, boy, and get started. We are paying a call on Colonel Ware this morning." He hoped his voice sounded reasonably unhurried. Adam waited until he heard Will leave the dressing room. He normally allowed the boy to shave him but not to dress him, unusual as that was for someone of his exalted station.

The second the outer door closed, Adam leapt from bed and began dressing himself. In his haste he almost forgot his padding. Shoving it into his waistband with a curse, he threw open the inner door for Will to enter with the basin of steaming water.

Resigning himself to the useless half hour he would have to spend being shaved and powdered, Adam jammed his most outrageous wig onto his head and sat down in the shaving chair. He kept his mind carefully blank, trying not to think of Lily being interrogated by Ware. Mostly, he tried not to think about last night and the colossal mistake it had been to make love to Lily.

Lily sat in an elegant wood-paneled library, the home of one of Williamsburg's wealthiest citizens. Evidently, the room had been commandeered for Ware's office. Lily noticed very little of the extensive library or the silk-hung windows. She was trying her hardest not to show her growing sense of despair.

"You are very much mistaken, young lady, if you think to cozen me with this tale of being at odds with your brother. I have been told that the two of you are very close, since you helped raise the lad after you were orphaned," Ware said after Lily had told him for the tenth time that she had no idea where Peter was.

Lily did not reply. Thank goodness Adam had not answered her question about where he had taken Peter, because she could truthfully claim to know nothing.

Not that the colonel would believe her.

Colonel Ware looked askance at her relieved expression. "I assure you your situation is quite serious, Mistress Walters."

"I do not doubt that, Colonel. 'Tis ironic that my recent associations with Loyalists have left me persona non grata with my former friends. All the Patriots think—"

"Rebels," he interrupted.

"The Patriots," she continued stubbornly, "no longer believe I hold their interests at heart. So you see, Colonel, I am neither fish nor fowl, trusted by no one, reviled equally by both sides. If you see me as a key to information about Patriot activities, then you are not questioning the right person."

"Who, then?" Ware asked, leaning forward over the inlaid mahogany table between them.

"I told you, I am no longer trusted." She directed her gaze to her lap. She knew her semblance of modesty would not fool Ware, for had she not shouted at him earlier while half clad to boot?

"But you know them, do you not?" Ware persisted. "You know who the rebels are, from the activities of your brother and of this mystery man." Lily must have started inadvertently, because Ware narrowed his eyes, tapping the quill pen he held against one long, narrow finger.

"You do know him, I see."

Lily shook her head, mute, afraid she had already betrayed Adam by the look on her face.

"Oh, come, my dear, 'tis common knowledge that the Sons of Liberty have a new leader who prefers to remain hidden. Not a local man, hmmm?" Lily thought he was bluffing. So far as she knew, Adam's presence was a secret closely kept among the Sons of Liberty.

"Certainly the other members of the Sons of Liberty know. And you know who they are." His pale eyes gleamed with intelligence. Lily knew she had to watch her words carefully with this man, lest he turn them back on her and wring something from her that he actually had not known.

"I assure you, Colonel, I know nothing. Though I am the elder, as I told you once before, my brother has not seen fit to keep me apprised of his activities." Lily allowed some of the bitterness she had felt at being excluded to creep into her voice.

Still, she knew too much. She knew who trained the Sons of Liberty at night. She knew who had planned the raid on the ship. She knew who had freed the prisoners.

Adam Pearson—and the colonel seemed to know him.

Suddenly, someone flung open the door to the library and a vision in lace and vermilion strode in. "I've come to save you, my dear," cried Squire Sotheby. Lily and the colonel exchanged surprised glances, causing Lily to nearly giggle.

The expression on Colonel Ware's face was indescribable. Revulsion, annoyance, and fleeting amusement warred with anger on his patrician features. Had Lily and the colonel been friends, the glance they shared might have been conspiratorial.

But they were not friends and never would be. Ridiculous or not, Lily had never been so glad to see anyone in her life as she was to see Squire Adair Sotheby, rose-tinted glasses and all.

She began to rise to her feet, but the look on Ware's face stopped her. His amusement had passed, and what remained was chilling. His cold fury could be dangerous for both her and the squire.

Lily said nothing, but the mute anguish in her eyes infuriated Adam, overcoming any remaining concern about confronting his former commander face-to-face. Brute force was not Ware's style, but his interrogation skills were formidable. Lily was right to fear him.

Adam recognized the signs of strain in the man who had been his advocate and mentor. He had last reported to Ware when he'd been sent to infiltrate the Sons of Liberty in Boston, a mission from which Adam had never returned.

Traitor? Spy? Adam knew the answers in his heart, answers Ware would never understand.

Pray Ware did not know who stood in front of him now.

"Colonel Ware, such a pleasure to see you again. What are you doing with my lovely florist?" Adam said in the squire's squeaky tenor voice.

"I'm questioning her. What does it look like?" Ware snapped, his usual composure fled.

Good, Adam thought. He had half a chance with Ware

off balance. "Whatever would you want to do that for?"
Adam asked offhandedly.

"I do not believe this concerns you, Squire," Ware
said politely enough.

Not politely enough for the rich, influential squire. "As
I have made it my business to circulate among our loyal
Tory community here, Colonel, I assure you this does
concern me. Mistress Walters is plagued with a scapegrace brother whose antics have been quite distressing."

Adam saw Lily grit her teeth at his choice of words
but knew she was intelligent enough to figure out what
he was doing. God, she must be frightened to let him try
to assist her, he reflected briefly.

"Scapegrace, you say? My dear Squire, Mistress Walters's brother is a traitor to the Crown and a fugitive from
its justice," Ware replied.

"Such harsh words in the presence of a lady," Adam
said in a languid voice, examining the elaborately carved
head of his cane. "Whatever her brother may have done,
the Crown would hardly wish to subject one of its loyal
subjects to such unpleasantness, I daresay."

Adam looked up, fixing Ware with a brief glance to
assess his mood. Then he resumed examining his splen-
did cane. He could not afford to meet Ware's eyes for
long, even with tinted spectacles, face powder, and a wig,
but he wanted to emphasize the point he was about to
make. "Do you have something to charge her with?" he
asked.

"Conspiracy . . ." Ware began.

"Conspiracy to do what? The brother is missing, is he
not?" Adam asked, watching closely to see if Ware
wanted to admit the prisoners had been freed, or if he
preferred to pretend they had embarked to be transported.

"Aye, he is missing." So Ware did not want the town to know the truth, at least not before news of it reached Williamsburg.

"Having unfortunate friends and relations is not a crime by itself, I believe," Adam continued, exulting inwardly when Ware looked away, discomfited and annoyed.

"The situation is unsettled here . . ." Ware started to explain, clearing his throat. Adam knew at that instant that he had him. He moved in to seal his victory.

"I know of the unfortunate events in Boston, Colonel, but I do not believe they prevail here." He moved toward Lily, who sat on a yellow damask sofa, hands clasped tightly in her lap. Nevertheless, he did not miss Ware's sharp glance in his direction. Had mentioning Boston been a mistake?

"You seem well informed about events in Boston," Ware commented.

"Just the usual gossip, I assure you," Adam replied, avoiding eye contact. He ignored the knife-edge tension emanating from Ware, holding out his gloved hand to Lily.

"However, as a Loyalist, someone with a certain amount of influence in this community," he said with an insincere humility he knew would antagonize Ware and perhaps distract him, "I assure you Mistress Walters is just an unlucky young woman with a brother gone bad."

He was gambling on the fact that Ware would not want to alienate one of the richest, most visible Tories in the area. Adam had assumed no overtly political role as Adair, but he had entertained lavishly, providing invitations that were not always forthcoming in a town turning increasingly toward Patriot sentiments.

Adam bent over Lily, urging her silently to rise with a tug on her hand. As she did so, he swiftly tucked her arm into the crook of his elbow, moving her steadily toward the door.

Ware watched them keenly but had not stopped their progress toward the door. "Let me suggest something, Colonel," Adam said, presenting Ware with the side profile that emphasized the squire's supposed bulk. "I understand that you may not know the lady as well as I do." He smiled fatuously, aware of Lily's grimace at his side.

He patted her hand. "She has done up absolutely the most marvelous floral arrangements for me. I will be hosting an entertainment the night before Mistress Chalmers's forthcoming wedding and will need her exclusive services to help prepare Oak Grove. I will also be able to consult with Mistress Walters about my sadly neglected flower beds."

Adam felt the brass handle of the door brush the back of his frock coat. There were guards outside the room, not that he entertained any hope of their making a run for it, certainly not in his present persona. "So I propose to take Mistress Walters with me to Oak Grove," he glibly continued. "She will be well chaperoned there, in every sense," he said, with what he hoped was subtle emphasis. "I am certain I need not expand upon that point."

Would Ware take the bait? Adam had just promised to keep Lily under the squire's care and out of trouble. Lily would no doubt be furious, but he knew Ware would never agree to simply release her. Adam had to get her out of Williamsburg.

"You may rely upon me, Colonel," Adam continued.

"Feel free to let me know at any time how I might be of further assistance to you and to the Crown. Good day, sir. I look forward to seeing you at the wedding."

This was the moment he would be permitted to leave with Lily or prevented from doing so. Adam made a leg to Ware, tucked his walking stick under his arm, and replaced his hat upon the high wig he wore. With one hand at the small of Lily's back, he avoided looking at Ware as he opened the door.

"One moment, if you please, Squire," his former commanding officer said.

Nineteen

A proper man . . . a most lovely, gentleman-like man.

—William Shakespeare,
A Midsummer Night's Dream,
1596

Poised to leave, Adam halted in mid-stride. He felt Lily's hand clutch his sleeve. "Aye, Colonel?" he forced himself to say calmly. He looked warily across the room at Ware.

"You will take full responsibility for this action," Ware said in an icy voice. It was not a question.

"Absolutely." Adam bowed. "Your servant, sir."

"Yours." Ware inclined his upper body in a brief half-bow. "I look forward to seeing you soon, Squire. We can talk of Boston. 'Tis where I am posted. Perhaps we have friends in common."

"Indeed?" Adam feigned bored interest. "Perhaps." Every muscle in his body screamed to leave. Ware was coming too close to the mark. A word mistakenly uttered in his normal voice, a habitual gesture, could alert Randolph to his real identity. Adam knew only too well how sharp an observer the colonel was.

Adam gratefully drew his gaze away from Ware's

pinched, irritated face. Adam patted Lily's hand patronizingly instead. He walked with her across the outer room, past the soldiers, and into the wide entrance hall.

Her legs were going to give out at any moment, he was certain. After the stiff tension in her frame, he felt the wobbliness overtake her as he guided her out of the house. The aftermath of fear. He was familiar with the sensation himself.

The normal bustle of Williamsburg seemed to have come to a halt in front of the house. People had seen his carriage before. They had seen him and Lily together before. Why, then, did he feel this sense of hostility surrounding her?

As the crowd stared stonily at Lily, he realized he had not seen her with patriots before. They clearly believed she had transferred her loyalties. This was another consequence of her impetuous actions, of trying to insinuate herself into the trust of Royalists to glean information. But she was no spy.

"Sold your brother to them, did you?" someone in the crowd muttered as he paused beside her.

"And my Ethan?" A young woman who must have been Ethan Holt's wife pushed her way forward. "You told the British about . . . about what they were doing that night." She lowered her voice, looking around nervously, seeming to realize for the first time that British soldiers were nearby. "Now they are gone. To be transported." Her mouth remained open in silent anguish.

"But they are not, they have been res—" Lily protested, then stopped in midsentence. Adam knew she was on the verge of blurting out that the men were safe. He could not let her reveal her knowledge because it would jeopardize his identity as Adam Pearson, although he knew her desire to justify her actions in the eyes of her friends must be powerful.

His arm shot out to tap his walking stick against the shins of a youth standing near him. "Out of my way, you lot. Or I shall have to call on my friends inside," he said arrogantly. He clamped his hand down hard on Lily's arm as the impulse to flee him took root in her.

Running into the crowd would do her no good. He regretted that she had no choices, this woman who was so independent and resourceful, but she would find no protection there. And even if she hated him for it, the refuge he offered her was the only one available to her at present.

"Come along, my dear," he said, pretending to be unaware of the embarrassment he was causing her.

Will handed Lily into the carriage. The boy was fit to burst with questions. Adam laid a heavy hand on his shoulder. "Not now, Will," he said in a low voice. "Not here."

Will nodded his understanding, his gaze traveling from the crowd to Lily's pale face to Adam's set one. Mounting the box quickly, he told the coachman without having to ask that they were headed toward Oak Grove.

Lily began to protest. Adam silenced her, waving a gloved hand in the air. "All things considered, lovely Lily," he said, "were I you, I should not risk going back to your house at the moment. Ware might still change his mind and want you back. I will feel much better with you safely ensconced at Oak Grove, out of the colonel's easy reach."

"Oak Grove?" The look of confusion on her face cleared quickly. "How dare you?" she said. "How dare you take me away from my home so high-handedly, order me about . . ."

"You may recall you were not at home at the time I

found you," Adam pointed out in what he thought was a reasonable voice.

"But . . . but you have ruined me, ruined my reputation with my friends and neighbors."

Adam raised his brows, but not too high, lest the spectacles slip. "I? My dear, I believe you have ruined your reputation all by yourself. I did not see many friends in that horrid crowd we faced." Adam lifted his lip in an elegant sneer, the fashionable black patch on his upper lip curling as he did so.

"Although I cannot think 'ruined' is the correct word to apply," he continued, "when all you have been doing is so intelligently rethinking the radical rubbish your brother espoused. That is what I have heard you say at various soirees, is it not?" Adam said, challenging her with her own lie.

Misery filled her clear golden eyes. He had trapped her in her own deceptions and she could not take them back. He knew she longed to throw his words back in his face, but for good or ill, she could not afford to alienate him. He watched the struggle play out on her face until he could bear it no longer.

Adam turned his head to look out at the countryside as they rolled down the packed-earth road that led to his plantation. Sweet God, but he did not relish the prospect of having her under his roof.

Lily spent the rest of the day closeted in the elegant room she had been given at Oak Grove, trying to decide what she should do next. She had been so angry at Sotheby that she'd refused to come down for lunch, taking a tray in her room instead. After an hour she was bored and restless. Sulking was simply not her style.

Now it was almost dinnertime, and Mistress Steele, the housekeeper, had been sent to see if she would be coming down to dinner. When Lily tonelessly said yes, the middle-aged woman smiled with approval.

Mistress Steele was now showing her a clothes press full of gowns. "I can have needlework done to alter any of these, mistress," she said.

Lily stared, amazed. "Where did all these come from? From his mistresses?" She had never thought of the squire in any sort of sexual way. She was hard pressed to imagine him surrounded by women, or that he might have ordered such an extensive wardrobe to suit a light-o'-love.

Mistress Steele puffed out her lips, rushing to defend her employer. "Oh, I know he can be peculiar, miss, but he is quite the thoughtful one, he is. He entertains so much, you know, he says that people should be comfortable while they are here, and if they want to stay longer, why shouldn't they?"

"Well, I suppose," said Lily, who had never before considered the isolation of living on a plantation. "But these are such elegant things." She looked at velvets and jacquard-worked silks, fur-trimmed cloaks and pelisses. Even for a rich town like Williamsburg, these were beautiful garments.

"These particular items, they come from England, I believe, mistress."

"Does he have a wife in England?" Lily had never thought of the squire in connection with a wife either.

"No, madam," Mistress Steele said, taking out a silk gown trimmed lavishly with ecru lace. "These are his mother's."

"His mother's?" Lily touched the soft fabric of the gown, which slid through her fingers with an enchanting whisper. It seemed rather sensual for an older woman such as Adair's mother must be. "Does she visit often?"

"I am not certain about that, miss. You would have to ask the master. These things were here when I arrived, but I have never heard him speak of her. He can be quite closemouthed when he wants to be."

Mistress Steele draped the gown over her arm. "Listen to me, fair running off at the mouth, I am. Best I give this to one of the girls to press, then you can wear it down to dinner, miss. Will that be all for now?" she asked.

"Yes, thank you," Lily said absently. How odd. She had never heard the squire speak of his mother. Indeed, he never mentioned any family at all.

Adam gave Lily a sharp stare when she first entered the dining room. "Is something the matter, Squire?" she asked.

"No, no. You just gave me a start in that dress," he said.

"Is something the matter with it?" Lily asked with apprehension. Had the swift hemming of the gown somehow damaged it? Would he be angry? Obviously, his mother had been a few inches taller than she and more ample in the bosom. Still, Lily did not think she was showing too much of her bosom, but perhaps the dress hung too loosely on her. . . .

She pulled herself up with a start. While she was hardly a hostage, she was not here because she wanted to be. Even if he gave lavishly and was generous, she would not worry overmuch about the squire's loan of a dress. After all, were it not for him, she would have her own clothes to wear. Were it not for him, she thought with a surge of anger, she would not be there at all.

Adam saw her thoughts on her clear, expressive face.

Oh, it was his fault she was here, all right, but, dammit, did she have to look so beautiful in his mother's gown? Thankfully, Lily looked nothing like the Countess of Dalby. He had all but forgotten the clothes were here, the results of his mother's last ploy to win his attention.

He had sent them on from Boston months earlier, never thinking that he would claim so soon the Virginia plantation he'd bought several years ago. His thought at the time was that the clothes would be farthest from his sight there. He'd returned her jewels on a ship bound for England with a note that said: "Do not even contemplate the journey." She might actually have come to America after the jewels, but he knew she'd never miss the gowns.

Seeing one of those gowns now on Lily brought back the last time he had seen his mother, almost twenty years ago. With the ruthless efficiency he'd learned over the years, he suppressed the memory, concentrating instead on the lovely woman before him. Lily was nothing like the woman who had betrayed his adolescent love and trust.

Though she was neither so tall nor well endowed as his mother, the dress otherwise fit Lily beautifully. The rich golden-brown brought out the highlights in her tawny hair and eyes, and the lace gave her a delicate, feminine air.

The reminder of her femininity was not a welcome one in Adam's present mood. Still, he found himself moving toward her, drawn by both her fire and her uncertainty.

Bare moments before he took her chin in his hand to kiss her lips, he remembered who he was at present. He made her a bow, then said in a tinny voice, "Nothing at all is wrong, lovely Lily. And do stop calling me 'Squire,' if you please. You make me feel like even more of an old man than I already am," he said, pursing his lips in a ridiculous semblance of a pout.

His gesture worked to some extent, because Lily

stopped scowling and seemed to be suppressing a laugh. Adam was relieved. When he was being foolish and she was laughing at him, it was not hard to remember which role he was playing.

"Please, sit," he said, indicating a chair at one end of the long dining room table. He sat at the other, ignoring her look of dismay. It pleased him somewhat, however, that even if she was angry at him and thought him foolish, she was still disappointed to have him sit so far away.

He did not think he could endure her closer, not if he wished to maintain his own composure. And that was essential to keep his identity hidden. During the intimate hours he had spent with her as Adam, his hands had followed the waves in her hair, smoothed the curve of her shoulders, traced the mole that nestled close to one breast. He did not have to close his eyes to imagine her beneath him on this very table, the silk gown hiked up to her waist. . . . Adam hastily took a gulp of water, as wine would only heat his blood further, something he did not need just then.

When dinner was concluded, Adam rose to excuse himself. He glanced at Lily. She looked so forlorn sitting there, the anger drained away by exhaustion. Her pain suddenly moved him more than concern for his identity. He found himself at her chair, helping her to rise. "Pray do not be sad, Lily. I shall look after you," he said softly.

A wild look of hope flared in her eyes. Then he watched it die as she took in his clocked silk stockings, elaborately brocaded coat, the uncomfortable wig puffing above his powdered face, his flabby middle and absurdly colored spectacles.

"I am sorry if I have made your position more difficult," he continued, pretending not to notice her scrutiny of him. " 'Twas not my intention."

"Oh, I know, Squire."

"Adair," he reminded her quietly.

"Adair," she amended. "Thank you for trying to help, but really, I must go home."

"And do what?" he asked more sharply than he'd intended. "Wait for that ne'er-do-well brother of yours? Be snubbed on the street? Suffer the insinuations of people you thought were friends? Who would want that kind of betrayal?"

She stared at him. In the silence that fell, Adam wondered just how badly he had damaged her slight affection for him.

"Has someone betrayed you, Adair?" she said softly. "Is that why you are so . . . so . . ." she searched for a word, failed to find one.

"My dear, 'tis my digestion that creates my ill humors," he said to avoid answering her. "Truly, I did not mean to offend."

She smiled, and the difficult moment was over. Adam bowed over her hand, kissed it, then looked up into her eyes, seeing her through a rose-colored haze.

"An impressive exterior is not always the best judge of worth," he said, more stung than he wanted to admit at the way she had perused and then dismissed him. Without waiting for a response, he tucked her arm into his elbow to escort her from the room.

At the foot of the stairs, he stopped. "I meant what I said, my dear. There is no reason for you to leave. Even if you were up to going back and facing your neighbors, I promised Colonel Ware I would keep you out of trouble. And if I do not, 'tis my hide he will be after."

Hating himself for manipulating her to feel sorry for the squire, he turned to ring for Mistress Steele. When his housekeeper bustled into the hall, Adam asked her to show Lily to her room.

Adam took the coward's way out and retreated up the stairs immediately, but it was too late. Her angry look lingered with him. Worse, so did the light floral scent that always seemed to cling to her hair and skin.

Memories of lovemaking with Lily rendered him sleepless as he lay stretched at full length in the huge, comfortable bed. There was only one remedy he had found for the powerfully sensual nature he had tried so hard to bury over the years.

He pulled on his riding boots, moving quietly down the hallway lest his footsteps give him away.

Twenty

*A bad neighbor is a misfortune, as much as a good
one is a great blessing.*

—Hesiod,
Works and Days,
c. 700 B.C.

A pretty bow. A pretty speech. Lily punched the pillow
with one fist, hearing the soft *whoosh* of goose feathers
shifting inside. How dare he appeal to her sense of guilt,
imply that he could get in trouble if she did not do as
he and Colonel Ware wished? She was grateful for his
rescue of her, but nothing on earth could make her stay
there as his "guest."

She had news to relay. Unless Adam had started paying
calls in daylight, which she doubted, no one had told the
Sons of Liberty that Peter and Ethan were free. Even if
Amy Cameron spit in her face, Lily was going to tell
Jack Cameron the news.

Lily waited until she was sure the household was quiet,
then crept down the shadowy stairs, holding the smooth
polished railing with one hand. Although she had a candle,
she dared not light it, in case a servant came to investigate.
She stole quietly through the entrance hall, finding the way
to the back entrance as she had once before.

The hunter was stabled in the same stall and seemed amenable to another nocturnal ride. She exercised the same precautions, walking him until they were well away from the house, although the time of night was much later.

A half hour later she was in Williamsburg.

She walked the horse carefully down the lane that led to the Cameron farm, veering off the track to come upon the house from the rear. Dismounting, she led the animal by the reins the last hundred feet.

She was stunned to see the dark shadow of a horse not twenty feet from the dwelling, grazing contentedly in the grass. The low hum of conversation reached her where she stood. Her heart thumped painfully in her chest. Given her current standing with the Patriots, she had hoped to come upon Jack alone. Based on her parents' long years of friendship with the family, she was sure he would at least hear her out, especially if Amy wasn't around.

Standing uncertainly in the dark, wondering if she should leave, she started to consider other ways to get the news to him. So absorbed, she failed to hear when the low murmur of voices ceased. Suddenly, she was jerked against a hard body, a hand pressed to her throat.

"By all things holy," muttered a deep, painfully familiar voice, "am I to spend all my time catching you eavesdropping?" His exasperated voice seemed to erase all the intimacy they had shared, and she was again nothing more than a nuisance to him.

She struggled to be free, but Adam held her fast against his body, his grip firm but not harsh. " 'Tis all right, Jack," he called softly as another shadow detached itself from a nearby tree. "You know this one." So much for riding as a cure for lust, he thought. Williamsburg suddenly seemed as small as an English country village.

Cameron approached, lowering his voice as he confronted her. "What do you mean coming upon a meeting this way, breaking the rules. . . . A woman? What the devil?" He broke off, confusion obvious as he stared at the pale glimmer of Lily's eyes.

Then Jack Cameron recognized her. "If you know her, then you know she is no longer trusted," he said in a surprisingly neutral tone. "Not by everyone, that is," he added.

"I will vouch for her," Adam said. "Everything she has done has been to further the cause. Have no doubt on that score." His arms around Lily relaxed slightly, but he did not let her go.

"What do you want, Lily?" Jack Cameron asked with rough kindness.

"I wanted to tell you about Peter. That Peter and Ethan are free," she said unnecessarily.

" 'Tis what *he* came to say. Was there anything more?" Jack asked, warmth in his voice this time.

"Just what he said." Lily motioned toward the hard wall of muscle behind her, forgetting for a moment that Jack could not see her gesture in the dark. "I am no traitor," she added.

"I never thought you were, lass. I know my daughter can be a little hasty with her temper. The red hair, you know," Jack said. "She is a good girl though. Loyal, like you."

Lily had no response for the Sons of Liberty leader, because with a shock she realized Adam Pearson was far from indifferent to her presence. He might consider her a nuisance to his work, but the pressure against her backside told her Adam wanted her.

As she wanted him, she thought, a thrill of forbidden pleasure racing through her. There she stood, not five feet from an old family friend, and all she could think about, all she could feel, was Adam's hardness against her.

Lily felt his hips move against her involuntarily before he brought himself back under control and moved away. He dropped his arms abruptly, but Lily knew his breathing was as hard and ragged as hers.

"If you know about the rescue, Master Cameron, then you know you have a great deal to thank him for," she said, concern to protect Adam's identity piercing the sensual haze enveloping her. She did not know whether Jack knew Adam's name, so she did not use it.

"Him?" Cameron asked in unfeigned surprise.

"Who do you think freed Peter and Ethan?" Lily asked, shaking off Adam's warning clasp on her arm.

"I thought there had been a party . . . a chosen few . . . younger men," he said self-deprecatingly.

"There was only one man involved, Master Cameron. I do not intend to be as modest as he is," Lily said. "And now I think I shall ride home. Good night, gentlemen."

She had found a tree stump to use for mounting when Adam, briefly engaged in a last word with Jack, suddenly stood before her. "Where exactly is home tonight, if I may ask?"

Had he looked for her in the gazebo? Another thrill coursed through Lily. Then she remembered the flower he had left on her pillow. It seemed a lifetime ago, although it was only that morning. There were two meanings. Which had he intended?

"Why do you want to know?" she countered, her voice cool. She was torn between shame that she had given herself to a man who would not reveal himself to her, who did not love her, and a consuming desire—to which she would not yield—to throw herself into his arms again.

Perhaps Adam regretted what had passed between them, because he made no move to touch her. "Because I must escort you," he replied, his voice even.

"I need no escort." She threw one leg over the saddle, wishing Master Cameron had not gone back into the house. If Adam insisted, she could have asked him to see her home instead.

He grabbed the bridle of her horse. "No, what you need is a chaperon. Did I not warn you about interfering?" His voice was low and angry. Sexual tension crackled between them. She doubted either one of them was discussing the facts at hand.

She was as furious as he. "Because I might run into strange men? 'Tis too late for that, is it not?"

"Damn it, Lily, do not twist my words."

"What words are there to twist? You have . . . been with me and disappeared twice without any words at all." She jerked the bridle rein gone slack in Adam's grasp. Before she could betray herself any further, she pressed her knees into the horse's flanks and bolted down the quiet lane.

Adam made no move to follow her. Like the flower he'd left, she wondered if there was more than one meaning to his inaction. The picture of the flower sprang into her mind again, and she could not erase it. Columbine. Tall, slender, its trumpetlike flowers on a stalk. I cannot give thee up, it meant.

But it also meant desertion. What had Adam wanted to tell her? When no hoofbeats pursued her as she pounded down the lane and toward town, she assumed she had her answer.

God, she was stubborn, Adam thought, exasperation mixed with admiration. He walked Mercury slowly toward the plantation road, then mounted, only to suddenly reverse the horse's direction.

He would sleep in town tonight to stay closer to her. He was virtually certain she had gone back to town. She had said "home," after all, and he did not for a moment believe she meant Oak Grove.

There would be trouble tomorrow.

It seemed the only thing more difficult than having Lily under his roof was not having Lily under his roof.

Lily tethered the hunter in the backyard, drawing a bucket of well water for him and promising oats when the livery stables opened next morning. She went into the kitchen to see if she had anything else to give him. Then she went upstairs to sleep and postpone the reckoning of what she was to do with her life until she had a clearer head.

The low, soft notes of a mourning dove woke her to a crisp spring day. Other than the unnatural stillness in the house that proclaimed Peter's absence, everything else seemed normal.

Until she went downstairs to open her shop. As she entered the room that had once been their living room, a rush of wind met her. Under other circumstances, a breeze would have been welcome, but not when it came from a rock-sized hole in her shop window.

The offending rock had a note wrapped around it. "Traitor!" it screamed. Lily buried her head in her hands. Blast him, the squire was right. Her reputation was ruined, and while she thought she was prepared to face the consequences, this hurt. She hadn't realized how much she'd relied on Peter and Adam.

She picked up the rock to toss it out the door, not especially surprised to find her sign hanging drunkenly from one metal chain. The other one had been severed.

Jack Cameron knew the truth about her. Would his word be enough to convince those who had once been her friends? She couldn't say anything herself, because it would raise questions about the source of her knowledge.

She might be desperate to lose her status as a pariah but not at Adam's expense. Whether she was angry at his high-handedness or not, his mission was too important to jeopardize.

Gathering her belongings, she stuffed them in a portmanteau and set out down the street for Adair Sotheby's town house.

Adam's surprise was boundless that Lily had come to him voluntarily. He opened the door himself, saying nothing as he stepped back to let her enter.

Her pride must be devastated and there was little he could do to salvage it. The best thing he could do was pretend that she had not broken the arrangement he had proposed yesterday to Ware.

"Have you breakfasted?" he asked in a softer voice than the one he usually affected as the squire.

Lily squared her shoulders, turning toward him with her portmanteau clasped in both hands. "No. Squire, I—"

"Adair," he interrupted. "Do not say anything." She shook her head, ready to speak again. He laid a finger on her lips. " 'Tis not necessary. I offered you my protection, such as it is, and the offer has not been withdrawn."

She looked bewildered. He drew his hand away hastily.

Had she felt it, the shock of recognition that went through him, the sense of elemental connection between them at that simple touch?

More shaken than he liked to admit, he tucked his hands behind his back, moving toward the drawing room door. "My town coach is here, although the coachman is at Oak Grove. If you do not object to my driving, we'll leave now."

"Thank you," she said quietly. He turned around to look at her, hoping the spirit had not gone out of her. He could offer her no comfort about the rigors of a life of deception.

"Do you have my horse?" he asked, keeping his expression blank with effort. As Sotheby, he supposed he should be peeved. As Adam, he could only admire her courage.

"Yes, he's still tied up in my yard." She did not apologize, though she looked a bit abashed. "Shall we fetch him?"

"I imagine he might want the comforts of home," Adam said dryly. "We can tie a lead rein to the back of the coach."

The ride to Oak Grove was quiet and constrained. Lily remained inside the carriage while he drove, high up on the coachman's box. The spring frolics of birds and forest creatures were lost on him as he drove along quickly, his thoughts racing in time to the pounding hooves of the horses that pulled the carriage.

The Sons of Liberty here were compromised. He had managed safely to remove Peter and Ethan from Ware's reach, but he knew Ware would not rest until he had caught the man responsible. It was only a matter of time before Ware and Dodgett found out what they needed to know about the Patriot group and unmasked him in the process. In this situation Adam might be doing the group more harm than good if he remained.

The front door opened as Adam guided the coach into Oak Grove's wide circular driveway. Mistress Steele and Will Evans hurried out.

"Squire!" Will shouted. "There is terrible news."

Twenty-one

*The gentlemen may cry, 'Peace, peace!' but there is
no peace. The war has actually begun.*
> —Patrick Henry,
> Speech in Virginia Convention,
> 1775

Breathless, Will ran toward them, skidding to a sudden
stop on the close-packed dirt. He appeared to have lost
all the sense of propriety that Adam had so laboriously
cultivated in him.

"Sir, Mistress Lily is missing," he said as he ran to take
the reins from Adam's hands. Adam climbed down from
the coachman's box, remembering to ease himself down
slowly.

"Will," he began in a warning voice, but the lad was
oblivious.

"We heard there has been a terrible massacre in Boston.
Oh . . ." Will's voice died suddenly as Lily emerged from
the carriage, portmanteau in hand.

"I am fine, Will," she said with a slight smile, her composure restored. Mistress Steele bustled forward to take
the portmanteau.

Adam thought he was the only one who detected the
fact that she had been crying on the trip here. Her nose

was slightly red at the tip and her brilliant eyes were just a bit too shiny. Adam kept his hands to himself despite a savage need to touch her.

About to turn and chide Will for his breach of decorum, he remembered the second thing the boy had blurted out. "What did you say about Boston?" he asked.

Will suddenly looked down, shuffling his feet. "I . . . uh . . ." Then patriotic fervor overtook him. "British soldiers fired on colonists in Boston's square," he shouted. "A peaceful gathering, sir. The redcoats fired first!"

Adam shared Will's feelings but could not express them. Such an outburst could only be condemned. He had long known war was inevitable and that it would most likely erupt in Boston.

Adam walked slowly into the house behind Lily as she questioned Will. His job here truly was finished. The colonists would organize a regular army soon, which would doubtless incorporate militias and groups like the Sons of Liberty.

He looked around the spacious entrance hall, at the mahogany banisters, the dentelle molding around the ceiling. In the short time he had lived there, he'd come to enjoy the beauty of this house, of the Tidewater area and its inhabitants.

Laying his riding crop on the foyer table, he snorted. Once he started lying to himself, he was in danger of losing his true self among his many roles. He did like Oak Grove or he would not have bought it years ago. But he realized he liked it best when Lily was in it. With her this house could be a home. She could be his wife.

A future suddenly presented itself, stretching bright and unbroken before him like the promise of spring. Then his own relentless logic brought him up short. Just whom would Lily marry? Adair Sotheby, the ostensible owner of this plantation? Or Adam Pearson, the fugitive?

Neither alternative was realistic. His heart as heavy as it had ever been, Adam climbed the stairs to his room slowly. It would take a little time to wind up his affairs here. Royalists would flee once war was declared, and he could use the exodus to return to Boston.

Assuming that was where the Committee of Safety wanted him next. Adam strode into his study. He had sent a coded letter to his Massachusetts contacts recently. He might as well show up in person once he was no longer needed here.

But first he had to do something for Lily, find some way to withdraw his sponsorship of her as Adair, to reingratiate her back into Williamsburg society. He propped his boots on the desk, uncaring that the act was not characteristic of Adair. Steepling his hands, he started thinking, trying to drown out the dull lament of his heart. He had to leave her. Oh, God, he did not want to.

In the courthouse across from Market Square, Randolph Ware pored over a document he should have checked weeks ago. Weeks earlier, however, there had been no reason to think of Adair Sotheby in connection with his rogue officer Pearson.

If Sotheby had not stepped forward to champion Peter Walters's sister, the colonel would never have investigated him at all. But his bold challenge was so out of character for the weakling Tory squire that Ware had started a discreet investigation.

Today he'd gone to the courthouse to find out what he could about the man. His first surprise was that there were no birth records for Sotheby, either there or at Bruton

Parish Church. For some reason he'd assumed the man was a native. A careless mistake, Ware chided himself. Second, Sotheby had not lived there very long, showing up just a few months ago to claim the plantation for his own. Third—and here the documents yielded their prize— Sotheby had bought the plantation from one Adam Pearson of Boston Town.

"I thank you for your assistance to the Crown," he said politely to the timorous clerk.

"Is . . . is something the matter with the ownership documents, Colonel?" he asked.

"Not at all. I will send one of my men to copy this document for me, however. Thank you and good day." Replacing his hat, Ware walked out into the spring sunshine with a satisfied air. A little more digging and he would be ready to confront Sotheby. How the devil could the man have met Pearson? He did not believe for a minute the gambling story the clerk had told him.

Pearson did not gamble. At least not when he had been a loyal servant of the king's. Who knows what had happened to him on his last mission, the one from which he had never returned.

Although Ware made certain his face had settled into its usual impassive lines by the time he returned to his office, inwardly he seethed. *Why, damn him?* he thought. His best officer, whom he'd treated him like a son. Took him in when he was a shell-shocked lad who had sworn off women at the tender age of fifteen. So traumatized that he'd nearly gotten himself killed in his first battle, until Ware had taken him under his wing and taught him that duty could substitute for love, if necessary.

Between them, duty had softened into a kind of father-son relationship that Ware would never know in his personal life. Stuck with a cold, aristocratic wife who never

failed to remind him of her higher station, he was not one
to preach the joys of women. But duty required that he
remain married, and Randolph had, over the long years of
military deployments and less than cordial domestic re-
unions.

No longer a boy, Pearson had betrayed his country, his
king, his mission—and Randolph Ware. And this Sotheby
was somehow involved.

"Do you play, Adair?" Lily asked as the squire showed
her to the music room after dinner. There was a gleaming
harpsichord in one corner, a tall harp in another. He'd
been an undemanding companion at dinner, never mentioning what would surely have caused an argument, the
death of American patriots on Boston Common. For once
Lily had no inclination to argue politics. She had asked
to sit closer to Adair, however, and he had acquiesced,
surprised.

"Once, long ago," he answered her now, running his
long fingers lightly down the keys.

"Would you play? This music looks recent." Lily
looked at the sheet music on the harpsichord.

"I have had a few things sent here from London," he
admitted, sounding embarrassed, "but surely you do not
wish to hear me—"

"Oh, but I do. Please, Adair." Anything for distraction,
Lily thought. As long as she did not have to hear him sing
in that gratingly shrill voice of his.

He escorted her to a blue-silk-covered divan, out of his
direct line of sight. Anticipating some half-learned melody, Lily smiled dutifully anyway. It did not matter. Adair
ceased to notice her once his hands touched the keys of
the harpsichord.

To her surprise, he played beautifully. With skill, feeling, and, dare she think it, with passion. As if there were things closed up in his soul that had no outlet save this. The precise, almost fussy tones of the harpsichord, which she thought would have suited his character perfectly, seemed deeper and more flowing.

She glanced at his profile as he bent over the keys, the tails of his vermilion frock coat spread out over the bench. Seen from this angle, he looked younger, more handsome. The line of his jaw was stronger than she had thought, his hands sure as they moved over the keys. He reminded her of . . . no, surely not.

They sat in silence for a moment after he finished, his head still bent over the keys. "Bravo," she said, applauding warmly. He turned to look at her, his eyes unreadable behind the colored lenses he favored. He had chalk-white powder on his face, a silly patch over his lip, and a piled-high wig on his head. Any thought that he reminded her of Adam vanished at once.

With all the strange events that had occurred, she must be losing touch with reality. "I believe I am tired, Adair," she said. "I will retire."

"An excellent idea, m'dear," he said, escorting her to the door. "I shall do the same myself shortly." But she saw the way he looked at the instrument as if it had unlocked his heart.

"Your playing will not keep me awake, Adair," she said. "I shall not hear a thing."

He bowed over her hand without responding. "Good night, fair Lily," he said lightly.

Later, as she lay in bed nearly asleep, she heard music again. The melody was familiar. Then a baritone voice, deep, rich, resonant, rose above the notes.

My soul retains thee still in sight,
When thou art far away,
Thou art my vision in the night,
My waking dream by day.

Surely not, thought Lily sleepily. She must be dreaming already. Dreaming of Adam. For who else had such a resonant voice?

But if he was, as she believed, a servant in Adair's house—for how else would he have seen her flower messages?—then perhaps she was not dreaming. Perhaps that was really Adam down there.

A servant allowed to play such a valuable instrument late at night? Her thoughts were too fanciful. Remembering that Adam had abandoned her, she closed her eyes, turned on her side, and placed a pillow over her head. She did not care who was out there or what he was doing.

But the next day she found herself scrutinizing all Adair's servants to see if one fit Adam's height, weight, strength . . . and voice.

Twenty-two

When shall I come to thee?
When shall my sorrows have an end?
Thy joys when shall I see?
— Anonymous,
The Song of Mary,
1601

Alicia Chalmers would be married the following week, on the first of May. Adair refused to allow Lily to return to Williamsburg but said his servants could gather the flowers she needed from her garden. The rest would come from his.

Lily accepted reluctantly. She did not need the notes that were in her house because she had already decided long before what flowers to use. A week gave her little time to work with the squire's neglected gardens, but she went to see what he had.

She remembered the roses from the night she'd been forced out there with Dodgett. On almost every bush bloomed a few good roses, but many were tangled. Most had not been pruned in a long time. Lily walked around, taking in the scents she so loved, noting the colors.

Seashell gravel crunched under the heels of someone

approaching. Adam? Lily's heart flared briefly, absurdly. Of course not. She saw Adair's wig before she saw him.

"Good morning," she said, summoning up a smile.

"Good morning, fair Lily," he said, sweeping his arm before him in an elaborate bow. "What do you think?" he asked.

She hoped he meant the gardens, not the silly amber-colored spectacles that matched his silk knee breeches. "Well," Lily began to say, focusing on the flowers, "these gardens were obviously lovely once. But before you came, I don't think they were well cared for. If you will let Will help me, you might see some results soon."

"How long?" he asked.

"Oh, before summer's end, I can assure you." She was surprised that Adair seemed unaccountably disappointed at that.

"Is there nothing you can do before the wedding?" he asked finally.

"Certainly, we can clean everything up and make it attractive for guests to walk here. But there will be no new roses for a while. The pinks have done well, however," she said, taking his arm to lead him to a different part of the garden.

"I'm sure you know pinks are all the rage in England," she continued as they stood before the ruffle-edged flowers. "You have many lovely varieties represented here. You see the white ones blooming now? And over there, the pink-fringed ones? The solid-colored ones start to bloom next month. They'll last until September. Do you know," Lily mused half to herself, "my father may have brought some of these to the previous owner."

"Your father?" Adair said in an encouraging tone.

"Aye. My father was a botanist. He brought plants to England and returned with Old World specimens to transplant here. The trade was wildly popular and paid well. 'Twas on one of his voyages that there was a storm." She swallowed to cover the sudden lump in her throat. "I imagine Father must have been in the hold, trying to save his valuable plants."

"How old were you?" Adair asked gently, his scratchy voice more quiet than usual.

"Nineteen. I started the flower business a year later, after Mother died."

"Your mother died as well?" There was real sympathy in Adair's voice now, and Lily warmed to it instinctively. She started down another path, where the borders were planted with viola tricolor, sometimes called johnny-jump-up. The bright purple and yellow flowers with their heart-shaped faces never failed to cheer her.

"She died the next winter," Lily continued as Adair continued to keep pace with her. "She had influenza, but I think her heart was broken." Lily kept her tone as matter-as-fact as possible. She abhorred pity. "And yours?"

"What?" Adair was clearly startled by the change in topic.

"Your mother. Mistress Steele told me the clothes were hers. Did she die?" she asked, perhaps too frankly.

"No." Adair turned away.

Well, he was not getting off that lightly, Lily decided. She kept her hand in the crook of his arm, tugging to turn him toward her. "I told you my family history. May I now hear yours?"

He looked down at her for a moment, his eyes shielded by the spectacles *du jour*. He came to some kind of internal decision, for he resumed walking. "There is not much to tell. I caught my mother in flagrante delicto with my uncle. I left the house that night, since I could not kill my uncle and I obviously could not tell my father. I joined the . . . ah, I moved to London, got bored, and eventually came here. My mother has been trying to get me to come home and assume the title ever since my brother was killed in a duel."

"Oh." Lily could not think of much to say. No wonder the man was so peculiar. What a hellish family history he had. "How old were you?"

"When I left? Fifteen." He disengaged her arm gently. "Now, if you will excuse me, I have other business to attend to. Get Will and any other help you need." He turned back a moment and handed her a cluster of flowers he must have plucked when she wasn't looking.

"These remind me of you," he said. Then he left without his usual elaborate bow or extravagant compliments. Lily watched his retreating back. She hardly had to look down to see what he'd given her. The scent was so strong, there was no need.

Lilacs. She sniffed the air with pleasure. *Youth, love, beauty.* She planned to use white lilacs in Alicia's bouquet. Surely Adair did not know their meaning.

Thinking about what he'd said tugged at her own orphaned heart. Adair's parents had not died, but he had been orphaned just the same. Given the harshness of the betrayal he had witnessed, Lily found herself forgiving much of his peculiar behavior.

Perhaps she viewed him now in a different light, but it seemed to Lily that Adair acted in a much more relaxed manner. Even his voice no longer seemed so high pitched. He was a charming table companion, his conversation light and never taxing. Although they had never reached a formal agreement, all talk of politics between them was suspended.

Instead, Lily relied on Will to tell her the news. A decision on what to do about the attack in Boston was referred to the Continental Congress, meeting in Philadelphia. Lily was worried about Peter. Will had no information about what had happened to him or Ethan. It seemed only the enigmatic Patriot leader knew, and no one had seen Adam since the night he'd visited Jack Cameron as far as she knew.

Was Peter safe where he was? If Virginia took some kind of defiant action to support Massachusetts, might that cause the royal governor to flee, paving the way for Peter to return home?

Lily decided she would leave after Alicia's reception and wedding. But first she must discharge this commitment. If she had not heard from Adam by then and could not contact him, she would . . . Well, she had not exactly decided what she would do. Charming as Adair had become, she could not continue to stay with him.

The day before Alicia's reception, she met Adair early in the music room to go over the final plans. Lily had moss soaking in buckets in the kitchen, and she had already cut the longer-lasting flowers. Will was going to her house today to cut some flowers not available in Adair's gardens. Adair's roses she would cut last, since roses tended to be fickle.

"Well, Lily, are you satisfied?" Adair asked as she frowned down at the list before her.

"Mostly," she answered. "I do need to look for something outside though. Will you excuse me? I may be a few minutes."

"I can use the walk. Let me accompany you," he said, patting his comfortable stomach. "What are you looking for?" he said as they walked along the garden paths.

"Here," she said, turning toward the folly. Stone statues

stood scattered around, with a small, vaguely Grecian rotunda in the center. To one side was a pond, and over it weeping willows draped. "I need ferns. I also want to use some willow branches."

Adair bent down gamely to help her cut ferns, but she noticed he had trouble doing so. " 'Tis all right, Adair. I can manage. Can you cut the willow branches? You are tall and those I cannot reach."

"Fine." He straightened. They both finished their tasks at the same time. As she stood, he reached down a hand to her. She came upright, her arms full of soft, damp ferns, almost colliding with his broad chest.

Adair reached out, but instead of taking her bundle of ferns, his arm went around her, drawing her closer. "Lily," he said, his voice suddenly deep.

She watched, paralyzed, as his mouth descended toward hers. Then he was kissing her, and something in her suddenly responded to the pressure of his warm, full mouth. He brushed his lips lightly against hers, gentle and undemanding. When he pressed her closer, she came in contact with his soft middle, the torso that in Adam was hard and firm.

Adam! Oh, God, what was she doing? This wasn't Adam; she was kissing Adair. Lily pulled away, pushing hard against his chest with the force of her panic. He staggered but did not fall. When he bent down to look for his expensive spectacles, Lily's ferns scattered as she turned and fled.

Early that afternoon Lily finally finished the last table arrangement. As she looked down, tucking the last bits of dampened moss out of sight, she noticed her hands were shaking. She pressed them to her temple as if she could control her limbs and bring order to her jumbled brain.

There were certainly other parts of her body she was having trouble controlling. How could she have let Adair kiss her? Worse, how could she have begun to enjoy it? She had forgotten who he was, only enjoying the firm touch of his lips on hers. Something had reminded her of Adam.

No, it could not be possible. Adair was nothing like Adam. Even had their politics not been so completely different, Adair was a strange and difficult man. She looked again at the jonquils she held that meant I desire a return of affection.

Should she put them in the bouquet? Lily plucked out the ones she had already placed within the arrangement. She held the strong green stems in her hands indecisively, fingering the bright petals. She reminded herself she wanted to speak to Adam only to find out if his words to Jack had restored her reputation. If not, she must ask him to help her return home no matter what. The news about the massacre in Boston had surely stirred up Patriot anger, and she had to know where Peter was.

She could stay here no longer.

Lily did not want to think about other reasons for summoning Adam. Not after he had abandoned her. But try as she might to push them to the back of her mind, her traitor body knew she wanted him. So recently awakened to love, Lily's body hummed with sensuality. Her breasts felt heavy, as they had in the garden, aching to be caressed by warm, strong hands.

But not Adair's. Never with Adair.

She heard a noise and quickly inserted the jonquils back into the bowl next to the iris. Lily placed the arrangement on the hall table. If Adam was in this household, he would see it.

She could not look at the bold lines of her creation. She hurried out of the foyer, fearing at any moment to see Adair. He had to come in soon for the evening meal.

Adam had spent the afternoon riding the fields of his plantation, inspecting crops, failing miserably to concentrate. He cursed himself for his lack of self-control, for being responsible for the misery in her eyes when she had broken their embrace. He groaned at the memory of her face when she realized she was kissing Adair Sotheby, the Tory fop. Worse, that she had liked it.

He, stupid, uncontrolled idiot that he was, had wanted only to touch her soft skin, to feel her hair against his hands. He'd forgotten he was Adair and allowed himself to become Adam, her lover. He had almost lost all restraint, almost turned the kiss into blazing intimacy, an intimacy to which he had no right even as Adam Pearson.

He had intended to leave her, to disappear now that circumstances called for his departure. He had intended to leave her alone, to give her the chance to hate him for not coming to her, then to forget him.

The columbine with its double meaning came to mind. *I cannot give thee up.* How ironic, how true.

Adam was still berating himself when he entered the front hallway. God, he hoped he had not driven her away as Adair. Not only was it dangerous for her to go back to Williamsburg without his protection, but he could not bear this house without her presence in it.

He threw his riding gloves and crop on the hall table. He was on the verge of climbing the stairs to change before dinner when he saw the flowers. On the hall table, in a blaze of color and glory, was an arrangement containing flowers whose meaning he knew. Iris for a message.

Standing out near the taller flower, nearly as tall, were the bright yellow and white of jonquils. Did they have a meaning, or were they just for color?

Jonquils . . . He had it.

For a brief moment all Adam's iron will broke. The restraints, the subterfuges, the masks, fell. Adam grinned with a joy and good humor that were completely out of character for the cranky Adair. Sweet, brave Lily! Even though she might be signaling Adam Pearson to help her escape the ogre Adair Sotheby—and he would have to consider what his response would be to such a plea—she wanted him. Wanted Adam.

He would go to her. She would want to know about Peter, at the very least. Perhaps her boldness was only for her brother's sake. But he would not think of that now, preferring the more positive interpretation.

He took the stairs three at a time, demonstrating more energy than Adair had ever possessed. He would go to her tomorrow night, after the reception. He roared for Will to bring him bathwater at once.

He was hard pressed to be surly to the young man today. But he had to, if only to prevent himself from breaking into an idiotic grin.

Lily spent the hour before dinner with a churning stomach, not knowing how she would face Adair again. She had almost decided to ask for dinner in her room, or else forego it altogether. No, that was the coward's way out.

Adam read Lily's agitated state as she entered the dining room. To quell his own ardor and not seem threatening to her, he retreated into his most foppish mannerisms. He chose to ignore the incident in the garden, prattling on about new harpsichord music he had received from London.

After a few brief moments of utter panic in which Lily cast him glances like a frightened doe, he saw her settle down. With his heightened awareness of her, he knew the instant she stiffened her spine and stopped being afraid of him and what he might say or do. *Bravo, Lily,* he thought, although he wondered for a moment why she had not marched over to him and slapped him for his effrontery.

Over the dessert of stewed pears it came to him, and he once more cursed himself roundly. He was her only protector, having saved her from the redcoats and ruined her reputation simultaneously. She was here on his sufferance. She did not know where her brother was. Adam, her only source of information, had not put in an appearance recently.

Finally, he added to himself, biting fiercely into a pear, she'd had no word of Adam since the morning he'd crept out of her house like a thief, one step ahead of the redcoats.

He had been a thief indeed, for he had stolen her innocence.

Adam bit his tongue as his teeth sliced through the fruit. He cursed fluently, this time aloud. Lily looked at him with some surprise.

"Damned fruit, 'tis not well cooked," he said sulkily. "Can't a man get a decent meal in his own home?" He threw his napkin down with more violence than was necessary, even in his supposed fit of pique.

At the door Adam halted. He turned and made her a leg. "I give you good evening, Mistress Walters. Tomorrow will be a busy day. I trust you will rest well." Then he was out the door before he could jeopardize himself again by doing something else stupid.

For a moment Lily thought she heard him whistle as he walked through the hallway where her flowers stood and then bound up the steps, but she discounted that immediately. Adair was in far too foul a humor to whistle, and she had never observed him to leap, bound, or exert himself in any physical way. It would be beneath his dignity.

Still, his departure relieved her, although the evening had not been as difficult as she'd feared. Adair had apparently chosen to ignore the afternoon's incident, which probably was good sense. It would have been awkward any other way.

She did not know how she could continue to stay there, but by not forcing the issue, at least she had some time to think. Indeed, from Adair's perfectly appropriate behavior this evening, she wondered if he had been seized with some strange mood in the afternoon that was now gone.

Certainly, he had not shown the least bit of interest in her that evening. He was a strange man, indeed, but not a dangerous one. She had only one more day to get through. After the reception, with or without Adam, she would leave.

Twenty-three

Though I look old, yet I am strong and lusty.
—William Shakespeare,
As You Like It,
1599

In the waning sunshine of a perfect spring afternoon, carriages swept up the graceful circular driveway. Other guests had traveled by boat from their plantations on the river, stopping at Adair's private landing. They would attend his festivities, then head into Williamsburg the next morning for the church service.

Lily watched from behind a lace-paneled window. She had received the flowers brought from her garden at home, made sure all was in readiness for tomorrow, but Adair had sent Will with the arrangements to the church. Almost as if he divined her thoughts, she fumed mentally.

Well, the wedding was one affair she had no desire to attend, but as the florist, she had to water the arrangements before the ceremony. She would go early, leave before Adair, and once finished at the church, not return. It would be simple, she told herself.

As for today, she could tolerate it. Mary would be there, and they could visit. She knew she also needed to put in an appearance for Colonel Ware's benefit. Adair had not asked her—he had never even mentioned it—but Lily knew he had challenged the colonel, a man who clearly did not like his authority questioned. It was the least she owed Adair, to show that her "host" had taken adequate care of her.

And tomorrow? Lily pushed away thoughts of her planned flight resolutely. Jack Cameron could surely be persuaded to tell her where Peter and Ethan had been sent and she would follow. If townsfolk still did not want her around, and the colonel caused problems by his inevitable fury at Adair, better by far that she simply disappear.

Lily refused to think about where Adam might be. There had been no sign of him the previous night. Nevertheless, she took special care dressing, and for the first time accepted the services of one of Adair's maidservants.

"Mistress, you look beautiful!" was the girl's predictable statement. Lily shifted in her seat, tired of sitting for an unprecedented hour with nothing to do. The girl, Betsy, had taken great care to arrange a coiffure that was elegant and elaborate without looking fussy.

She saw the girl advancing toward her with a powder puff and ducked her head inadvertently.

"Oh, no, don't do that," Betsy squealed. " 'Twill get on your dress."

"Sorry," Lily said, laughing, "but I will not have that thing near me."

"The squire, he loves this stuff, mistress," the girl declared, although from the wrinkle on her pert nose it did not appear she thought much of it either.

"Well do I know it," Lily said. "But I am no English queen, and I refuse to wear it."

"You don't need it, mistress," Betsy said sincerely.

Lily glanced at the full-length looking glass, surprised and actually quite pleased at the transformation wrought by a hairbrush, a curling iron, and a new gown. In this case, a made-over gown.

Lily had altered this gown belonging to Adam's mother since the sight of another dress had brought him painful memories, the source of which she now understood. In addition to taking up the hem and taking in the bodice, she had added lace to cover her upper arms a bit more. The housekeeper had also helped her substitute the showy scarlet bodice over the heavy yellow silk skirt with a stomacher of dark emerald jacquard. Lily refused the painted silk fan Betsy offered her and headed for the door.

She met Adair coming from his rooms at the other end of the house. He stopped. "You look stunning, Lily," he said in a quiet voice that bore none of his usual high-pitched flattery.

Starting toward her, he seemed to recollect himself, making a sweeping bow more characteristic of his flamboyant style. Lily studied him covertly. Perhaps he had lost some weight from helping her in the garden and from his riding, for he didn't seem quite so bulky to her. His figured silk burgundy frock coat was elegant, as were his striped waistcoat of light blue and his midnight-blue breeches. The spectacles perched on his nose were tinted blue, but his wig was merely normal for a change. That is, as normal as one could expect from someone who invariably added a good four inches to his height when wearing the elaborate creations. But at least it was all white, with none of the tints he occasionally used.

Then he straightened, and Lily saw that he was wearing a heart-shaped face patch—in honor of the wedding no doubt. Any thoughts of Adair's incipient normality vanished. His silk stockings were clocked, of course, but he had not worn the high heels she had seen him in before, thank goodness. Any more height and she would barely be able to see him. For the first time, she realized he was actually quite tall.

"Shall we go down, fair mistress mine?" Adair asked. Lily hesitated for a moment, then, remembering his silly words and ridiculous wig, she placed her hand very lightly upon his silk-clad arm.

Nervousness assailed her at the sight of guests crowding the porch below. She saw Ware alighting from a carriage with Alicia's fiancé and stiffened. Adam followed the direction of her glance, then murmured, "A little powder would not have gone amiss, fair Lily."

It distracted her, as he intended it should. "Why on earth would you say that?" she answered, the alarmed look gone from her eyes with the rise of her annoyance. Adam hid a smile.

"Well, it does wonders for the complexion, hides spots and whatnot . . ." he said innocently.

Lily's gaze shot pure amber fire at him and he was hard pressed not to chuckle. "Not that you need have any concern about that, dear girl, but I always say what others cannot see, they cannot judge."

"Such as?" she shot back, clearly outraged.

"Nervousness, anger, fear," he said blandly. "You look a bit pale, m'dear." They had almost reached the bottom of the wide, curving staircase. "But a touch of annoyance does wonders for the roses in your cheeks."

She was speechless at last, surprised at his manipulation. Her color high, her dander up, as he had probably intended, together they moved toward the open front door.

Ware had seen them, of course, and moved briskly to the front of the receiving line forming around Alicia and her parents. As for Ware's young officer, Adam could read the lust on Dodgett's face from where he stood when the bastard spotted Lily.

His hands itching to wipe the look off Dodgett's smug face, all Adam could do in his present guise was pat Lily's arm reassuringly.

God, that was the last thing he wanted to do when he saw her looking like a ripe spring bloom herself in her finery, her innate elegance complementing the graceful ensemble she had made out of his mother's showy silks.

He wanted to bury his lips in her lustrous shining hair, take down the curls, and spread the amber silk between his hands while his lips traced a path down her throat to her discreet décolletage. His body instantly uncomfortable thanks to his wayward thoughts, he forced himself to soothe Lily's nerves with inane comments. If only she knew that he longed to do what William Dodgett's lecherous gaze so clearly indicated.

That thought brought him smartly to his senses. He channeled the lust into pure liberating anger, so that by the time they reached the foyer, Adam's eyes glowed with rage. Fortunately, no one would see them due to his spectacles.

He realized Randolph Ware was staring at him just about the time he turned his own burning glance on Dodgett. *Blast and damn,* he thought, *I am a fop, remember? I would not dream of running Dodgett through.*

Softening his ire with effort, he released Lily and turned to Alicia, offering her painted cheek a tentative buss as if he rarely approached females and was uncertain how to kiss one properly.

"Welcome, darling Alicia, and your lovely family," he cried in his lightest, most effete voice. "My poor little house is graced so charmingly by your radiant presence."

Lily moved away from him as if she had been shot. He let her go without a backward glance. He had revealed too much of himself already. Ware was no fool, and the man knew him better than anyone alive. Adam had to mind his mask tonight, and wear it closely.

Randolph Ware took a good long look at Squire Sotheby descending the stairs with the lovely Mistress Walters beside him. The man was simply too ridiculous, he thought. Pearson could not have gone to pot so quickly. How could a fugitive acquire the sort of belly that went with soft living?

And that walk, the face powder. No, he could not countenance it, this man could not possibly be Pearson in disguise. But he must know something of Adam if he had bought the plantation from him. When the hell had Pearson had time to buy an estate in Virginia anyway? he wondered. Something else he had never mentioned to Randolph.

Polite conversation gave him the opening. As Dodgett's bride gushed about the beauty of the plantation after the charmingly self-deprecating speech the squire had delivered, Randolph moved in to kiss her cheek.

"I agree with Mistress Chalmers, this plantation of yours is quite elegant, Squire," he said, joining the little group around Alicia. "Have you owned it long?"

"Not long at all, Colonel, but 'tis amazing how quickly one can settle into a place." Sotheby's tone was bland, his facial expression undetectable under a thick layer of rice powder. Christ, his complexion is paler than the woman's, Randolph thought, although he saw Alicia had not missed an encounter with the powder brush either. Her pallid face was the correctly fashionable shade of white.

"I heard a traitor owned this place before you," Randolph said, aware the squire was about to move on to another guest.

"Mmm, I just won a lucky hand at cards," Sotheby said offhandedly. "If not here, I suppose I would be in the Carolinas."

"Oh? Why?" Ware felt a sudden surge of hope. Perhaps Sotheby had helped Pearson flee, although that made little sense for a Tory sympathizer such as the squire.

"Why Carolina? I like the southern climate, and there was another fellow about to put his place on the table as a stake," Sotheby said dismissively.

"Where did the man who sold this place to you go after the game?" Ware knew he was no longer making polite social conversation but did not care. He had to get to the bottom of Pearson's disappearance. Sotheby was the first definite link he had found.

"Why, he stayed in Delaware, I imagine."

"Why do you think so?"

"Once the game was over, he had no money left that I know of. Else why deed the place to me to cover his losses?"

Alicia, bored at not being the center of attention, had drifted away to claim Dodgett, whose interest in Mistress Walters was too glaringly apparent for a man on the eve of his wedding.

Ware refocused his attention on Sotheby. "Perhaps you had an arrangement. Perhaps Pearson meant to come here later to claim his property."

"Really, Colonel, that is a bit over the top."

"In what way?" Ware refused a servant with a passing tray of champagne-filled glasses. Adam took one, his palms sweating. Thank God for the spectacles. Lily had not known him before, but Ware would have recognized his former subordinate immediately due to the strange color of Adam's eyes. As it was, he was nervous that the colonel would see through his disguise.

Adam took a sip from the long-stemmed glass. "Why would I hold someone's property for them? I have put quite a bit into bringing this place up to snuff. I have no intention of giving it back to that Pearson fellow, assuming he ever shows up."

There was no apparent link between the two men other than opportunity, just as the squire had said. Ware had to concede this round, but, damn it, there was something here. He just had not gotten to the heart of it yet.

"Were you acquainted with the Earl of Dalby before?" Ware asked.

"No, not before that night—" Adam closed his mouth abruptly, making an awkward gesture that spilled champagne down his waistcoat. Dammit, Ware was sharp. He was one of a very few men who knew Adam's title. In the army, Adam had rarely talked about his past.

Ware would also know that Adam Pearson would never have acknowledged his privileged heritage to a stranger such as Adair Sotheby.

"Excuse me, Colonel, I have made a mess here." *God, was that the truth,* he thought. Adam turned swiftly on his heel and walked away, not daring to look back. Had Ware noticed his slip?

Of course he had. Ware missed nothing. Adam cast a quick glance behind him as he opened the door to the hall. Ware was staring after him with a look of frustrated triumph. Adam did not have to read Ware's mind to know what was going through it. Adair Sotheby knew Adam Pearson better than he should from a simple night's acquaintance. Ware already knew there was a link between the two men. He was more than halfway to discovering Adam's secret, and he knew it.

It was only a matter of time until he finished putting the pieces together. And when he did, Adam had best be well away from there. There would be no sentence of transportation for his treason. There would only be a death sentence.

Mary had not come after all, and Lily missed her friend. Mistress Hardison had explained in a rather roundabout way that Mary was suffering from the female complaint. How ironic, Lily reflected, that Mary actually had the malaise Lily had invented for her the night Adam lay wounded in her bed.

"But you think she will be able to come tomorrow?" Lily asked.

"Yes, child, she would not miss it for the world." Mistress Hardison's rather trembly chin was set, suggesting she would make sure Mary would attend, "female complaint" or not. Probably to make her daughter realize that she had best apply herself to finding a husband, Lily thought.

Lily kissed Mistress Hardison dutifully, then went in search of needed fresh air. A few minutes with Alicia—whose arch comments left no doubt that Lily was intended to feel melancholy about her spinsterhood—had irritated her to the point where she felt like screaming.

The roses in the garden had all been cut for the flower arrangements, but Lily had no objection to thorns at the moment. She had an agreeable fantasy of Alicia pricking her thumb on her bouquet tomorrow, letting out an unladylike curse while blood stained her pale yellow gown. Lily was smiling rather wickedly and did not hear the man come up beside her.

"What do you find so amusing, my dear Mistress Walters?" said a voice she recognized only too well. Lily's shoulders stiffened. She wished she had a thorn long enough to turn and stick into that self-satisfied face.

"Lieutenant Dodgett, do you make a habit of accosting ladies in gardens?" she said.

"Are you a lady?" he replied. Lily's anger rose like tinder to flame. He had gone past smirking now into sheer insult.

"What gives you the right to say such things?"

"You, my dear. You have obviously found yourself a protector, clever girl. But that old curmudgeon cannot give you what I can, so once you tire of him, we can come to an arrangement," he said, taking her arm firmly.

She yanked it free. "You are going to be married tomorrow," she said, aghast at his intentions.

William grabbed her wrist, turning her forcefully to face him. "She will not be a problem, I assure you," he said, his handsome liar's face a combination of greed and lust.

Lily noticed she had strayed too far from the house. Only someone looking for her would see her now, because plants obscured most of the view from the house. "What makes you so sure of that?" she said, trying again to get her arm free and failing.

"She is marrying me for the title I shall have someday, and I am marrying her for her money. She has no illusions, a practical girl, my Alicia. Ambitious too." Evidently tired of talking, he pulled her closer to him, circling her with his other arm. Lily was effectively imprisoned.

"No need to wait, then," he continued. "There will be no trouble from Alicia. So you can give me a little taste of what you are giving that old fool," he said. His face descended toward her like a nightmare.

"No," Lily said, and bit down hard on his lip when he tried to close his mouth over hers.

"Ow! You little bitch," he yelled.

"Louder, William, do. It will be interesting to see whether your future father-in-law will be as practical as you say Alicia is." Lily's triumph was short-lived, since William tightened his grip on her wrist.

He was drawing her back toward him, malicious intent in his eyes, when footfalls on the dark path attracted their attention.

"What do you think you are doing?" came a quiet, deadly voice behind them. Lily used the moment of surprise to pull free of William's grasp. She looked beyond the lieutenant's shoulder to her rescuer with surprise. Adair had never looked so efficient or so serious, even with his silly spectacles on.

He looked, she thought fleetingly, capable of murder.

William's thoughts must have been similar. But after a moment in which panic crossed his face, the habitual smirk set in. "Just chatting with your fancy piece, Squire," he said. "No harm done, eh?" he said in a man-to-man tone.

"Mistress Walters is not anyone's fancy piece, Lieutenant Dodgett," Adair said with more steel in his voice than Lily had ever heard. "Moreover, she is under my protection and you are quite clearly bothering her."

"Here now, Squire, we all know what kind of protection you have going," William said, taking an involuntary step back. "She is just a Colonial. Surely a few words will not offend her."

"I think they can and they do. Mistress Walters, did he hurt you?" Adair asked, his gaze softening as it rested on her. Lily did not want the men to come to blows, because she knew Adair had no chance against a young army officer in good condition.

"No, Adair, really, I am fine," Lily said, trying to hide

her sore wrist in the folds of her skirt. Adair saw the gesture. Reaching out, he seized her arm lightly. Even the gentle touch hurt. Lily winced.

"You hurt her once, you bastard, and I should have killed you then. By God, you will not touch her again," Adair growled in a truly menacing voice. William lost some of his smirk, but his stance altered subtly, tensing with a fighter's readiness.

Lily tried to step between them, but Adair would not allow it. Without further ado he made a fist and belted William in the jaw with a force she had never suspected he possessed.

William went down in a flurry of ungainly sprawled limbs. He obviously had not expected such strength either, for he touched his jaw gingerly, pain contorting his surly expression.

"Why, you bastard," he said. "This little colonial tart ain't worth it." He rose to his feet, ready to lunge for Adair.

Adam's punch this time hit William in the gut. Then he brought up his knee and caught William in the groin. "Never impugn the honor of a lady," he said, making no move to help the lieutenant up from the oyster-shell path, where he sprawled again, groaning and cursing.

"Adair, I did not think . . . I never thought you could . . ." Lily babbled, stunned at the raw power Adair had unleashed.

The sound of a lone man clapping caused both Adam and Lily to look down the path behind them. "Neither did I," said Colonel Randolph Ware, whose gaze raked Adam from head to toe. Lily followed the colonel's glance, saw for the first time that unpadded shoulders filled Adair's coat. That taut muscles ran the length of his strong calves and up his thighs through the silk breeches. That his hands were large and powerful, not the soft white hands of a pampered aristocrat.

How had she failed to notice all that? Not quite sure what was she was seeing, Lily missed Ware's penetrating look at Adam's features. But she heard him say, "Perhaps you learned more from Pearson than how to defeat him at a hand of cards, eh, *Squire?*"

Adair seized Lily's other hand, not the one that hurt, half dragging her down the path in another direction. He did not break stride or look to see if the colonel followed them. Lily looked, and saw Ware help Dodgett up from the ground. As the colonel whispered urgently to the younger officer, she watched the two men follow Adair's progress with interest. Too much interest. And their intent seemed menacing, even at this distance.

Adair marched past the folly and its statues, never slowing or answering her efforts to ask him what had just happened and what Ware's strange words meant.

They arrived at the back entrance to the kitchen. He thrust her inside unceremoniously, then turned on his heel and headed in the direction of the stables.

Cook did not seem perturbed by the arrival of Lily in her kitchen. "That man loves to ride," she said. "I hear tell he rides sometimes half the night." That did not fit with what Lily knew of the indolent Adair.

"Why?" she asked, allowing Cook to look at her wrist when the woman noticed how Lily held it awkwardly at her side.

"Why? Honey, I don't know. I just know that when a man is troubled, he takes it out some way he can. Some men, they drink. Some gamble. And then there be some so lovesick, they can't do nothing but ride out their frustration. That Squire, there is a lot more to him than most folk think." Her brown eyes gazed at Lily assessingly. "And he been riding a lot since you come here."

"I'm beginning to realize there is more to him than I thought," Lily said, refusing to respond to Cook's blatant interest. *But I do not know what to make of all this,* she thought. *Or him.*

Twenty-four

O never say that I was false of heart,
Though absence seem'd my flame to qualify.
                                    —William Shakespeare,
                                    Sonnet 109

Lily did not see Adair again that night. Someone put about the story of his troubled stomach, but she did not believe it for a minute, although she said nothing. Dodgett did not so much as glance her way again, but she felt Ware's eyes on her from time to time. Lily stuck close by Mary's mother and father until they left, then sought her room.

She did not know whether Adair returned to entertain his guests at dinner, but the crowd had certainly seemed merry enough when she left. Cook thoughtfully sent Betsy up with a tray piled high with delicacies, divining somehow that Lily didn't intend to join the others for dinner.

Lily packed, sitting down to eat only when Betsy pressed her. She hid her portmanteau when the knock came. No one needed to be alerted to her plans, so she told the girl that her services would not be needed. Will could surely be persuaded to drive her into Williamsburg early on the pretext of checking on the flowers at the

church—something she would need to do in any event—
but there was no need to alert the other servants, who
might tell their master. Assuming he returned.

The problem of Adair troubled Lily all evening, but it
was only one more preoccupation crowding the others in
her head. With her other pressing concerns, eventually she
forgot the mystery of his sudden burst of power and Ware's
strange reaction.

Her chief worry was what to do if Jack Cameron would
not tell her where Peter had been sent. What if he did not
know?

And what if the only man who did was Adam Pearson?
Where had he gone and who could find him? After all,
Lily thought, he had been among them for months without
anyone ever discovering where he kept himself during the
day. She realized, of course, that he wanted it that way.
The fewer who knew details of his activities, the less there
was to give away to the redcoats.

Worrying only tired her and advanced her plans no further. Lily forced herself to stop pacing and fretting. She
laid out the simple gown in which she had arrived at Oak
Grove, not intending to take with her any of those belonging to Adair's mother.

Lily started to undo the emerald silk bodice, when a
rustle of sound at the open window behind her attracted
her attention. Before she could move toward it, a hard
male body pressed against hers. Strong arms held her
around the waist, and the voice she would know anywhere
murmured soft and deep, "I received your message."

"Adam!" Lily tried to turn, started to ask him about
Peter, about where he'd been, but he held her where she
was.

"You are angry," he said against her ear. She nodded.

"You have a right to be." He braced his legs, drawing her more closely against his body.

"There have been so many lies," he said in his deep voice. Not her sadness, it was his she felt. The heat from his body, the solidity and power of his frame, melted her resistance.

"Adam, we have to talk . . ." she started to say, trying to turn and face him despite the lassitude engulfing her limbs. Where had he been? Why was he there now?

"Aye," he said, his grip tightening so she could not turn. He nuzzled her hair aside to brush his lips against her neck. "We will talk. I will explain everything. But not now. I have to know how you feel."

It was the same thing she wanted. How could she know so little of him yet find their thoughts ran as one? Adam lived in isolation, bearing secrets. Perhaps he, too, was entitled to uncertainty.

She knew how she felt. "Touch me," she said, "and know." Lily held her breath, waiting for his response. Suddenly, she desperately wanted to see into his extraordinary eyes, to see the effect of her bold words. Too late. She could not take them back.

Adam's body tightened, and Lily trembled, wondering what she had unleashed. She felt his breath at the nape of her neck a moment before his lips covered it, and his hands began to move on her.

He stroked her body, first her curves through silk, then sliding under her clothing to skim her shift. His hold was light, tantalizing, and when his hands reached her breasts, they remained distant, touching only the sides. Her nipples peaked on their own, and she felt a surge of desire.

At last his fingertips touched her, plucking erotic music with the most delicate of caresses across her hardened crests. A low moan escaped Lily. Keeping her chest perfectly still so as not to lose even the too-light, torturous contact with Adam's hands, she swayed back against him with her lower body.

Her backside, covered only by the delicate shift she wore, rubbed against Adam, and the moan this time came from him. He yielded, sliding her nipples between his fingers, filling his hands with her as she had longed for him to do.

Lily died ten deaths when Adam's hands retraced their path, leaving her breasts, skimming the indentation of her waist, her navel. His fingertips passed just as lightly over the triangle at the junction of her thighs.

Then stopped. Lily squirmed, but his hands did not move. Her soft curls, which had known his touch, were damp. But he couldn't feel that because he had not touched them.

"Adam, please," Lily said.

"Do you want me?" His voice was as dark and seductive as she'd ever heard it, his hands poised over her motionless. All at once Lily was tired of waiting, tired of wanting, tired of his control. She wanted him to lose himself, to forget that he was anything but her lover, to own him fully, at least for that night.

For answer she placed her hands over his, pressing them against her. Boldly, she kept her hands over his, urging them downward. When she exerted pressure on his fingers, they slipped inside her folds, startling them both with the wetness dampening his fingers, even through the barrier of cloth.

"God, what you do to me," he muttered. Her hands left his then to reach back toward his wrists, pulling the ties that held his sleeves closed. She ran the cloth up his arms as far as she could, eager to touch his warm skin. Adam moved the cloth between her legs, her tiny cries like water to his parched senses.

The testing was forgotten, his control a shattered veneer.

There was no doubt she wanted him. He did not even think he could wait to undress them both, when all he had to do was lift her hem to plunge inside her. One hand went to the buttons at his breeches, while he slid the cloth away from her legs with his other.

"Lily, bend over," he urged softly, taking her hands from his forearms to place them on the mattress in front of her.

"What . . ." she started to ask, but he shushed her gently, using both hands to gently fondle her breasts while he brought his hips into complete contact with her.

He did not think she understood, not yet. He lifted the bunched-up material of her shift. He bent over her, his mouth near her ear to whisper what he wanted.

Lily felt his blunt manhood probing her core at the same time his dark, heated words reached her ear. Although this was not the Adam she thought she knew, her heightened intuition told her this was a facet of himself Adam worked hard to keep concealed. Like the night he confessed he hadn't wanted to stop touching her, this powerful sensuality was a part of the inner self he guarded so closely.

And whether he had denied his sensuality for years, or never allowed it expression, still he knew exactly where to touch, how to wring from her a response she hadn't known existed in herself. The cry wrung from her matched his own deeper one as he slid into her in a heated rush. Lily succumbed to the utter sensuality of it, the unmatched depth of him inside her, his hands cupping and holding her breasts as she thrust back against him to take him deeper.

"Cannot . . . hold on," he panted, his thrusts quickening. She didn't want him to, so she pushed back again. Although his hands tightened on her breasts, he withdrew almost all the way. "Have to . . . slow down . . ."

"No," she moaned in frustration. He was not going to control this encounter. Lily leaned forward even more, planting her elbows on the bed. Adam had to surge deeper into her or lose contact altogether, and she hoped he was too far gone for that.

She had gambled correctly. He followed, his hands sliding down now to grasp her hips, his hard length sliding into her again.

God, what was she doing? Adam thought. He had never been so deep inside a woman, never felt so tightly held. Adam bent over her again, his teeth closing lightly on her ear. He felt the shudder that wracked her and urged her fully onto the bed just before her knees collapsed.

A final deep thrust home and she climaxed, which led to his own. He emptied himself into her, his pleasure so intense that only her name emerged from his lips, a cry that contained his soul if she but knew.

He reached behind him to close the shutter, then followed Lily onto the bed, bringing her to his side as if to shelter her from a storm. His lips, meeting hers for the first time that night, were gentle, cherishing, as he acknowledged the bittersweet truth.

He loved this woman as he had never loved, would never love another. Like the columbine, he could not give her up. He could not abandon her. How to manage it, he had no idea. Hearing her soft intake of breath beside him, about to take up the thread of interrupted conversation again, no doubt, he turned to kiss her before she could speak.

But this time he was not quick enough.

"I love you" was the sentence he cut off with his kiss.

He did not lift his lips from hers. He wanted to tell her he loved her, wanted to give her the choice of whether she would believe him, forgive his deception, come with him. *Where?* his mind continued, relentlessly logical. *As what?* tore at him as he increased his gentle pressure against her lips.

Years of repressed sensuality reared up, a thousand desires longing to be fulfilled. Whether he left her or not, whether the soldier or the lover won out by morning, at least there would have been this.

One hand tangled in her thick hair, which he rubbed softly across her breasts, the crests still pebbled in the aftermath of their passion. His other hand cradled her head, and he opened his mouth over hers in a blatantly carnal kiss.

If he hoped, in some part of him that still wanted control, to shock her with sensual excess, to have her reject him to justify a leave-taking, it wasn't working. Her tongue darted into the warm recesses of his mouth with alacrity, she being just as relentless, just as inventive, as he.

He rolled over her, wondering if she could stand a second joining so soon after the first. She parted her thighs under him, nudging him close so that there was no decision to be made. As her legs closed around him, he entered her.

Home. He was home. He had not known he spoke aloud until her soft voice answered in the dark.

"With you, Adam. Wherever you are." More erotic than anything they had done or said, her words triggered his release. Helpless again where she was concerned, he tightened immediately, and she came with him until it seemed to him they had gone on climaxing forever, ripples of pleasure and love spreading through them, inside and out, their oneness absolute.

When he awoke later in the night, they were still joined. Lily woke as he tried to ease himself off her.

"Did I hurt you?" he asked, stroking her hair.

"No. Adam, did you ever . . ." Suddenly, he knew what she was about to say and it was important to him that she not have to ask.

"No, I never thought it could be like this," he said, smiling at her start of surprise.

She shifted, and he found himself still joined with her. They both felt him hardening. "You are incorrigible," he said. "And quite likely to be sore," he added, trying to be considerate.

"And you are quite willing to be encouraged," she replied, laughter in her voice, sweeping away his doubts. But he did move in her gently, so gently that even before his urge for tenderness had been fully satisfied, she swept her arms down his back, raking him lightly with her nails to urge him on.

What could he do but answer the lady's wishes?

Twenty-five

At every word a reputation dies.
—Alexander Pope,
The Rape of the Lock,
1712

The knock came early, more a warning than a request for permission. As the door flew open with restrained violence, Lily felt a weary familiarity about it all. What was it about Adam that attracted so many visitors, usually unwelcome, when he was with her?

Her sleepy annoyance did not last long. Even as she savored the realization that for once Adam's warm, heavy body lay beside her, the door slammed against the wall.

"Mistress Walters, once again you are the only link between Sotheby and Pearson, both of whom have disappeared." Colonel Ware's stern tones were openly disapproving as he took in her disheveled state. The sheet Lily clutched to cover herself hid her companion for the moment.

Adam heard a familiar voice and sat bolt upright, years of training interrupting the deepest, most pleasant sleep he had enjoyed in years. Over the top of the sheet, which Lily held high under her chin, he saw cold blue eyes boring into him. Suppressing the instinctive urge to stand

and salute, he reached down to the floor, grabbing the first piece of cloth that came to hand. Fortunately, his breeches.

He slid into them at the same time as he stood up. Lily's head turned. Her gaze slid up to his face as he fastened his breeches. A blush warmed her cheeks. Adam tossed his shirt at Lily. Despite her shock, she had the presence of mind to dive into it. Adam turned to face Ware.

"There's Adam Pearson, gel, as if you didn't know," Ware said. "Your notorious Patriot leader is my second in command. And 'Adair Sotheby,' I'd wager a year's pay."

Lily did not answer, her gaze riveted on Adam. As she read the truth in his face, the shock in her wide golden eyes was unmistakable. Oh, sweet God, not this, Adam thought. Not now.

"Adair?" she said, shock, horror, disbelief all a jumble on her lovely face.

Ware laughed. "You never noticed, and you his mistress?"

"Adair wears spectacles . . ." Lily said in a weak voice.

"Now you know why. Do you think there was any other way he could have fooled me as long as he has, any other way to conceal those strange eyes of his? But he gave himself away with Dodgett last night. Oh, I confess, I was fooled for a time by the padding and the disguise, but I bloody well know an officer who served with me for twelve years."

Ware reached one arm behind him to lock the door. At the sound of the click, Lily started to scoot out of bed away from Ware. Realizing she was moving toward Adam, she turned back.

With her movement, Adam knew he had a way out. It would not be easy on Lily, but at this point nothing would be. He grabbed her elbow, hauling her out of bed. He dragged her against his chest, her cloth-covered buttocks and bare legs a brief reminder of last night, when they had begun a journey of discovery in this position.

From her desperate attempt to keep from touching him, he guessed she was remembering—with loathing. "I intended to explain this morning, Lily," he murmured to her rigid back, "but we were interrupted."

"Explain that you are a Tory spy?" she asked incredulously.

"What are you doing with the gel?" Ware interrupted.

"Do you want her running to her Patriot friends with this tale?" Adam asked Ware.

Ware waved a hand. "Of course not. You know, even I might not have tumbled to your disguise until you betrayed yourself last night," Ware said.

Lily was mortified, shame painting her cheeks scarlet. *How had she not known?* It was not that obvious, she thought, but she was in no mood to spare herself. She had never seen Adair's eyes uncovered, or touched him except . . . except for that kiss. She should have known then. God, what a fool she'd been.

Ware was onto another topic. Thank heavens she did not have to answer. "Disguises are all very well, but why in the name of hell didn't you contact me, Adam? Christ, I had begun to think you'd spent too much time infiltrating them and had gone over to their side."

" 'Tis been most irregular," he complained irritably. "Not to mention getting stuck with that ass Dodgett when I was sent here to investigate the doings of this mysterious Patriot leader. I should have known 'twas you at once. These damned colonials cannot normally keep their activities secret past a fortnight."

"Speaking of Dodgett," the colonel said, running his

finger around his uniform collar. "Christ, Adam, he is straight over from England and he's a bloody fool. I wish I knew who let him buy his colors."

Adam had felt Lily's spine stiffen with each damning word of his story exposed, but there was no way he could explain, not in front of Ware. Yet he could do something about Dodgett.

"Ah, yes, your young lieutenant, the one having trouble keeping his breeches buttoned. Get rid of him, Randolph," Adam said, knowing Randolph would still rely on his judgment in this.

Lily's indrawn breath at this statement sealed his doom. He hardly needed to read her thoughts: Why would he address Ware in such a familiar way if he hadn't been working for him all along?

The prospect of losing Lily was hell itself. Life had not looked bleaker since he'd witnessed the infidelity that shattered his adolescence. Discipline rose reluctantly to take the place of what had been his heart.

"Get rid of him," Adam repeated, not looking at Lily.

"You've not exactly kept yours buttoned, have you?" Ware asked, lingering anger at Adam's long silence evident in his sarcastic words.

"Wrong target, Randolph," Adam said, moving swiftly. "Take your bloody anger out on me, not her." By the time he finished speaking, Adam had Ware's uniform jacket in both fists, his face inches from Ware's own. "Dodgett molested her knowing she wanted nothing to do with him. Until now Mistress Walters's actions have been of her own accord. There is no comparison."

Lily had frozen in place. Ware seemed to scent the danger. "Easy, my boy," he said. "My apologies, Mistress Walters," he said without a trace of condescension.

Adam stepped back, snagging Lily's arm as she swung into motion, trying to dart past him to the door.

"Damn you, let me go," Lily said vehemently. "I don't need you to defend my honor now that you've made sure I have none."

"I can't let you go, Lily, you know that."

"Why? Who would believe me if I told them you were Adair? I am no threat to you." Adam held her firmly. She was safely imprisoned within his grasp again, but her loathing was every bit as deep as he had feared.

Ware stared thoughtfully at Adam. "Very clever ruse, Pearson. Quite unorthodox, as I know you like things. But why go to such great lengths to keep your disguise a secret from me? Frankly, why risk a court-martial? I would have been happy to approve this, although I have to wonder what you hoped to accomplish as that silly fop Adair."

Lily tried to pull away. "You . . . lying bastard," she said in a low voice.

"Not a bastard," Adam said, no inflection in his deep voice. "As far as I know," he said, remembering his mother.

Lily's next words wrenched him back to the present. "You do not even deny you were spying?" she asked, outraged.

"No." He wished he could say more. But their only chance to get out of there rested on Ware believing Adam Pearson was still a loyal officer. Explaining to Lily would have to wait.

"Adam," Ware broke in, "what do you plan to do with her?"

"Randolph, leave this to me. 'Twould be awkward to reveal my disguise at this point. I'll come see you Monday to discuss this, after the Chalmers wedding. I'll take care of Lily, you get rid of Dodgett, then we can talk."

God, he sounded cool, Lily thought furiously. As if this were all just a game to him. Which it was, obviously. Adam could now reveal the identity of every Sons of Liberty member between here and Richmond. But why hadn't he told Ware everything? How could his commander not have known Adam was masquerading as Adair?

"Very well." Ware nodded in agreement. "I suspect young William's bride will not be reluctant to return to England." The colonel doffed his uniform hat and turned to go. "One thing, Adam. If this were anyone but you, and if I weren't so bloody furious with that idiot Dodgett, you would be in serious trouble. 'Tis only because I assume you have a good reason for all this irregularity that I am allowing you to end it in the same fashion."

He opened the door, then turned back. "What word of the squire do you want put about? The guests will be leaving for the wedding soon."

"The squire's stomach leaves him indisposed this morning." Adam's voice was still cool as he delivered his latest lie.

"Very well. Until Monday, then."

Lily turned on Adam the moment Ware left. "Let go of me," she said. To her surprise, he did. She moved immediately to the door.

"I think you will find Ware took care of that already," Adam said.

He was right, Lily found. The door was locked.

"Do you want to advertise?" Adam asked, a thread of amusement in his deep voice.

"What?" she said, then it hit her. She was wearing Adam's shirt, which came halfway down her thighs, and nothing else. She swept past him to the bed, daring him silently to laugh.

He did not. Instead, his magnificent eyes, the startling blue-green gaze she had wanted to lose herself in, rested on her assessingly.

"Deciding which room to lock me in?" she asked, bitterness pervading her voice. "Turn around," she said, not waiting for him to answer. "I want to get dressed."

"No to the first," he said imperturbably, "and as for the second, 'tis a bit late to worry about your modesty with me."

"Turn around," Lily repeated, torn between anger and tears. He was in control of everything again. All he had to do was say no, and there was nothing she could do to salvage her modesty or her pride.

"Nay, 'tis not too late for modesty," she said. "For it seems I do not know you after all." Adam turned on his heel, searching out the rest of his clothing without saying another word. She hoped she had wounded him.

Lily dressed hastily, not caring if her bodice was properly laced or not. She turned around, ready to demand her release. She found herself staring at Adam's very naked, very male chest.

How did you ever masquerade as Adair? How did I ever believe it? She did not realize she had spoken the words aloud until Adam replied.

"The real question is, how did it take Randolph so long to unmask me?" Adam said.

"You *are* working for him," said Lily, handing him his shirt as if she performed this wifely task every day. She watched him button his waistcoat over it, noting for the first time that his own clothes were simple but well cut, with nothing of Adair's foppish style evident.

"If I were, I would have told him what he wants to

know instead of playing for time," Adam said in a distracted tone. Lily wondered what he was looking for, just as she wondered what on earth she was still doing there. The door was locked, of course, but she should be screaming down the house.

Screaming what? she asked herself. That she had slept with Adair Sotheby and had not known it? That she bedded a British spy posing as both a British Loyalist and a Patriot? That sounded insane, and she knew it.

"Ware will wonder soon enough why I told him nothing. We had best be long gone before he realizes it," Adam continued, expertly tying his stock. "Which I reckon will be in less than half an hour's time. If he is in Bruton Parish Church when he realizes I cozened him, we will escape. If he is still stalking about my house trying to puzzle things out, we will not."

He shrugged on a bottle-green frock coat that emphasized the breadth of his shoulders and the clean lines of his frame. It was all Lily could do not to stare. How could she ever have thought Adair flabby . . . and middle-aged . . . and effeminate?

His words sunk in only as he held out his hand. The sense of cozy domesticity had affected Adam as well, for he looked startled when she slapped his hand aside. "Go somewhere with you? Not on my life!"

"It may very well be both our lives. Come, Lily, I will explain," he said, the beseeching note so well hidden that only she, who knew his voice so well, sensed the plea in it. *She, who knew him so well?* What a fool she was, Lily thought bitterly.

"I will not go anywhere with you. Why do you want to leave anyway if you have to report to Ware?" Lily darted a glance at the windows. They were closed. "I don't know who you are or what you want, but I've no intention of leaving with you," she repeated.

Adam moved toward her then, and she was fleetingly reminded of the implacable stranger who had dragged her from the forest the night she stumbled on the training. Although she was more uncertain than ever what he was capable of, she knew he would not harm her. "There is no time to argue now. I cannot leave you here."

"Why not? Who will harm me? Other than those who were once my friends, before association with you ruined my reputation."

Rueful amusement crossed his expressive face. Like an echo off a cliff, the thought continued to resound deep within her. *How could I not have seen him in Adair?*

"Which reputation, little flower?" he said. "Your maidenly one or your Patriot one?"

She lunged at him then, engulfed by a purely feminine sense of rage. He absorbed the blow of her small fists against his chest, then captured her hands, still fisted, pulling her gently against his side.

He transferred control of both wrists to one hand, while with his other he tilted up her chin. "Forgive me, Lily," he said in a grave voice. "Now is not the time for lightness, but there is no time to explain. There are a hundred reasons why I cannot leave you here. You would bring the Sons of Liberty down on me as a traitor—if you could get them to believe you—and I must avoid Ware. There will be confusion over who I really am, Patriot spy or Loyalist spy, and that in itself is dangerous."

"But you *are* a spy," she said flatly, shocked to find she secretly hoped for his denial.

"Was," Adam replied, grateful that she had cut him off. His last reason was that he loved her and could not leave her behind. Although he had planned to do exactly that before his identity had been revealed, last night had changed him. She might no longer trust him, but he had at last found a woman he could trust, a trust he had not known since his mother's betrayal.

Yet he could not bring himself to say so, to expose his vulnerability to her—the woman who had without doubt just become his most fervent enemy.

Under the brown wool cloak, Adam held Lily's arm tightly but not uncomfortably. Would he tie her up when they reached the stables? she wondered. With the hood over her face and Adam unrecognized—of course, now she knew why he took such pains not to be seen—they passed through the early morning hustle and bustle of Oak Grove unnoticed.

Lily hoped to spot Will Evans, knowing him for a friend and perhaps the only person who would listen to her story before condemning her. Everyone else was a servant of Adair's.

Adam's.

Whoever.

A low sound of frustration tore from her throat. Adam's grip softened slightly. Lily prepared to bolt, to seize any possible advantage in this unequal contest.

"Think, Lily," he said softly. "Imagine yourself explaining how you discovered my disguise. Not even someone so careless with her reputation as you would want to describe the circumstances of my unmasking." His low voice was relentless but not harsh.

"Careless . . . ?"

"Yes, my love, careless. Oh, I know why you did it. I know you wanted to help the Patriot cause. But to the eyes of Williamsburg, you apparently changed sides. You frequented Tory revels, danced with British officers, accepted Adair Sotheby's hospitality. . . ."

"When I had no choice," she flung at him as they entered the deserted stables.

"Forgive me, little flower," he said softly when he bound her hands behind her with rope and looped it around a hitching post on the stable wall. As she opened her mouth to scream, he shot a turbulent blue-green glance at her. "How will you explain?" he asked again, cinching the girth under Mercury.

Lily shut her mouth, glaring. "I am not sure I care anymore," she said finally, her jaw clenched.

Adam held her scornful gaze, but his expression was bleak. "I care," he said, his last words to her before lifting her bodily to the saddle, then mounting in a single fluid motion behind her.

Twenty-six

*Cease to ask what the morrow will bring forth, and
set down as gain each day that Fortune grants.*

—Horace,
Odes,
23 B.C.

All the traffic on the road was heading toward Williamsburg. Adair's guests going to the wedding, no doubt. *Adam's* guests, Lily thought, reminding herself of the shocking truth.

Turning Mercury's head, Adam urged the horse through the bracken and into the forest. He had not allowed them to come within a hundred feet of a carriage.

Lily was irritated by the solid feel of Adam's big body behind her and by her own reaction. She did not loathe having him at her back, his arms clasped around her waist—far from it. She should not feel this way. To distract herself, she blurted out the first inane thought that came to her.

"My flowers," she said.

" 'Tis why you did not see Will this morning." Lily gave a guilty start, forgetting how easily Adam was able to read her before. Although she now felt disoriented and uncomfortable around him, he had always known who she was and what she felt. Another reason to resent him.

". . . so I sent him into Williamsburg to water the arrangements," he finished. Gracious, did he think of everything?

"When did you ask him to do that?"

"Last night."

"You planned to seduce me, then?"

"That was your request, or did I misread your message?" he countered.

"Request?" Her voice quivered in outrage. "When did I ever ask you to—" She stopped, assailed by the memory of inviting Adam to touch her as he stood behind her.

"With your bouquet." His steady, unemotional voice indicated he had not meant to embarrass her. And yes, she had asked him to come to her, although she would rather die than admit it now.

Lily's thoughts seesawed wildly. Unwillingly, she remembered how he'd defended her to Ware. His game was too deep for her to fathom, yet something fundamentally honest about him remained.

He untied her hands as soon as they cleared Oak Grove—but his hold around her waist was secure. He had forced her to go with him—but he'd said the reason was to keep her safe. He had lied to both sides and she did not know who was his true master—but he had rescued Peter.

Peter! Her own troubles forgotten, Lily twisted around to look up into Adam's face. "What have you done with my brother?" she demanded.

Her question crystallized Adam's intentions in a swift, searing rush. What he was going to do was as much for her as for himself, though if he told her that, she wouldn't believe him—not now, and perhaps not ever.

"He is safe," he answered, unable to stifle the pain that stabbed through him at the mistrust in her voice. "Safe, Lily," he said, willing her to feel his sincerity.

"Why should I believe you? You probably betrayed them to the British." Mercury danced uneasily in response to his too-tight grip on the reins. He forced himself to relax before answering.

"If I had done that, why would I have risked—" He had been about to say "risked my neck" but realized that she would not give a damn about the difficult rescue. "Why would I have rescued them?" he substituted. "They were already in British hands."

"How do I know you risked anything? Perhaps 'twas all part of your plot."

It would have been so easy to take offense at her accusations, to be angry with her, but Adam refused to allow himself an easy exit. He had created this mess.

"He and Ethan are safe. I have proof."

"The only proof I would believe after this morning would be to see them with my own eyes."

"And so you shall," he promised. From the stiff set of her back, he knew she did not believe that either. They rode on in silence.

Ware strode toward the stables. Damn, had it not been for the girl, he would have had it out with Pearson then and there. There was more going on here than he'd realized at first.

Pearson had never been one to flout command. Oh, Ware had seen the growing restlessness, known that playing the spy did not appeal to Pearson's moralistic nature. Adam had always wanted to call a spade a spade and be done with it. That business with his mother had a lot to

do with it. But disappearing the way he had was tanta-
mount to desertion.

Something still was not right. Why the devil play at this
"Squire Sotheby" when he had successfully established
himself as a Patriot leader? To have spent all this time
among the rebels and not to offer him a word of information was deuced strange.

Even as Ware surveyed the quiet stables and noticed
the empty stall, his suspicions grew. Perhaps Pearson had
truly been in hiding. He had not infiltrated the Patriot
band in Virginia: He was there because he had joined the
rebel cause.

Ware swung around, seeing a stable lad creep from a
bed of straw where he had been enjoying a few extra
winks.

"You, boy," he said. "Which horse is missing?"

The lad jerked, ashamed at being caught, then straightened manfully. "The horse that has gone is the master's,
sir. Mercury."

"What sort of horse?"

"A big black gelding, sir."

"Black with a blaze of white on the rump?" Ware remembered the flash in the forest as the would-be rescuer
escaped the jail ambush by an instant.

The carrot-haired boy rubbed his eyes sleepily. "Blaze
of white, yes, sir, that's Mercury."

Ware yanked a coin from his pocket, cold fury and certainty replacing his confusion. "I am one of the squire's
guests, lad. I may be late for the wedding. Saddle up the
swiftest animal you have, and quickly." Where would
Pearson take the girl? he wondered. If he was in love with
her, it was unlikely he would tie her up here in the house,
then leave.

Pearson in love with a colonial? But this was no more

fantastic than what he'd learned that morning. Perhaps she was the reason he had abandoned his principles. . . . No, the girl had been as surprised as Ware about Adam's disguise. But they were obviously lovers.

He had not thought Adam was a man to be led around by his male organ. Ware had taught him to know better. Moreover, Adam had his own painful boyhood experience to consider.

Ware found the trail without much difficulty, due to Pearson's haste, no doubt. Adam was too well versed in Indian ways to leave much of a trail behind. They were headed north.

His luck had finally broken. He had little doubt that when he found Pearson and Mistress Walters, he would also find Peter Walters and the other escaped prisoner. Bringing down four at one time was not a bad hunt. It might even erase some of the censure sure to fall on him when the general learned one of Ware's most trusted men had turned traitor.

Traveling with the woman was sure to slow him down. He'd catch up.

Lily awoke from a doze. In her dream she had imagined Adam at her back, warm, strong, solid. Then he'd turned her. They were body to body, skin to skin. Best of all, face to face.

While his blue-green gaze held her, he bent his head to kiss her. "Look at me, Lily," he ordered gently. "I want to see you." She complied, color mounting to her cheeks, modesty forgotten, his intense gaze locked with hers in this intimate moment.

"Look at me, Lily," he said again. Stomach lurching, Lily realized that this was no dream. Adam was indeed warm and solid, damn him, but they were not lying together in a warm bed. They were riding through the Virginia countryside.

"Are you too tired to ride on?" he asked.

Lily turned, dazed. The expression in his eyes was searingly intense, bluer now than green. Then she remembered where she was and how things were between them. "I can keep going," she said.

Adam sighed. For a moment, when she'd gazed at him with those huge amber eyes, his body heat had risen from simmer to boil. Some parts of him were already far from indifferent to her, his thighs where they cradled her hips, his arms where they brushed against her upper arms. But that had been nothing next to the moment when she looked at him with that sleepy sensuality she was not aware she possessed. Then, as quickly as his manhood leapt to life, her contempt doused it.

"We will ride until noon, then," he replied just as curtly. He'd been careful not to overtax Mercury, but the animal would need water soon. He and Lily would need food; Lily needed clothing. She wore only her shift under the wool cloak, a fact he tried not to focus on.

Hours later the sun was high overhead. Adam was thirsty, Mercury tired. He imagined Lily was both, though she had not spoken a word in hours. She might be sore too, after last night. But he could not ask her that now.

"We'll halt soon," he said.

"Why?"

"You need clothes and we need food. We'll have to steal them."

"The owner of Oak Grove stealing food?" Lily asked scornfully.

"You may recall we left in a hurry," he said, refusing to be provoked.

"What is to prevent me from telling everyone who you are?" she asked hotly.

"The same as before. Who would believe you?" He watched her wilt before his eyes as she realized how absurd her tale would sound.

" 'Tis better than tying you up," he pointed out. He hated cruelty, did not want to tie her up, but he'd have to do something tonight to keep her from fleeing while he slept.

" 'Sufficient unto the day is the evil thereof,' " he murmured to himself.

In the end Adam tied Mercury to a tree. Lily came with him, protesting the whole way. At the outskirts of a farm he turned to her. "You can help with this or do it the hard way." Her furious posture promised eager battle.

"The hard way, Lily, means bound and gagged."

She did not bother saying "you wouldn't" because she knew he would. "Do not expect me to make this easy for you, Adam."

His gaze trained on clothing drying on a line, he said, "Clothes first or the chickens and pie?"

Lily felt stirrings of humor but repressed them sternly. "Unless you want me riding about the countryside in my night rail, Adam Pearson, then clothes first."

The heated look in his eyes brought a blush to her cheeks. She watched him gather the shift and gown, then return to the shelter of the trees with barely a sound.

"Where did you learn to do that?" she asked.

"The last war," he said, handing her the garments while indicating a pine with huge branches that nearly swept the ground. "My lady's dressing chamber," he said, sounding very English.

"Am I to trust you'll be a gentleman about this?" she said.

At the word "trust," the light in his eyes faded. "It works both ways. If you agree not to run off, I shan't have to supervise."

Thinking of the night to come when he surely could not watch her and sleep, Lily nodded. "I'll see to dinner, then," he said.

When he returned, the chicken's neck already wrung and dangling from one hand, a fresh-baked strawberry pie in the other, Lily had struggled into the too-tight muslin shift and dress.

"This was meant for a child of sixteen," she grumbled.

"I see what you mean." His gaze lingered on the bosom of her dress, then dipped to her ankles. She knew far too much of everything was on display.

"Lucky for you I am so trustworthy." He did not smile when he said it, and she knew she had offended him. What did she care for the feelings of a spy? she reminded herself.

Lily plucked and cooked the chicken efficiently and in silence. With the roots and greens Adam had gathered, their dinner was quite tasty, all in all.

Adam pulled out several things from his saddlebags. He knelt by her, a blanket in one hand. "Now, Lily, the hard part. How do we sleep tonight?"

"Nowhere near you," replied Lily, her outrage stirred anew.

"Calm down, love, 'twas not what I meant," he said. "Do you need to be tied to something to prevent escape, or can I trust you to sleep alone?" he continued.

"I am as trustworthy as you are, Adam Pearson."

"Since that was obviously meant to be an insult, I take it I shall have to tie you to something." His gaze traveled around the clearing while Lily hoped silently that her plan would work. He wouldn't tie her up in an awkward position. Surely she could work herself free of the knots while he slept.

To her surprise, Adam tied one end of the rope around his wrist. Before she could react, the other end was around her wrist in a neat knot.

"What are you doing?" she demanded, the touch of his fingers on her wrist making her sensitive and jumpy.

"As long as you are going to act this way, Lily, I have to prevent you from leaving. If I tie you to a bush or tree with enough leeway to make yourself comfortable, you will be able to undo the knots." He swept a lock of hair off her brow while she fumed.

"You can work yourself out of this one, too, with a little effort," he said, "but you will wake me doing so." She heard the regret in his voice but said nothing. "Now stand up," he said, "and let's find a way to make this blanket comfortable before we lie down."

Adam continued talking of inconsequential things, paying no apparent notice to her stiffness or silence. Certainly, he wasn't about to test last night's passionate declaration against today's developments. She had no idea what she'd do if he did.

Twenty-seven

No mask like open truth to cover lies,
As to go naked is the best disguise.
                              —William Congreve,
                                    The Double Dealer,
                              1694

Morning found Lily uncomfortable in a distinctly intimate way. In sleep she had snuggled up to Adam. She and Adam were pressed together all along the length of their bodies in a warm and cozy nest. Her fingers were nearly touching the rigid manhood that pressed against the front of his breeches.

Lily started to draw her hand back. Adam's eyes opened, and for a moment she forgot everything but the joy of being bathed in that awakening, luminous gaze. His hips moved slowly, sensuously, as if he wanted to press himself into her hand.

Lily snatched her hand away, reaching the end of the rope and lifting Adam's hand with it. She jumped to her feet. Adam followed her in a swift, contained motion that prevented the rope from chafing her.

His gaze no longer lambent, green sparks of annoyance flared amid his aquamarine irises. "Lily, a man cannot control his thoughts when he's asleep." He bent to lift the blanket off the ground. "That part of my anatomy does not seem to have been informed that things are different between us."

"Oh, you have no manners, you brute."

"This from my little eavesdropper? Ah, Lily. I have many sins, but believe me, I can control myself. Even when my body is urging me toward something different, something that, as recently as the night before last, you welcomed, even . . . invited."

She wanted to slap him, but angry as she was, she could not strike him when he spoke the truth. Lily backed to the limit the rope allowed, then seized the other edge of the blanket. She helped him fold it in silence. Adam stuffed the blanket back into the saddlebag, then untied her.

She looked at him, surprised. "I may be a brute, but not an insensitive one, I hope. I assume women experience the same call of nature in the morning as men," he said, smiling faintly.

Lily blushed despite herself, a sudden glimpse of a future with Adam unfolding. Waking every morning, sharing the natural, inevitable facets of a life together. She went off toward the bushes, subdued and thoughtful.

Because Adam couldn't leave Lily alone when he needed to scout, he hadn't covered their back trail well and didn't know how far behind them Ware might be. Feeling guilty about keeping her bound, Adam took extra care at mealtimes to see she had enough to eat, to give her the greater part of the blanket at night, to hold back branches on the trail so they did not slap her. He doubted she noticed. She scarcely spoke to him at all.

Besides, he could hardly say "Look, Lily, will you stay

here while I double back and check our trail to see if there's pursuit?" She had to relish the idea of anyone, even Ware, coming after them to free her.

Lily watched Adam one night as they made camp, and he skinned the rabbit he had caught for dinner. She wondered if his courtesy was artificial, to try to win her over, then felt ashamed of the thought. His behavior now matched what she knew of Adam . . . and reluctantly, she admitted, Adair.

Thoughts of him laughing at her while he masqueraded as Adair still made her furious. "That story you told me about Peter and Ethan, was that just to get me to come along with you willingly?"

Adam did not look up as he impaled the rabbit on the spit. "No, that *is* where we are going. 'Tis where we've been headed all along."

"We are?" Suddenly, she flung her arms around his neck and stood on tiptoe to hug him.

Adam relished the feel of the soft curves pressed against him but set her away from him. There was so much more he wanted, but taking advantage of her sudden good humor wasn't enough. It had to be all or nothing from Lily.

Either she came to him willingly, offering herself, her life, her love, or everything had ended back at Oak Grove when she learned he was also Adair Sotheby. He kept his arms at his sides and did not kiss her. From the swift intake of her breath and slightly parted lips, he thought she had been expecting it.

"We're going to Pennsylvania, Lily. To Philadelphia, to be precise." Where the men for whom he had agreed to spy should be meeting by now. "That's where Peter and Ethan are," he added.

"But they are in a redcoat jail," she said, her brief flare of enthusiasm gone.

"No, they were not betrayed. I sent them to safety, to shelter with other Patriots. Philadelphia is a free city."

"Why didn't you tell me this before? I'd not have even thought of escape." She dragged the rope out of the saddlebag. "You didn't need this," she said, flinging it aside in disgust.

Had the scales fallen from her eyes, or was it her ears? There was only so much a man could take. "Damn it Lily, this is what I told you at Oak Grove. Why do you believe me now? The truth is no different now than 'twas then."

"Then tell me the truth," Lily challenged.

He saw that she expected him to make up a story about being converted to the Patriot cause and knew she was not ready to hear the truth. So he didn't bother with explanations.

"This is the truth," he said simply. "Peter and Ethan are safe in Philadelphia. I am taking you to them."

"And what is your part in all this?" she asked. But he turned away, dropping to his knees to check the progress of their dinner.

That night, without the constraint of the rope, Lily did not have to sleep next to Adam. He used her cloak and gave her the blanket. When she looked at him later, she was certain he had slept no better than she. The cloak came no farther than his knees and did not cover the wide expanse of his chest.

Lily turned over, pretending not to care. Adam was right. What was different about today, when he'd told her about Peter? He had not truly mistreated her, and had extended her as much courtesy and freedom as the strained situation allowed.

What had changed was her acknowledgment that she believed him. There had been so much hurt and humiliation to overcome. The knowledge that she had been deceived had been too much. She had not been ready to hear him out then. She was now.

But the emotional chasm between them was a mile wide. She did not know how to bridge it or whether she wanted to. Why, then, was she so disappointed to find that Adam didn't want to either?

Early the next morning when she woke, stiff and cramped, Adam was gone. Her first thought was of her own physical discomfort. How in heaven's name had the ground become harder since the last place they camped? Then she realized that Adam had been sheltering her at night, supporting her all these past nights.

Adam reentered the clearing noiselessly a few minutes later and crouched down beside her at the fire. "We have to move on," he said. "Someone is tracking us." He drew her to her feet, looking surprised when she hastened to the saddlebags to pack their few belongings away. "Isn't this what you wanted, to be rescued?" he asked.

A quiet devastation broke over her as she looked up at his unsmiling face in the misty spring morning. " 'Love unchanged by adversity,' " she quoted softly from her flower vocabulary, turning away so he would not see the pain in her eyes.

Why should he trust her feelings anymore? She was not sure she did herself.

The days passed in a blur. Adam spent as much time backtracking to cover their trail, it seemed, as they did actually traveling north. Never close enough to see who it was, always hoping to lengthen their lead, still he had no doubt who followed them. " 'Tis Ware," he said.

"In that case, there should be a whole troop of redcoats with him," Lily said.

"Normally, yes. But this is personal, it's clouded his judgment," Adam said.

That afternoon they splashed through a streambed to hide Mercury's hoofprints. Lily waited until they reached a quiet meadow, where Adam gave Mercury his head and let the animal stretch his legs. Then she placed her hands over Adam's on the reins.

"Why is this an obsession, Adam? What are you to him?" she asked quietly. She dared not look at him, afraid to see refusal in his ocean-blue eyes.

He tensed but after a moment began to speak. "What I told you when I was Adair . . . about my mother and my uncle. 'Twas true." In a flat, unemotional voice, he described the scene that had met his fifteen-year-old eyes. He might have fooled others that he had overcome the pain, but Lily relied on the sound of his voice as her guide.

She heard in it the betrayal, the wrenching pain of his world falling to pieces on seeing his mother naked under his uncle's body, urging him on. Lily felt his shudder as if it were her own. "What could I do? I could not tell my father. I wasn't certain he'd believe me, and the idea of a duel between my father and my uncle was too horrible to contemplate.

"I rode away that afternoon, leaving a note saying I had decided to buy my colors. I never went home again. Father eventually died of the same heart trouble that killed Uncle Harry, then my older brother, Tony, the heir, was killed in a duel over a married woman. How ironic. Mother begged me to return, to take up the title of Earl of Dalby. She even tried to come to America once she learned I was in Boston."

Adam's hands relaxed somewhat on the reins. Lily stroked her hands over his lightly, though she doubted he felt it. He was too far away, reliving his own private hell.

"I bought Oak Grove when I came back to the Colonies from India. I intended to muster out, perhaps read law at the college here. But things did not work out that way." He fell silent. Lily turned to look at him once, but he had retreated behind the facade of his formidable control.

"Mercury grows tired of the double load," he said later as they prepared dinner together. "We need another horse. When I scout, I could use the other animal to lay down false tracks."

"Where would we get an extra horse?" Lily asked. The countryside through which they traveled now was forested and rural. There had been no real towns past Baltimore, as they headed into Maryland toward the Pennsylvania border.

"I don't know where to find a horse wandering around loose. If you see one, let me know." Adam tried a smile, but even across the firelight separating them, the effort failed.

Lily asked again about Ware. Adam's sigh stirred the fire's low flames. "He sees me as his surrogate son."

The words stabbed through Lily. She feared she had been right about Adam back at Oak Grove. Perhaps he was a Loyalist through and through and had undertaken to spy for Ware not only from duty but out of affection.

She must have flinched, because she saw pain flicker in Adam's face. "You don't believe me, do you?" he asked, firelight emphasizing the sculptured planes of his face.

"I don't know what to believe," she said.

"Will what I say make a difference?"

"I don't know," she answered honestly.

If what he said had no effect on her contempt for him, why was he bothering to tell her? Adam asked himself. She hated him now, she would hate him when he finished. Ah, well, he had nothing more to lose, having already lost her.

"Ware noticed me during the French and Indian War; he was a major, I was a green lieutenant. Then our unit was posted to India. He was married but had no children. He saw that I found India a bit overwhelming and invited me to dinner. When it became apparent after a while that his wife would not produce the family he wanted, he took me under his wing, and our relationship became almost father-son."

"She could not have children?" For the first time, Lily wondered if she might be carrying Adam's child.

"Could not, would not, I don't know. Over time, he resigned himself to his life being his work. He let himself be drawn into espionage. I preferred a clear, open battle, had no interest in this murky spying business. When the posting to Boston came, I wasn't particularly happy to learn we were to be its occupiers.

"I was fed up with army life. I'd talked to Randolph about mustering out to practice law when he came up with this project for me. 'You only have to try it this once,' he said. 'If you don't like it, go ahead and muster out, no hard feelings.' "

Adam rubbed his face tiredly. His beard was growing in thick and dark. Lily thought he looked a bit like a pirate that way. She wondered briefly how his beard and mustache would feel against her skin, before she caught herself.

"Randolph wanted me to infiltrate a Patriot group. Boson was in an uproar and reacting badly to our occupation. The Adams brothers had been stirring the pot every chance they got.

"We made it look like I mustered out for real—I put on civvies again, made a show of getting interested in law. Twas how I met John Adams. One thing led to another, and suddenly I was frequenting places where the Sons of Liberty gathered."

Adam stirred the fire's embers with a stick, preparing to bank it for the night. "By the time they got around to planning the 'tea party,' as 'tis called now, Randolph was practically frothing at the mouth. He saw his promotion to brigadier in this, I think. He encouraged me to participate.

"I realized what this was leading to, that I'd never be able to muster out. Randolph planned to get me involved in this so deeply that I would have only his word to vouchsafe that I was really still a British army officer. And by that time I no longer wanted to be.

"I liked America from the first time I came here. I like your independence, your forthrightness, your hurry to get things done, have them done right, and on your own terms." Adam reached back to lay out the blanket. His back was turned, so she did not see his eyes, but Lily had a sense that he was not just talking about "America" in a general sense now.

Lily moved around the tiny fire until she was sitting next to Adam. "I accepted his next assignment," he continued, "but by then I had spent weeks convincing the Sons of Liberty that I was serious about joining them. They approved my plans, agreed that getting out of Massachusetts where people knew me was essential. Only with distance could I get away with not reporting to Ware. So they contacted the leaders here, told them I was coming, but nothing about my background. They trusted me."

There was no accusation in his voice, but Lily felt that she had been found wanting. Adam had not judged her, though, as she had judged him. He'd been hurt by her rejection yet had not turned on her in anger. But she found *herself* wanting, her lack of faith in him had poisoned their relationship as surely as if she had found him with another woman. And after what he said about his family history, she knew that was one concern she need never have about Adam.

"So you came here, and to hide from Ware. . . . Is that why you adopted the role of Squire Sotheby?" she asked.

"Yes. I could think of nothing less likely for me to do, or for Ware to think of. I believed that by hiding in plain sight, using the money, clothes, manners to which I was born, I could help the Patriot cause and keep Ware off my trail. Until now."

They were both sitting on the blanket. Lily saw Adam reach for the cloak to make his solitary bed. "Do not go. 'Tis . . . more comfortable when we are together," she said haltingly, wondering as she did so just what she was inviting. Simple human comfort, or something more? Would Adam seek more than she was prepared to give?

"Nay, Lily." His deep voice was somber. "You still are not certain about me. Without trust there is no love. If I have learned anything, 'tis that." His lips brushed the top of her head, his hand clasped her shoulder briefly. Then he pulled the cloak over him with dignity and quietly turned his back.

Lily lay alone by the fire for a long, long time.

* * *

When she opened her eyes, she thought the morning sunlight through the wood's thick canopy played tricks on her eyes. The eyes staring down at her were not the ones she dreamed of. These were cold, pale blue, and merciless.

"Colonel Ware." Lily heard him cock the hammer, watched the pistol move into her field of vision.

"Good morning, Mistress Walters. I assure you this is the last time I shall have to wake you."

Twenty-eight

It is man's peculiar duty to love even those who wrong him.

—Marcus Aurelius Antoninus,
Meditations,
A.D. 160

Adam was nowhere to be seen as Lily sat up slowly. She spoke first, possessed of a desperate urge to seize control of the situation, although, of course, that was impossible.

"What do you want with him, Colonel? To kill him for his betrayal or take him back to face justice?" Ware actually looked blank for a moment, as if he had not thought past the moment of reckoning.

Before he could answer, she saw Ware's head snap forward. "Oof," he grunted as his torso bent. Over his shoulder Lily saw a flash of dark hair and knew it was Adam. She knew enough about weapons after watching Adam's training to realize Ware's pistol was not primed.

Swiftly, Ware recovered, straightening. In one motion he half turned, slamming his pistol into Adam's gut.

Adam had not tried to take Ware down, Lily realized, because she had been directly beneath the older man.

Ware, and possibly Adam behind him, would both have fallen on her.

While Adam doubled over in pain, Ware drew the pistol butt down hard against the back of Adam's neck. Adam went down face first, sprawled in the dirt. Lily watched, horrified, as Ware stood, panting.

Adam turned over with agonizing slowness. Ware allowed Adam to do so, never moving. Adam lay flat on his back, looking up at Ware through half-closed eyes. Both men were breathing hard. Reassured that Adam was all right, Lily found she could move her limbs again. She reached for a large branch.

Ware turned slightly. "Do that and he dies, Mistress Walters."

"You don't want him dead, Colonel," she said. But she froze, which gave Ware time to prime the pistol.

"Whether I want him dead or not will not prevent me from shooting him," he said.

Bold words slipped from some secret well inside Lily. "Then you will have to shoot me too." She raised the branch.

With Ware's attention divided between the two of them, Adam lunged swiftly from the ground. He didn't try to seize the pistol, just knocked it from Ware's hand before Ware could attack or shoot Lily.

It fired, showering dirt high in the air. Adam lunged again, reaching for the pistol. So did Ware. Lily launched herself at the older man. Acting on pure instinct, she drove her arms into his knees from behind. He hit the ground heavily, headfirst, just as Adam reached the weapon.

Adam's shoulders were wet with blood, but his gaze was steady. "The rope, Lily." She ran to the saddlebags to withdraw the hated length of hemp. Ware had not moved when she returned seconds later. Either he was unconscious or had given up the struggle.

Lily hoped Adam wouldn't wait to make sure but she needn't have worried. He handed the pistol to her, took the rope, then dropped to his knees swiftly to tie Ware's arms behind his back, reserving the rest of the rope to bind his ankles.

Only then did Adam risk turning over his former commanding officer. A bump the size of an egg bloomed on the colonel's high forehead. His eyes were closed.

Lily breathed a sigh of relief, turning to Adam. Adam looked up at Lily, mouth open to say something. He started to rise but then fell rather dramatically to his side.

If Adam had not been bleeding, Lily might have laughed. The two men lay side by side, both unconscious: a perfect opportunity to escape. Instead, she fetched the flask to clean Adam's wound.

The bleeding was minor, but the bump on his neck was larger than the colonel's. There was little more she could do to bring Adam around. So she sat down, drew Adam's head gently into her lap, and waited.

Her stomach was growling with hunger by the time Adam opened his eyes. This time she welcomed the sight of those arresting eyes under dark, heavy lashes, staring at her as if he'd been merely asleep.

"Are you all right?" were his first words.

"I believe I'm supposed to ask you that." Lily smiled. Adam's lips curved in a half-smile that despite his injuries told her he remembered exactly when he'd asked that question before.

To cover her blush, she ran her fingers through his hair. Although the thick, springy feel of it delighted her fingertips, she was checking to see if the swelling had spread. Adam relaxed against her for a minute, submitting to her ministrations with a low growl of pleasure rumbling in his chest.

Then he tried to move his head. "God above, Lily, if I've died and gone to heaven, 'tis not supposed to hurt so bloody much, is it?" he asked.

"Don't move. Ware hit you with his pistol, remember?"

"Not really. I can only remember coming into the clearing and seeing that gun pointed at you. I charged him and 'tis all I recall until now."

His peripheral vision caught the bright vermilion flash of Ware's uniform. Adam turned his head to look, provoking an inadvertent moan so loud that Mercury whickered anxiously at him from across the clearing.

"I told you not to move!" Lily chided, imprisoning his face between her hands.

"Did you do that, tie Randolph up? Nice work," he said.

"You do know who you are and where we are, don't you?" asked Lily, beginning to worry that his oddly festive mood signaled a serious head injury.

His smile faded. "Of course." His complexion had gone ashen. Sweat beaded his skin beneath her fingertips. He closed his eyes.

Lily wondered if he would pass out. She thought he had gone to sleep as his breathing slowed and lengthened, until she felt a hand close over hers.

"Oh!" Lily nearly jumped out of her skin but managed not to dislodge Adam's head.

"You mustn't let me rest. We have to move on," he said. "Can you take Mercury to find Randolph's horse?"

"No need. They've been whickering at each other. I'm sure it's nearby." She bent over him, probing the bump lightly before she was willing to leave.

"Go torture Ware instead," he barked. There was pain under the gruffness.

"Wait until I start cleaning it," she threatened, laying his head gently against the cloth she had torn from her petticoats. Lily found the horse in a nearby clearing. She recognized it as a gelding from Adair's . . . Adam's stable. No wonder the horses had been "calling" to each other.

By the time she returned, Adam had forced himself to a sitting position against a tree trunk. His eyes looked glazed but focused on her well enough.

"I have to stay awake, Lily," were his first words. "I don't think I have a concussion, but we can't take any chances."

"Are you able to mount Mercury?" she asked.

"Not as I usually do," he replied. "But I can if we find something to use as a mounting block."

"What about him?" Lily indicated Ware with a jerk of her head.

"I intended to tie him to his horse and let them go. We don't need an extra mount anymore. I'm sure he pursued us alone."

"But eventually he'll untie himself. You're going to let him go?" she asked, incredulous.

"I shan't kill him in cold blood, if that's what you mean," Adam said in a voice that brooked no dissent. "What did *you* want to do with him?"

Belatedly, Lily realized that despite the struggle, Adam probably still had some lingering affection for Ware. Or was there more to it than that? Adam must have interpreted the look on her face, for he interrupted her thoughts uncannily.

"No, Lily, this was not part of some prearranged plot," Adam said.

"I didn't say that!"

"You had no need. 'Tis written all over your face."

"At least I never hid my face from you."

"Touché," Adam said, then, with an effort, pulled himself to his feet. "Come on. We haven't much farther to go. Bring his horse here, please."

Lily complied. Adam untied Ware's ankles, then used the extra length to tie Ware's hands to the saddlebow. "Get Randolph's saddlebags," he directed while he led Mercury to a huge log across the clearing, half obscured by a cluster of blooming dogwood trees.

Lily removed the canteen, then hooked its leather strap onto the saddlebow of Ware's mount, not checking to see whether Adam approved. She had not wanted the man's death either, just to see him stopped.

"Home, Apollo," Adam said, slapping the animal lightly on one flank. The gelding moved out of the clearing in the direction from which they had come.

She moved over to Adam where he leaned heavily against Mercury's flanks. "You mount first," he said slowly. The log was tall enough for Lily to swing one leg over the saddle when she grabbed the stirrup. She scooted as high as she could on the saddle to leave more room for Adam.

He made it, although without his usual agility. She already had hold of the reins. He made no move to take them from her. "This way," he said, indicating a path through the trees she would not have noticed on her own.

As they left the clearing, Lily wondered if her suspicions had shattered irrevocably the tiny shoot of trust that had begun to grow again between her and Adam.

Lily feared Adam would lose consciousness. Finally she forced Adam to recite the flower vocabulary to keep him awake. It seemed they had been riding for hours, although the sun was still high in the sky. Adam slumped heavily against her, his head almost touching hers. Her shoulders ached. Their one brief stop for food and water had been on horseback after Adam warned her that he doubted his ability to remount Mercury.

They were about halfway through the list. "Iris," she said, her voice deliberately staccato.

"Means there is a message. Lily, let me rest a little."

That alarmed her more than anything he had said— Adam forgetting his own injunction to remain awake was not a good sign. She wished she knew how long he was supposed to stay conscious. Surely not past a day and night, but nightfall was still hours away.

"Lilac," she said.

"Love."

"Almost everything has a meaning for love, Adam. White lilac is for youth, love, and beauty. Purple lilac represents love's first emotions."

"Mmmpph. What I said."

"All right," she acquiesced, not wanting to argue. "Love-in-a-mist."

"Foolish love."

"No."

"What flower again?" His words were slurring slightly as if he'd been drinking.

"Love-in-a-mist. 'Tis long and purplish, remember? Droops slightly."

"Means purplishity."

"Perplexity," she repeated carefully.

" 'S what I said. Have to rest soon, Lily," he muttered, his mouth near her ear, her shoulders carrying much of his weight.

"How long do you have to stay awake, Adam?"

"Hmm? I can sleep now, but y'have to wake me every hour . . . to make sure . . . I still can. We can stop now," he said, his voice taking on more of its accustomed air of command.

Lily thought frantically. Ware had attacked them that morning. The sun had been nearly overhead when they left. Now it was on its descent, shadows lengthening. They should ride at least another hour.

When they stopped to make camp, Adam slid from Mercury so quickly and into sleep that Lily barely had time to pull the blanket from the saddlebag for him.

Fearful of attracting attention in case Ware had somehow managed to follow them, Lily decided against a fire. Dried beef and fruit from Ware's saddlebags would do fine for a cold supper.

Lily unbuttoned Adam's shirt while he slept, to inspect his torso. The pistol butt had made its mark. An ugly bruise marred the smooth ripple of muscle and light pelt on Adam's chest.

Yet he roused easily enough when she woke him for dinner. Still, she was worried about the night. "Are you afraid I will not wake up?" he asked her, his gaze dark and pain filled.

"No, me. I fear I shan't wake every hour."

"Is there a stream nearby?" The apparent non sequitur confused Lily.

"Well, yes, not far from here. I watered the horse there earlier."

"Good. Can you fill our flask and Ware's?"

"I left his on his saddlebow," Lily said.

"Why?"

"I didn't think he should be completely without resources," she said.

"Thank you," he said, his voice warm. "I've no wish to see him die, and I knew he'd come to the attention of a farmer or trapper shortly. Ware had no way of knowing we were going to Philadelphia, so I think we are safe from pursuit." The short speech seemed to have exhausted Adam. His long lashes flickered over his eyes, lingering longer each time.

"I'll refill this flask, and I can always go back for more. Why do you want so much water?" Lily asked, relieved that there was no conflict between them on the subject of Ware, at least.

He smiled, the first relaxed expression Lily had seen on his face since Oak Grove. "If you aren't certain you can wake me often enough, I have to supply myself with a reason to do so."

Lily blushed as comprehension set in, warming despite her embarrassment to the rich sound of Adam's laughter.

Twenty-nine

No man is born unto himself alone;
Who lives unto himself, he lives to none.
                                        —Francis Quarles,
                                              Esther,
                                              1621

They rode into Philadelphia on a fine spring morning in the middle of May. Bedraggled and saddle weary, Lily scarcely noticed their surroundings. She knew the city hosted the Second Continental Congress and that Peyton Randolph of Williamsburg presided over it, but her attention at the moment was focused entirely inward.

Peter. She would see Peter soon. That thought sustained her. It was difficult to know what the situation was between herself and Adam. He'd retreated from her, whether to save his strength or to focus on completing their journey, she could not tell. He was polite but distant.

Lily did not begrudge Adam one minute of sleep or rest, for heaven knew he needed it. But when they camped, he never placed the blanket closer to hers than was necessary for safety. She found bedding in Ware's saddlebags, so they no longer had to share. Neither his touch nor his glance indicated that he cared to remember the intimacy they had once shared.

Her heart leaden and confused, Lily looked forward now to the reunion with Peter as to a lifeline anchoring her to a world where she had lost her bearings. For she had realized in the last few days that not having Adam in her world was unthinkable.

Despite fatigue and the lingering pain in his head, Adam guided Mercury through the busy streets. They passed near the hall where the Continental Congress met. He needed to see certain people in the Massachusetts delegation soon.

Besides welcoming him, they would establish his bona fides. Now that the possibility of vindicating himself in Lily's eyes was within reach, he found himself strangely disinclined to do so. Perversely, he thought, if it took this for her to believe him, then perhaps she was not the woman he loved.

Perhaps he would just reunite Lily with Peter. Then they would leave. He had little doubt that Lily wanted only to return to Williamsburg with Peter and resume her life there. With the disappearance of the squire and the reappearance of her staunchly Patriot brother to vouch for her, Lily would be able to return to her old life.

"This way," he said, turning down a wide street. Adam dismounted first, but when he lifted his arms to help Lily down, bright lights flashed across his eyes. Dizziness swept over him in a wave.

"Adam," Lily said, pushing him back and dismounting on her own. "Are you all right?"

"We're here, so now I can say it," he said, leaning against Mercury's flanks. "No. I need to rest. Would you see if you can get a room for us?"

"What is your hurry?"

"I'd planned to stay at the tavern near Carpenter's Hall," he said. "There are people I need to see among the Massachusetts delegation," he said. As she made arrangements to stay with the innkeeper's wife, Adam gave the innkeeper a bit of folded paper.

"You aren't going anywhere until you rest," she said firmly, opening the door to the room they'd been given and pushing him inside. "When you've done that, you can go anywhere you want." She did not even ask about Peter, only walked slowly to the door next to his.

As if she somehow sensed his scrutiny, his fears, she turned. "You still hold everything dear to me in your hands, Adam," she said softly.

"Until I see Peter, I won't be going anywhere." Her golden eyes lit up, fierce and teasing at once. "But then, neither will you."

Adam removed only his boots before he fell asleep fully dressed. Lily haunted his dreams. He had not expected anything else.

Hours later, a cool cloth against his face brought him around. He struggled to sit up. Small, delicate hands, slightly roughened, pushed him back.

He knew those hands. "Lily?" he croaked, his voice hoarse with the dust of travel still in his throat.

"Aye," she said. "Are you always going to need looking after?" she teased.

He stilled her hand where it pressed the damp cloth against the bump on the back of his neck. "Always." A firm rap at the door interrupted what they might have said next to each other.

"Who is it?" Adam called, hoping they would go away.

Ethan's head poked through the door first, followed by a taller youth with dark gold hair. "You are here, then," Ethan said. "Look, Peter."

At the word "Peter," Lily turned. The cloth plopped wetly against the neckband of Adam's shirt, dripping, while Lily rushed into her brother's arms. As he watched them embrace, Adam wondered how it was possible to feel great sadness and throat-choking joy at the same time.

Lily reached out to squeeze Ethan's hand while Peter hugged the breath out of her. "Peter, I was so worried. I'd heard nothing, nothing about you and Ethan," she said, her tears springing from every crazy emotion she was experiencing.

Peter dabbed at her eyes with his fingertips. "Messages were sent to the Sons of Liberty," he said, awkwardly patting her back.

"Oh, I knew you were alive, but not where or any other news," Lily said.

"Adam didn't want our whereabouts known in case of treachery, so no one else was told, including Jack Cameron," Peter said.

"He probably wouldn't have told me anyway," Lily said.

Peter drew back, looking surprised. He searched her face. "What happened, Lily?" Peter asked, an authoritative note in his voice. Lily realized her brother had finished growing up in the weeks they had been parted. The confident set of his head and shoulders, his manner, all indicated that he truly was no longer her baby brother.

She took a moment to sigh and absorb a little of the bittersweet joy of that realization before replying. " 'Tis a long story, Peter. For now, let me just say that we've traveled for days to get here. Colonel Ware caught up with us along the way, and he and Adam fought."

"I knew he had it in for Adam the night he questioned me at the jail," Peter said. "The man was frantic to know whether the leader of the raid on the ship at Yorktown was Adam. I didn't tell him anything," Peter added proudly. "Actually, once Ethan said no one had seen Adam except at night, the colonel didn't press."

"You knew who Adam was?" Lily asked.

"The very first day he arrived. I was his contact. I met him out at the edge of town. He gave me a tongue-lashing, too, for lacking caution. He said we were never to meet that way again."

"What about Squire Sotheby?"

"Who? Oh, that idiot you did flowers for out at the plantation. What about him?" So he didn't know about Adam's disguise, Lily thought, not sure how much to tell him.

As Lily hesitated, Adam sat up. He opened his mouth to speak, closed it again. Let Lily choose what she would say. He waited, pain forgotten in the tension of waiting to hear her denounce him as she had done that morning at Oak Grove.

"A lot of things happened in Williamsburg," Lily said lamely. She'd had her moment and hadn't taken advantage of it. But soon she'd be alone with Peter, and then . . . Her heart contracted in desolation. Was it the thought of turning Adam in—or the prospect of no longer being with him?

Lily was silent, but Peter seemed not to notice. "When we got your message, we came at once. You won't believe what is happening! You'll have heard about the slaughter at Lexington and Concord?" Adam nodded yes, conscious of Lily's eyes upon him.

"The Massachusetts men demand a declaration of war! The Congress is trying to create an army and turn some of the militias into units for it. John Adams has proposed that Congress name the units around Boston the Continental Army."

"Has he?" Adam asked, the wet cloth falling to the floor as he pushed back the covers. Lily turned her face away but did not blush.

"Never fear, sweetheart," Adam murmured as he passed her on his way to pick up his vest and coat. "You've seen worse."

Observing that Peter was watching this exchange with a puzzled frown, Adam realized that brother and sister needed to talk. Peter Walters would no doubt then come after him, but Adam was prepared for that. Whether he would be an outraged brother or an outraged Patriot, however, was up to Lily.

He willed Lily to look at him as he walked by, but she did not. When he picked up his travel-stained coat and found it brushed, however, he marveled at her thoughtfulness despite being so angry with him.

Adam shrugged on the coat. "Are you going to return to the Congress this afternoon?" he asked the younger men. Ethan said yes, while Peter looked indecisive.

"Peter, we have to talk," Lily said, her hand resting for a moment on Peter's coat. Though he was her brother, Adam still felt jealous that she touched Peter so freely and willingly. She hadn't reached out to him since— He stifled fiercely the memory of the night in her room at Oak Grove.

"Go on, then," Peter said. "I'll see you later."

"Yes," Adam said, leaving with Ethan, feeling as though he were going to his doom.

A muscle in Adam's jaw spasmed as he walked with Ethan to the door. Otherwise his face was set, remote. Lily thought he gave nothing away when he was like this, until he looked at her before the door closed behind him and Ethan. Turbulent, powerful, compelling, his blue-green eyes were charged with suppressed emotion. She felt the impact run through her.

Then he was gone, and Peter turned to her. He was nearly as tall as Adam and no longer anyone's little boy. His first words were not what she expected.

"All right, Lily," Peter said softly. "What has happened between you and Adam?"

"I tell you, 'tis not so. He cannot be a traitor," Peter said an hour later after listening to her story. They had moved back to her room. He sat, elbows on his knees, running his hands through his thick blond hair in anguish.

She hadn't yet said anything about her personal relationship with Adam. "How do we know?" she asked. "What do we know of him, really?"

"Ethan and I would not be here if not for him!" Peter said, sitting up straight. "Come on, I'll take you to John Adams. He will confirm Adam's story, because I have heard most of it myself. Once we arrived here, they were glad to see us but even happier to hear Adam was safe. When they learned Ware had gone to Virginia, they were worried for Adam's safety."

"But how do we know he wasn't still . . . isn't still working for the British?" Lily asked, knowing the last of her protective anger was being shredded in the face of Peter's logic.

"Oh, for heaven's sake, dear sister. You watched Adam fight Ware. If they were in league, the whole charade would have stopped once he caught up with you."

"I know, I know." Lily crumpled over, hugging herself. "Oh, Peter, I distrusted him, I said terrible things to him.

And look at everything he did for the Sons of Liberty, for us, for—" She stopped.

Peter bent down to take her chin gently in his hand, turning her anguished face up to his. "You love him," he said.

She nodded miserably. Peter went down on one knee to match their heights more closely. "Then tell him," he said.

"Oh, Peter," she said, shocked, "I tried but that simply is not done."

To her consternation, her brother roared with laughter. "Since when has the constraint of polite manners ever stopped you from doing what you wanted?" he teased.

Lily batted his hand away, indignant. Then she seized Peter's ear, pulling him toward her as if to box his ears. She smiled. "I missed you. Even if your manners leave much to be desired."

"Everything I know I learned from you," he said, grinning. Her heart was lighter but not for long. Peter couldn't solve the problems between her and Adam. She had to do that herself.

But how?

Thirty

So court a mistress, she denies you;
Let her alone, she will court you.

— Ben Jonson,
The Forest,
1616

Ethan came back at dusk to tell them Adam was behind closed doors with members of the Massachusetts delegation and that they were all invited to dine with members of the Virginia and Massachusetts delegations. "Thomas Jefferson will be there," Peter added proudly, mentioning the brilliant Virginian who had read law in Williamsburg with George Wythe.

Lily wasn't prepared to dine with anyone. "Peter," she said, dragging him into her room and shooing a puzzled Ethan away. "I have nothing to wear."

"Women always say that," Peter muttered with new-found masculine exasperation.

"No, I mean it. We left Oak Grove hastily," Lily said without elaborating on her state of dress at the time. There were some things little brothers didn't need to know. "This dress is too small and I could not possibly wear it anywhere. You dine alone, and maybe by tomorrow I will have found a milliner's. 'Tis too late tonight."

Peter was not happy but was about to agree, when something made his warm green eyes light up. "I know! The innkeeper's daughter is about your height and shape. I'm sure she will have something."

"As long as she is parting from a dress for my sake and not yours," she said. Peter was still young enough to blush.

"This is not an inn," Lily murmured an hour later as they alighted from a hackney carriage in front of a large Georgian house where azalea bushes blossomed beneath graceful windows topped by fan-shaped arches.

"No," Peter agreed, " 'tis rented for the length of the Congress. Some of the delegates who were here last year found lodgings such as these more to their liking."

Lily hiked up her skirts a little as they crossed the threshold. The innkeeper's daughter was taller than Lily, but otherwise the dress fit her perfectly. On the arms of the two young men, Lily entered the house. She saw a few familiar faces immediately, former burgesses from Williamsburg and other residents. Thomas Jefferson was easy to recognize, his flame-colored hair a contrast to the many men who still wore wigs. Neither Peter nor Ethan did, of course, and she saw the Adams brothers, radical Samuel and plain-spoken John, with their dark hair similarly unadorned.

Then her breath caught, and she dropped the boys' arms. Deep in a knot of men in intense discussion, one man snared all her attention. Dark, thick hair was pulled back in a queue that did little to disguise its tendency to wave. His face was in profile, a study of pure masculinity in clean, sculptured lines. A hunter-green frock coat hugged broad shoulders, while a dark blue waistcoat and breeches clothed the rest of his powerful frame.

As if he sensed her scrutiny, Adam turned to meet her gaze. She watched as his eyes, a calm blue-green, turned turbulent, plunging her into deep and hidden waters. Drowning in his gaze, she realized she had seen that look only directed at her. She shivered with the sudden certain knowledge that Adam had always looked at her this way, even when she had not known who he was.

Then Adam stood before her, suffering being pounded on the back by an exuberant Ethan, Peter's thanks ringing out heartily. Could they start over again, Lily wondered, and pretend to forget all that had gone before?

Adam bent formally over Lily's hand, hesitating briefly. Then he turned it over, placed a kiss directly on the sensitive palm. He felt her shudder and looked up to see her amber eyes gone smoky with memory and desire.

Fierce exultation leapt through him. Even if he never had another moment with her, he did not regret what had happened between them. He would have taken her in his arms then and there, forgetting everyone, but she stepped back. Her color was high, her voice cool. "You look well, sir," she said.

He glanced at her sharply. Had her lips trembled? "Thanks are entirely due to you, mistress," he said politely. The moment of connection was gone, and he regretted that they were not alone. But her exquisite responsiveness just then, as when they had first met, bolstered his hopes. He only hoped she knew herself as well as he knew her body's responses.

Lily locked her knees from pure weakness when Adam kissed her hand. Such a small gesture, his kiss, but it opened a floodgate of feelings and memories. Then John Adams came up and took Adam off with him to a far corner of the room. Lily looked around to find Peter regarding her comprehendingly.

"No, Peter," she said, not waiting for his question. "We haven't been able to talk." *I scorned him. I swore I would denounce him. How do I tell him I was wrong? How can he ever trust me again?*

Trust. The word cut her like a sword. The one thing he wanted, needed, she had denied him.

"After the way he looked at you, I'm not sure you need to tell him you love him. I think he knows." Peter was sweet, but even with his new maturity, he didn't know what had transpired between her and Adam.

At the dinner that followed, the table was awash in the latest developments. Fort Ticonderoga's fall, General Gage's movements in Boston, excited talk of who might lead the Continental Army. Lily followed it with less than rapt attention.

The reason was half a table away. Adam was seated with the Massachusetts delegation. She had no need to question John Adams. The esteem in which these men held Adam was obvious from the questions they asked and their careful attention to his answers.

Although Adam participated fully in the intense and heated discussions flowing around the table—for many in the Virginia delegation were more cautious than the Bostonians—Lily knew he was aware of her.

His gaze crossed hers on occasion. Every time, she felt something wrench within her when their gazes no longer met. Memories lingered, and she had trouble reconciling Adam with Adair, their vastly different personalities, their opposing politics.

Then she chided herself, for there was no Adair, only Adam. "Only" Adam? There were so many sides to him. The Adam she knew was the man who had made love to her, the Patriot leader who risked his own life to rescue others, the shadowy figure who preferred to operate in the dark. The Adam she did not know was this brilliant, intense, learned man.

Adam looked her way during a moment when Samuel Adams was at his most bombastic. The slow smile he sent her displayed another side, one reserved for her alone. The lover, the sensual man so carefully concealed beneath the self-control. The man who with one glance could make the fine hair on her arms stand up, while her heated blood sang a song of desire throughout her body.

Despite the wave of desire, she smiled. Something about her look transformed his expression. Feminine fancy told her that the fierce gaze he directed at her now would have magically stripped her clothing from her had they been alone. Then he would touch her, kiss her. . . .

She nearly laughed when Sam Adams resorted to plucking at Adam's sleeve to regain his attention, so intense was the look of frustration Adam directed at the older Patriot leader. Then she experienced the same frustration, bereft when his blue-green gaze was gone.

Later, Lily returned to the inn with Peter. Ethan lingered, while Adam had not been seen since he had been drawn into a group debating who among the colonists had enough military experience and respect to command an American army.

"What are you going to do now, Lily?" Peter asked.

Lily hugged her elbows but not because the evening air was cold. "I thought we would go home to Williamsburg," she said.

"Ah." Peter was silent the rest of the way back to the inn.

At her door she turned to Peter as he bent to kiss her good night. "Are you not going home with me?"

"I . . ." He hesitated, his green eyes troubled. "Do not misunderstand me, Lily. 'Tis wonderful above anything to see you, but you know as well as I do that there will be a war soon, and I mean to be in it."

"Oh, Peter." Lily had known the moment would come but not that she would feel so unready. Her fledgling was ready to flee the nest. She didn't relish the prospect of war but knew that America would never find its freedom without one. Still, to have Peter declare himself ready to leave home and fight, all on the same day she found him . . .

Her tears spilled over, tears she had held back so long and for so many reasons. The terror of Peter's loss, the flight from Oak Grove, her anger at Adam, and now her fear; fear that like Peter, Adam would march off to war and she would never seen him again. There was obviously a ready place for Adam in Massachusetts. Surely he would be offered a command in the colony from which he had come.

Peter eased her into her room, then held her against him. She allowed herself the luxury of crying for several minutes against Peter's shoulder. And because he was grown up and a man, she no longer feared burdening him with her own worries, as she had when he was younger. Now that she did not need to be strong, she found it comforting to let her tears flow and know that for once, the stronger shoulder was that of her very capable brother.

" 'Tis all right," he murmured. " 'Twill all work out, I know it will." She had whispered these phrases to him over the years. They had been designed to comfort him when he'd skinned a knee, broken an arm, when his pride had been wounded, when she had administered a necessary scolding.

If only things were as simple now as they had been then.

A red tulip lay at her door the next morning when Lily emerged to break her fast with Peter. A declaration of love? There was no sign of Adam, no note, no letter. She caught sight of him later in Carpenter's Hall—and the next day and the next—but he was always at a distance, and always among a thick crowd of delegates.

Every morning a new flower appeared at her door. Although she never saw Adam, Peter assured her he still had a room there.

The next day she found a pink, the most popular of all flowers and so highly sought after in England. The red color of the pink meant pure love.

The next day brought a lilac. A purple one. First emotions of love.

That night, a forget-me-not. True love.

The next morning, a red carnation. Alas for my poor heart.

If Adam looked at her across the distances of the hall and its environs, it was difficult to tell. Tempers were heating as names were proposed, discussed, rejected. Couriers from beleaguered Boston brought news of military movements, of General Gage's actions.

Adam never approached her, but then, he was never alone. She thought they wanted his views about Virginia's military leaders, for Colonel George Washington's was a name much bandied about these days. Then they heard that Governor Dunmore had fled Williamsburg for a British sloop on the river, and Peyton Randolph, leader of the Virginia delegation, returned home.

With the governor gone, Adam Pearson could return to

"reclaim" Oak Grove, Lily thought. With Dunmore's flight, other Tories had fled too. There need be no complicated explanations about what had happened to "Squire Sotheby." But Adam himself was still maddeningly out of reach.

She would have thought he'd forgotten her existence except for the flowers at her door every day. That morning it had been a red rose. Peter, who had stopped by to take her to breakfast, cocked an eyebrow. A red rose needed no translation.

"Are you enjoying this?" Peter asked.

"I am not sure," she said, twirling the rose slowly between her fingertips. "I feel like I'm waiting for something, but I'm not sure what."

"We're all waiting," Peter said. She knew what he meant. The air in Congress was expectant; a nation struggled to be born. Her own fate was nothing next to it, and she felt no urgency to return to Williamsburg.

After all, her heart was here with Peter. *With Adam,* the thought rushed in, unbidden.

Still, the day could not be put off much longer. She couldn't fight in a war, but there were things she could do at home to help organize the women. She would make a place for herself again among the Patriots no matter what. She had to cut her ties, say good-bye to Peter. And, it seemed, to Adam.

Her heart quailed at the thought. Nevertheless, she was beginning to be annoyed by the silent, constant parade of perfect blossoms at her door. Did he want her to come to him? Did he tantalize her with what they could have been together had she trusted him more? What was he trying to tell her?

That night she picked up a tuberose, its white flowers blossoming along the length of its stem. She shivered, expectation cresting inside her in a wave of pure desire. Dangerous love.

She was done with this teasing and taunting. Or courting and wooing, whatever it was. His choice of increasingly more flamboyant, direct flowers meant one of them was going to crack under the sensual strain.

Two could play this game.

Thirty-one

And ruin'd love, when it is built anew,
Grows fairer than at first, more strong, far greater.
　　　　　　　　　—William Shakespeare,
　　　　　　　　　　Sonnet 119

Walking along Philadelphia's shady streets that morning, she found an early primrose. She laid it at Adam's door that afternoon before supper. As their name suggested, evening primroses opened at night. This blossom could mean wait for me. However, since they only opened capriciously, they also symbolized fickleness.

Adam was not the only one who could give a flower with a double meaning, Lily thought smugly. She rather hoped he stayed up all night waiting for her.

Then again, perhaps he didn't know the double meaning, because he continued in the same vein the next morning. She knew a honeysuckle was at her door even before she opened it, its heavy, sweet scent wafting upward to greet her.

It meant generous affection. There were two ways to read that meaning too.

Pointedly, she placed a small bunch of violets at his door that night. Modesty. That should cool his licentious thoughts.

A yellow tulip greeted her the next morning. She almost laughed aloud. Hopeless love.

She relented slightly. That night she placed a daffodil at his door. It was very late in the season for one. It meant affection.

She did laugh when she saw the mulberry branch lying listlessly at her door the next morning. I shall not survive you.

Carpenter's Hall was crowded, and observers like Lily were even farther away than usual. As she and Peter arrived, Ethan came racing up to them.

"You will never believe it! John Adams has proposed George Washington for commander in chief of the new Continental Army!"

"But I thought his name was put forward last month and he refused," Lily said.

"I think he wanted more consensus. There was no general agreement when the Congress first convened, you know. The Bostonians didn't want a southern colonist as their leader. They said we'd been too slow to support them," Ethan said.

"I wonder how much Adam had to do with this," Peter mused.

"Why?" Lily asked.

"Why? Well, things have progressed since the two of you arrived. Adam learned a lot about our people during his months in Virginia. You saw how they surrounded him the other night, how we have hardly seen him since. I wonder where he will serve."

"What do you mean?" Lily asked, her heart in her throat.

"He has his choice of where to raise a unit. He'll get

a plum command with his military experience. He could
go back to Boston or—" Peter's eyes glowed with a new
excitement. "I'll wager Washington asks him to form a
regiment in Virginia."

Peter seized Lily's hands in his enthusiasm. "Perhaps I
will return with you after all, Lily!"

"And I," declared Ethan.

"I thought you wanted to go to sea," Peter said.

"There were fishermen in my family for generations
until we came to the Colonies," Ethan confessed. "I do
feel the call of the sea. Sure you don't want to be a sailor,
Peter? We talked about it, you know," Ethan said.

"Aye, I know." Peter looked torn.

She patted his arm. "Choose what you will, Peter. You
need not accompany me home."

"But you and Adam . . . I thought that you—" Peter
stopped, looking confused. Ethan wisely stuck his hands
in his pockets and wandered away, whistling a sailor's
hornpipe.

"He's said nothing, and now there is war. No, I'll go
home, Peter."

"Do you want me to . . . I mean, has he . . ."

"No. I don't want you to do anything, Peter. What is
between me and Adam will remain that way. You're my
brother, not my father, and I don't need cosseting," she
declared.

After she packed her few things and returned the bor-
rowed dress to the innkeeper's daughter, Lily walked outside in the gathering twilight. At last she found what she
was looking for. Snapping the stem carefully with her fingers, she placed the flowers in a shallow bowl because
once cut, these particular flowers quickly died.

There was sadness but no bitterness in her heart as she laid the blooms at Adam's door. Oh, she wished for a bit more courage, and some of the boldness that proximity to Adam seemed to produce in her, but in his absence she had none.

Adam had clearly invited her, day after day, to come to him. He had told her as much during their journey. Until she made up her mind about him, he would not pursue her, he had said.

Although the look in his eyes at the delegates' dinner had exerted an irresistible pull, and although his flowers recalled and promised the sensual delights she'd found with him, she needed more. A rose might mean I love you, but she needed words.

As she unfastened her gown and prepared to climb into bed in her chemise, the epiphany struck her. She wanted words, he had given her actions. He wanted a declaration from her, she had given him her feelings in flowers. They were both doing the same thing, both avoiding the same thing.

Lily threw back the covers.

Adam held the delicate stems between his big hands soberly. The blooms were already half spent, white turning to tired brown. Was she gone, then? She must be if this was how she had chosen to end matters between them.

Departure. Apparently, she intended to leave matters at a stalemate. The wilted flower curled limply between his fingers. Sweet pea died quickly once cut. Was that another statement about her feelings for him?

No! It couldn't be. He'd hardly had a moment to collect his thoughts since their arrival, but he had told them all that he wouldn't spy again. As for Lily, yes, he'd held a part of himself aloof, waiting for her to admit she was wrong about him.

They had struck sparks off each other so strongly that night at the delegates' dinner, it was a wonder he had been able to rise from the table. He had started the flowers then, putting his love and his yearning into the fragrant, ephemeral messages, but there was nothing ephemeral about his feelings.

Then had come that damned primrose, and he'd waited for her that night like a green schoolboy. When she delivered the violets, he realized she had used the primrose's second meaning, the little minx. By then he had no doubt that had he run across her, he'd have pressed her against a wall and kissed her until she melted in his arms and begged him to take her.

He made damned sure he didn't see her after that, because he couldn't trust himself not to do exactly that. His control where she was concerned was a joke.

But this . . . He crushed the delicate stem between his thumb and forefinger. The rose-and-white blossom dropped to the floor.

He must face facts. He had decisions to make about the future. He did not want to make them without her. If that meant he sacrificed his pride to see her, to ask her if she loved him still, then he would do it. After all, what was pride compared to the emptiness in his soul without her?

Adam strode to the door. If he had to clip red roses from every matron's bush along Philadelphia's streets until dawn to give her the flowers, he would do it. She couldn't leave before sunrise, which gave him some time.

This time he would deliver the message in person.

He smiled at a mental image of Lily, surrounded by

roses, her ivory skin glowing against a backdrop of velvety red.

Before he could open the door, a knock sounded. He could not have been more surprised if his thoughts had conjured her directly into his room.

There stood Lily, her cloak slipping open to reveal a flash of white that must be her night rail. "What are you doing here?" He was gruff with surprise, but she did not appear put off.

"May I come in?" This wasn't a good idea, but his body wasn't interested in his brain, so his arms obligingly held the door open, then shut it firmly behind her.

"Adam, I don't know what to say," she said.

Say you love me, he thought.

"I was wrong about you," she continued. "I knew that even before we got here. You didn't have to prove to me who you were."

Say you love me.

She looked down. "I said some terrible things to you."

"You had every reason to," he said. He seized her hands. "I meant to tell you who I was, Lily, even before Ware found us. I couldn't go on with the disguises anymore. But we fell asleep, and I thought there'd be time to tell you in the morning. I couldn't be Adair and Adam both."

"I believe you," Lily said.

"Are we still at an impasse?" Adam asked softly, seeing the confusion on her face.

She took a step toward him. "No, I think not," she said in a voice so low he could hardly hear her. "But you have to help me with this. 'Tis quite . . ."

". . . socially inappropriate?" he finished with a smile. He took a step toward her. They were only inches apart. "Lily, Lily." He shook his head in mock sorrow. "Your manners leave much to be desired. An eavesdropper, a forward baggage, a willful woman. What am I to do with you?"

"Love me," she said, stepping toward him, sure now that his arms would go around her and she would be home.

"I do, oh, I do, my love," he breathed into her hair, wrapping strands of honey around his fingers until he tugged gently to turn her face up to his.

Their lips met in a kiss that renewed their bond with the simple pressure of their lips. As he took her mouth again and again, his sensuality overwhelmed her, and he gathered her against him until he no longer knew where she ended and he began.

Then he felt the wetness against his cheek and broke off. "What is it, little flower?" he asked.

"I love you so much," she confessed helplessly. "I can barely stand the thought of saying good-bye." He set her on her feet abruptly.

"You are still leaving?" he asked, incredulous.

"I have to go home," she said. "After all, you're leaving too."

"Yes. But not the way you think." He pressed a quick, hard kiss against her lips. "Stay right here until I get back. I mean it, Lily. Don't move from this room." He snatched his cloak off the wall and jammed his three-cornered hat onto his head.

"Where are you going?" Lily asked, wondering at the purposeful look on his face, where a moment before she had seen only passion.

"Just stay here." He locked the door from the outside. She heard the lock click and started forward in surprise and anger. Hearing his booted feet already on the stairs, however, she knew she could not call him back without a scandal.

Damn him, she thought, for always leaving her in compromising positions. The more fool she for allowing herself to be maneuvered into them. Here she had been, ready to sacrifice her virtue—what was left of it—for the sake of saying good-bye to the man she loved, nobly departing in the morning to leave him to his life unfettered, and what did he do? Kiss her and walk out!

Two hours later Lily's eyes closed despite her efforts, and the chair had long since ceased being comfortable. She curled up on top of his bed, her cloak pulled firmly around her.

"You are quite mad, my good man," said the Reverend Muehlenberg, woken from a sound slumber by Adam.

"No more than you, sir, since you lead a double life," Adam replied. Muehlenberg, who was also a secret member of the Sons of Liberty from Williamsburg, had heard of Adam Pearson. He gave Adam a look that had quelled lesser men. "You do have that expression about the pot and the kettle, hmm?" he said in barely accented English.

"Absolutely, *mein Herr.*" Adam smiled. "I know firsthand how difficult is the life you lead. But I am done with secrets. Will you assist me?"

"I am rarely accosted by men bearing roses—and really, you shouldn't have," he said dryly. "I suppose I must help you. You are certain of the lady's intentions?"

Adam did not answer. He hadn't given Lily a chance to answer, since he hadn't asked. But she loved him. What else was needed?

"I need help with these thorns," he said instead.

"A rose without thorns? Impossible," said Muehlenberg.

"She is," Adam said with such conviction in his voice

that Muehlenberg abandoned his misgivings and reached for a prickly stem.

Lily awoke from a dream of Adam pressing his lips against her hair, stroking her cheek, while the scent of roses filled the air. They had moved into Oak Grove, its flower beds beautifully restored.

Then a velvet petal stroked her cheek and a deep voice whispered in her ear, "Wake up, little flower, we have company."

"Company? In the garden?" she murmured sleepily.

"Here in my room," he whispered back, aching to stroke the rose's soft petals over more tender flesh. But he had a mission to accomplish and would not be distracted.

"Your room?" Lily gathered her sleepy wits, then sat up. Adam pulled the edges of her cloak together, then helped her to stand.

Lily gasped. Adam's other arm was filled with roses. More roses lay on the table. All were red. He must have raided a dozen gardens to find so many blooms. The pale-gray light of morning seeped into the room. He must have been up all night. "Oh, what have you done?" she cried.

"Nothing that can't be forgiven," he whispered, his voice resonant. He held her with one arm, while the other, filled with roses, was between them.

"These flowers say I love you, Lily Walters," he said. "But in case you still have doubts, I give you the words I held back for too long. I love you. Will you marry me?"

"What about the Continental Army and your command?" Lily asked.

"Hang the Continental Army," Adam said. As he shook

his head, Lily saw a man standing in the doorway behind him.

"I thought you knew the lady's intentions," the man said.

"Give me a minute, Muehlenberg, would you? Fetch her brother, please. You know him, Peter Walters."

"Oh, this is Mistress Valters, your brave courier and informant?" he said with great interest. " 'Tis a pleasure indeed to meet you, mistress." He bowed.

Lily was hopelessly confused. "What is all this? Flowers, this strange gentleman, your leaving last night, and—"

Adam silenced her with a finger on her lips. "One minute, give me one minute, little flower."

"So I'm leaving," came the good-natured grumble from the door. "Which room is her brother's?"

"Third down on the right," Adam said. "And shut the door on your way out."

"Don't push your luck, Pearson. You aren't married yet."

"For the lady's sake," Adam said with offended dignity. But Lily saw the twinkle in his eye as he said it.

Lily pushed herself away from Adam with an effort. "What is all this about? You disappeared and never came back, and—"

"Do you know how hard 'tis to gather six dozen roses and strip their thorns in the middle of the night? Even with help?" Adam demanded with a smile. "Little flower, I want to marry you. I wanted to make sure you knew, and I could not think of anything better than red roses. *One* did not seem to make enough of an impression on you," he said with mock plaintiveness.

Lily crossed her arms, feeling joy bursting within. "I'm impressed," she said, trying to keep her expression severe.

Adam went to one knee, a huge bunch of roses still clutched in one arm. "Dear Mistress Walters, would you marry me? I feel I must warn you that there is only one acceptable answer to this question," he said, looking up at her with laughter in his eyes.

Lily concentrated on the roses he held, but the desire to tease vanished when she saw the carefully, painfully scored stems. He had gone to such effort to take off all the thorns.

"What of the army?" she asked instead. "Who is that man?"

Adam rose, putting the flowers on the table with the others, dusting off his breeches. "That man, my love, is the Reverend Muehlenberg. He is also from Williamsburg and is a secret Sons of Liberty member. George Washington gave Reverend Muehlenberg a commission when he offered to raise a unit from among his parishioners. I asked him to marry us."

He advanced toward her, his gaze charged with intense emotion. "I asked General Washington if I might raise a unit in Virginia myself. Although he offered me a command in Boston, I told Washington I considered myself a Virginian now."

He circled his arms around Lily's waist. "I want to live at Oak Grove, Lily, with you. I want to make it a home, see you restore the gardens, raise our children there. Will you be my wife?"

"Oh, I . . . This is all so irregular," Lily managed to say.

Adam threw his head back, a deep, natural laugh emerging that Lily found immensely appealing after so many days of tension between them. "My dearest love, etiquette is not your strong suit. Let us go on as we have begun, shall we?"

The door swung open and a sleepy but determined-looking Peter rushed into the room. "What do you mean having my sister in your room at dawn, Pearson?" he asked in a more dangerous voice than Lily had ever heard from him.

Muehlenberg lounged in the doorway, his robust face alight with amusement.

"You didn't tell him why?" Adam demanded, sheltering Lily behind him as he turned to face Peter.

The minister shrugged. "Saying his sister was in your room and he should come quickly had all the necessary effect on him."

"This is your revenge for plucking off all those thorns, I suppose," Adam said, appearing unconcerned that Peter was advancing on him with balled fists.

"And waking me up at an ungodly hour," Muehlenberg affirmed.

Lily stepped out from behind Adam. "Really, this is too absurd," she said. "There is no propriety at all in this, but here is what happened, Peter. Adam decided that it was easier to pluck thorns off six dozen roses, wake up a minister, lock me in his room, and compromise me than simply ask me to marry him. And I was worried about *my* lack of social graces!"

Lily was not about to tell her baby brother that she had come here originally intending to pass one final night of passion with Adam, much less that there had been other nights. He was not that mature, and what an example she would set for him!

Adam moved to stand beside her, and she welcomed the solid warmth of him, his unwavering support. "We're returning to Williamsburg, Peter. I intend to raise a Virginia regiment for the Continental Army. And as I do not intend to be parted from your sister for one more night, I asked the Reverend Muehlenberg to marry us now."

"I wanted to be married at Oak Grove," Lily complained halfheartedly.

"We will have a regular wedding when we get back," Adam assured her. "But I do not think we need create any more scandal when we arrive than necessary."

Peter looked from one to the other, then at Muehlenberg, who shrugged. "One *more* night? *More* scandal?" he said, bewildered.

"We will explain everything," Lily said, crossing her fingers behind her back.

"Almost everything," came Adam's soft voice in her ear.

" 'Tis a long way back to Williamsburg and a formal wedding," Lily said. "But will you take our father's place and be our witness for now, my dearest brother?"

Seeing the radiance on Lily's face and the happiness in Adam's, Peter smiled, his doubts resolved. "Of course, Lily. But I should tell you I've decided to remain in Philadelphia with Ethan. We Americans will need a navy as well as an army, and the two of us intend to join."

He frowned in mock seriousness. "So 'tis just as well you decided to wed and reduce the scandal of a *second* trip in each other's company."

Lily sighed. Peter really did not miss much. Adam chuckled. "I take it we have your approval, then?" he said.

"Of course!" Peter shook Adam's hand and pounded him on the back.

"At least let me get dressed," Lily said, seeing the minister pull a worn black Bible from his coat pocket.

"Why bother with propriety now, little flower?" Adam said, turning Lily to face him.

"I do not even have a bouquet," she lamented.

Adam rolled his eyes. "What does it take, my love?" He strode to the table, scooped up an armful of flowers, and thrust them gently into Lily's arms. He settled the cloak more securely around her shoulders, hooked her arm through his, and turned them to face Muehlenberg.

"I'm not waiting any longer," he said into her ear, his voice a rich, dark velvet that raised the fine hairs on her arms. "Not one minute longer than necessary. Do you realize you spent all night in my bed without me in it?"

"Hush," said Lily, scandalized.

"Proceed, please, Reverend," Adam commanded politely, unperturbed by his bride's blushing a shade nearly as bright as the roses she carried.

The sun was well up before the two of them were alone again. They would breakfast with Peter and Ethan in an hour, then rendezvous with Muehlenberg for the trip back to Virginia.

But first things first. Adam divested Lily of her cloak and nightgown and proceeded to indulge his fantasies of covering her with roses. He wound petals through her hair, trailed them over her breasts, and teased her thighs with velvet tenderness.

Lily had never known a luxury richer than Adam's gentle, demanding strength above her, loving her, while the unmatched softness and fragrance of crushed rose petals lay beneath her.

They were exceedingly late for breakfast.

ABOUT THE AUTHOR

Corinne Everett writes historical and fantasy romance. She hopes you find the stories of these passionate couples—compelled to explore their own love while torn between conflicting loyalties to England and America—as absorbing to read as they were to write. Corinne reminds readers that "Virginia is for lovers" and welcomes letters (enclose SASE for reply). Write to Corinne Everett at PO Box 1055, Vienna, Virginia, 22183-1055, or visit her homepage at CorinneEverett.cjb.net for news about the DAUGHTERS OF LIBERTY series.

If you liked Corinne Everett's LOVING LILY, be sure to get the next installment of The Daughters of Liberty series, FAIR ROSE, available September 2001 wherever books are sold!

After the war, headstrong Englishwoman Rose Fairchild, daughter of the Earl of Lansdale, refuses to sell her family's land in Virginia to the Tidewater Nurseries run by Lily and Adam Pearson and Lily's brother Peter Walters. Peter has his eyes on the Lansdale property to build a dock and greenhouse for the nursery. But he, who wants nothing to do with the British, is stymied by Rose's determination to run Willow Oaks plantation on her own. Worse yet, Rose and Peter find themselves strongly—and reluctantly—attracted to each other. When Rose's brother forces her to return to England to marry and sell off the plantation, Peter must compete with the British aristocrats he hates and decide which he loves most: the land or his fair English Rose.

BOOK YOUR PLACE ON OUR WEBSITE AND MAKE THE READING CONNECTION!

We've created a customized website just for our very special readers, where you can get the inside scoop on everything that's going on with Zebra, Pinnacle and Kensington books.

When you come online, you'll have the exciting opportunity to:

- View covers of upcoming books
- Read sample chapters
- Learn about our future publishing schedule (listed by publication month *and author*)
- Find out when your favorite authors will be visiting a city near you
- Search for and order backlist books from our online catalog
- Check out author bios and background information
- Send e-mail to your favorite authors
- Meet the Kensington staff online
- Join us in weekly chats with authors, readers and other guests
- Get writing guidelines
- AND MUCH MORE!

**Visit our website at
http://www.zebrabooks.com**

Put a Little Romance in Your Life With
Betina Krahn

__Hidden Fire 0-8217-5793-8	$5.99US/$7.50CAN
__Love's Brazen Fire 0-8217-5691-5	$5.99US/$7.50CAN
__Midnight Magic 0-8217-4994-3	$4.99US/$5.99CAN
__Passion's Ransom 0-8217-5130-1	$5.99US/$6.99CAN
__Passion's Treasure 0-8217-6039-4	$5.99US/$7.50CAN
__Rebel Passion 0-8217-5526-9	$5.99US/$7.50CAN

Put a Little Romance in Your Life With

Jo Goodman

__**Crystal Passion** $5.50US/$7.00CAN
    0-8217-6308-3

__**Always in My Dreams** $5.50US/$7.00CAN
    0-8217-5619-2

__**The Captain's Lady** $5.99US/$7.50CAN
    0-8217-5948-5

__**My Reckless Heart** $5.99US/$7.50CAN
    0-8217-45843-8

__**My Steadfast Heart** $5.99US/$7.50CAN
    0-8217-6157-9

__**Only in My Arms** $5.99US/$7.50CAN
    0-8217-5346-0

__**With All My Heart** $5.99US/$7.50CAN
    0-8217-6145-5

Call toll free **1-888-345-BOOK** to order by phone, use this coupon to order by mail, or order online at **www.kensingtonbooks.com.**

Name_____

Address_____

City _____ State _____ Zip_____

Please send me the books I have checked above.

I am enclosing $_____
Plus postage and handling* $_____
Sales tax (in New York and Tennessee only) $_____
Total amount enclosed $_____

*Add $2.50 for the first book and $.50 for each additional book.

Send check or money order (no cash or CODs) to:

Kensington Publishing Corp., Dept. C.O., 850 Third Avenue, New York, NY 10022

Prices and numbers subject to change without notice.

All orders subject to availability.

Visit our website at **www.kensingtonbooks.com.**

Celebrate Romance With Two of Today's Hottest Authors

Meagan McKinney

__In the Dark	$6.99US/$8.99CAN	0-8217-6341-
__The Fortune Hunter	$6.50US/$8.00CAN	0-8217-6037-8
__Gentle from the Night	$5.99US/$7.50CAN	0-8217-5803-9
__A Man to Slay Dragons	$5.99US/$6.99CAN	0-8217-5345-
__My Wicked Enchantress	$5.99US/$7.50CAN	0-8217-5661-
__No Choice But Surrender	$5.99US/$7.50CAN	0-8217-5859-

Meryl Sawyer

__Thunder Island	$6.99US/$8.99CAN	0-8217-6378-
__Half Moon Bay	$6.50US/$8.00CAN	0-8217-6144-7
__The Hideaway	$5.99US/$7.50CAN	0-8217-5780-6
__Tempting Fate	$6.50US/$8.00CAN	0-8217-5858-
__Unforgettable	$6.50US/$8.00CAN	0-8217-5564-1

Call toll free **1-888-345-BOOK** to order by phone, use this coupon to order by mail, or order online at **www.kensingtonbooks.com**

Name _____

Address _____

City _____ State _____ Zip _____

Please send me the books I have checked above.

I am enclosing	$_____
Plus postage and handling*	$_____
Sales tax (in New York and Tennessee only)	$_____
Total amount enclosed	$_____

*Add $2.50 for the first book and $.50 for each additional book.

Send check or money order (no cash or CODs) to:

Kensington Publishing Corp., Dept. C.O., 850 Third Avenue, New York, NY 10022

Prices and numbers subject to change without notice.

All orders subject to availability.

Visit our website at **www.kensingtonbooks.com**.